BELLA COVE

BELLA COVE

A SECOND CHANCE ROMANCE

ROCHELLE KATZMAN

ISBN: 978-1-63161-050-9

Published by TCK Publishing
www.TCKPublishing.com

Get discounts and special deals on books at
www.TCKPublishing.com/Bookdeals

Sign up for Rochelle's newsletter to stay tuned on her latest releases and updates:
www.RochelleKatzman.com

For an additional free scene of Bella Cove, please go to
www.RochelleKatzman.com/BellaCove

DEDICATION

To my Nana, Grandmother, and Mom

CONTENTS

1

KAYLA HAD BEEN STARING at the contract before her for the last fifteen minutes.

"Sweetie, just sign it. I promise there isn't anything scary in it." Melody smiled softly.

Beside her, the lawyer who'd drawn up the papers glared.

"I'll sign it. I promised I would," Kayla said as she read the same words over and over. She wasn't hesitating because she didn't want to take over the toy store for Melody...but a part of Kayla's soul felt as if it was dying.

She kept clicking the top of the pen until the sound started to annoy even her. So instead, she glanced outside at the quaint street lined by cobblestone sidewalks and at all the old but well-kept buildings. Bella Cove sure was pretty. Too bad her heart was only half here.

Melody placed her hand on Kayla's. "What is it, honey? Are you tired of selling toys, too?"

"I like toys," she answered honestly. And she *did* like them. But at twenty-nine years old, she still didn't have any children of her own. Yet she sold toys. And with each one she sold, her heart died a little, especially when a mommy or daddy bought a doll for a little girl.

Melody's hand remained on Kayla's. "Sweetie, I promise, you'll be happy. I always was."

"I know," Kayla said as she smiled warmly. She never spoke that much about it, but everyone knew she'd left graduate school two years ago to take care of her family. When her nana had passed, Kayla had been assigned the role of family matriarch. Kayla never referred to herself as such. The word "matriarch" seemed too archaic. But her family needed her. When her nana asked her to take care of the family before she died, Kayla never realized it would take this long. Yet here she was, two years later, and she was still taking care of them. She had been so close to getting her degree and having her freedom in California. Leaving the love of her life to come back to Bella Cove had been the hardest of all.

Kayla sighed as she held the contract in her hands. Melody was right. Kayla had nothing to be afraid of; the terms were pretty straightforward. The contract said Melody Fischer was giving Magical Toys to Kayla Conway for the cost of one cup of coffee. It was a great opportunity, and her nana would have encouraged her to take it.

So, with shaking hands and her soul screaming at her to run back to California, Kayla signed her name on the dotted line.

"Oh, thank goodness. If you'd changed your mind, Harry would have been beside himself." Melody grabbed Kayla's face and kissed her on both cheeks.

"Thank you so much for giving me this opportunity." Kayla stood, hoping Melody hadn't left lipstick marks on her cheeks. When she put her chair back behind the register, she realized her palms were sweating like crazy, so she ran her hands down her yellow sundress. The last thing she needed was to shake that asshole attorney's hand and have him discover how terrified she'd felt.

Melody hitched her purse further up on her shoulder. Kayla hoped that meant her friend was leaving. She needed a few hours to cry and then get herself together before the celebratory dinner her mother was cooking tonight.

"Sweetie, you've been my only employee for the last two years, but you've also been my friend. Of *course* I want you to have all of this. Besides, you'll make this place even more of a success than I have. And Harry will be so relieved. Now we can finally use our lottery winnings to travel."

Melody's husband had played the lotto every week for the last ten years. Finally, he had won, and he wanted to travel the world. They no longer needed the income from the shop. Even if he hadn't won the lottery, he'd still pressure Melody to retire. Wanting to hand over the shop made sense, but at the same time, it affected Kayla's life. She wished *she* had won the lottery. Not for money, as Nana and Pop had made sure their family had enough of that. Kayla wanted only to live the life of her dreams. But such lotteries didn't exist.

"Thank you for your confidence. I hope I do this place justice." Kayla smiled, even though her heart was breaking.

"Of course you will. You're fabulous."

The rest of the meeting was a blur. Kayla shook the attorney's hand as fast as she could. He didn't like her for taking so much time to sign the contract, but he could go take a flying leap for all she cared. She turned and hugged Melody once more then walked them both to the entrance. When they left, Kayla shut the door behind them and flipped the old, white wooden *open* sign to *closed*. She desperately needed a moment to breathe. And this was her store now, so she could do whatever she wanted.

Kayla walked over to the little girl's section, where some sunglasses with mermaids on them were displayed. She picked up a pair and put them on, needing darkness. Then she walked into Melody's office—*my office*, she corrected herself—and closed the door.

Kayla sat and placed her hands and head on the empty desk. Finally, she allowed the tears to flow. With each day that passed, she was getting farther and farther away from Gabe. Her heart still craved him. Her body craved him, too. He was the last man who'd touched her and they'd had the most intense sex. God, she missed him.

"Kayla, come on! Mom's waiting for you."

Kayla jumped. She must have dozed off. Hadn't she locked the front door?

"Really? Your first afternoon as the owner and you're sitting in your new office with sunglasses on, and the store is closed. Way to make money, Kayla!" Her brother Josh ran his hands through his blond hair as if she had offended him.

It was a good thing she was wearing the sunglasses, so Josh couldn't see her rolling her eyes.

"Is there a reason you're here? Did you get me a congratulations present?" Kayla asked sarcastically.

Josh shifted his feet. At two months sober, he was a mess, but Kayla was the only one who realized that. Everyone else thought he was doing *wonderfully.* She knew better. The only reason he'd agreed to get sober was so their dad would buy him a new car. Josh had some grandiose plan that the moment he got the car, he would leave Bella Cove and never return. Kayla thought he would drive to the nearest bar and break his sobriety. He had put the family through hell, and he was part of the reason she had no choice but to stay.

It was a miracle he wasn't trying to get money from her, but he knew better. When she'd inherited Nana's millions, Kayla had also received specific instructions on how to use the money.

On her deathbed, Nana had made Kayla promise to keep the family together. Kayla didn't want the responsibility and had told her grandmother so. But Nana said the family wasn't stable. Kayla had to agree. She'd then confessed about falling in love with Gabe and how badly she wanted to finish her graduate degree back in California. Nana had grabbed Kayla's face and had kissed her, then said that one day, Kayla would have everything she wanted. Nana had said Gabe sounded wonderful, and if he truly loved Kayla, he'd wait until her family was back on its feet.

That had been the first time Nana had been wrong.

"Come on, Kayla. Mom's going to freak if you're late."

"Right." Kayla slammed her hands on the desk and stood.

She looked at the clock and saw it was already six. She had slept for two hours. Josh was right: She couldn't be late for her own celebratory dinner. Mom's one claim to fame was the meals she cooked for the family. Other than that, she was mostly anxious and scatterbrained, which was why the matriarch baton hadn't been passed to her.

Then there was Kayla's older sister Lauren, who wanted to do nothing more than get married and shop. At thirty-one, she was still single and living at home. Kayla didn't think that was such a big deal; Lauren just hadn't met the love of her life yet. If she met him at thirty-five, forty, or fifty, it didn't matter, as long as she found her true love. But Lauren disagreed. She worked in a real estate office, but only because she was trying to meet a rich man. She cried daily about being single. Nana hadn't thought anyone in the family other than Kayla was mentally balanced and strong enough to keep the family intact. In a way, it was a compliment, but if Nana could have seen the turmoil going on inside Kayla, no doubt her grandmother would have thought differently.

Kayla glanced at her brother. Josh seemed to be on edge. If he wasn't drinking, then he needed to eat, which was probably why he had walked all the way there to get her. He also lived in the family house. In fact, all the siblings did except for her oldest brother, Matt. His wife, Jessica, would never have allowed that.

Kayla took off the sunglasses, opened the bottom desk drawer, and grabbed her purse. She applied light-pink lip gloss and ran her hands through her long blonde hair. She glanced in the mirror behind her and thought she looked atrocious, but at least no one could tell she had bawled her eyes out two hours ago.

"Okay, I'm ready," she said.

She zipped up her purse and walked toward the front door with Josh following. Letting Josh exit in front her, she glanced back at the store once more. This was all hers. She'd promised Melody that first thing tomorrow, she would call the building's landlord and introduce herself. Melody had given her the toy store basically free of charge, but, unfortunately, she still needed to pay rent. Three days ago, Mr. Kleiner, the landlord, had passed away in his sleep and his grandson had inherited everything. So far, they hadn't heard from the grandson, which was why Melody thought it would be smart if Kayla contacted him instead. She hoped he'd be nice. On top of everything else, a mean landlord was all she needed right now.

"Kayla!" Josh yelled.

Kayla sighed loudly. Her alcoholic, two-months-sober brother was getting on her nerves.

She closed the front door behind her, making sure it was locked, and then threw her keys into her purse. Nana had been firm about the need for Kayla to look out for Josh, but she never told Kayla how to deal with him. Out of all Kayla's siblings, he was the hardest to handle. She missed how he was when they were kids.

Kayla sighed. It was smarter to numb out her feelings. She had learned the technique in one of her psychology classes in graduate school. If she allowed any emotion in, she would never be able to wake up in the mornings and be there for her family. She would also have to acknowledge how she really felt about leaving Gabe behind at school.

"Of course. Let's go before Mom calls one of us," she said.

In silence, they walked down Main Street. Kayla thought about being nice and asking Josh how his sobriety was going, but she wasn't in the mood. He wouldn't have told her the truth anyway. Instead of starting a useless conversation, she looked at all the pretty shops. The town had been founded in the late 1600s, and the stores had been built in the early 1700s. It was a beautiful place, like a picture postcard. Each store looked different but all of them had a New England feel. Magical Toys was a small, brick building with red shutters. The chocolate store next door had brown wood shingles with white shutters around the windows on the second floor. The knitting store, which they were passing now, was painted yellow and had flowerboxes filled with pink and yellow flowers below the windows. Most stores had white picket fences around them, and the streets were lit at night by tall lamps with flowerpots hanging from them in the summertime. She loved summer here. The few tourists who visited called the town "majestic and enchanting." But here, as in every small town in America, everyone knew each other's business, and few people had secrets.

When the stores ended on Main Street, the bay came into view. At this time of year, it was especially beautiful. There were hundreds of boats on the water and even one or two yachts. Bella Cove was perfectly situated an hour and forty-five-minute drive from New York City. The town was so small, most people didn't even know it existed, and even if they did know, it wasn't the Hamptons. Most folks went to the Hamptons or the North Fork for the summer. When Kayla was growing up, the North Fork had the same boring reputation as Bella Cove, but since the Hamptons were overflowing, vacationers had now claimed the North Fork as their own. Bella Cove sat a couple of miles west, but so far, the rich snobs from Manhattan hadn't claimed it. Part of her hoped things stayed that way. She enjoyed the peace and quiet—not that her family allowed her to have a lot of either. And part of her welcomed people from other areas. If tourism picked up a little, maybe the presence of more people would shake the stagnant feel that consumed this little bayside town.

Kayla enjoyed walking around the bay. The water soothed her and made her feel whole again. Josh and she were still quiet, but she could tell he was thinking about something. Probably alcohol. Her family members were hopeful he would stick with sobriety this time, but Kayla knew the chances were slim.

The path around the bay narrowed as they headed toward the community park. She had kissed a few boys in high school in the gazebo straight ahead, but those kisses had been nothing like Gabe's. She gave herself a mental shake. She had to stop thinking that way. Gabe's kisses made her think of sex. She craved having sex with him. But that was in the past now.

Josh was walking abnormally slowly, but she still didn't feel the need to talk. Unfortunately, he did.

"How come you're so quiet?"

"How come you're still sober?" she responded.

"I deserved that," he admitted.

He didn't look Kayla straight in the eye. Josh had a way of giving her the creeps, usually when he was up to something. However, she had so much on her mind, she wasn't in the mood to ask. Too bad he was so good-looking—six foot one with blond hair and twinkling-blue eyes. He worked out daily, so he had great muscles. Unfortunately, being that adorable was how he got away with so much.

Everyone in her family was good looking. They even all had naturally platinum-blond hair. Her ancestors on both her mom's and dad's side were from Sweden. She and her two sisters looked like girl-next-door types. She certainly did, with blonde hair, navy-blue eyes, ivory skin, and a height of five three. But Kayla never cared about her looks. She was always more concerned with how she felt on the inside. Her nana always said if you felt beautiful on the inside, it showed on your outside. These days, Kayla didn't feel beautiful on the inside, especially with how she'd left things with Gabe. It might have been two years ago, but with all the family drama, it felt like two minutes.

Once she and Josh made it through the park, they walked the final distance to her parents' house up a hill. She liked this part. The higher the hill, the more beautiful the view. Nana and

Pop had built this house. Her Pop had made furniture and sold the pieces throughout the country. He'd built interesting pieces, too, like couches that converted into beds, and coffee tables that doubled as wine racks. Each piece was unique. Her favorite was the coffee table with carvings from local artists. Her dad and brothers still made furniture. Pop had made sure they knew exactly how to craft each detailed piece. He'd made a lot of money and then invested in the stock market. Not only had Pop made a good living, but through his investments, he'd made certain future generations would never have to worry about money, either. Too bad he'd passed away seven years ago. She missed him terribly.

The furniture business was still going strong. The factory where the furniture was made was about five miles up the road. While the men in the family were building furniture, the women could do whatever they pleased. Kayla had always wanted to be a psychologist. Her mother was a stay-at-home mom, and her sister Lauren wanted to be a wife. The jury was still out on what Sarah wanted to be. Nana had taught Mom, Kayla, and her sisters how to cook and how to take care of a man. But most men weren't interested in wives like that anymore. Today, women had to do it all. Men liked women who were lawyers and doctors. They no longer wanted the responsibility of being the sole breadwinner. Times had changed from Nana's era. Yet, Kayla was a career woman, and the one man she wanted, she couldn't have.

The hill was an easy climb and not too steep. Large, postmodern homes came into view. Some overlooked the bay and some didn't. In between was a narrow road, barely wide enough for one car to pass through. She and Josh walked by her favorite house, which was white with pink shutters around the windows. The owners had even painted their porch pink to match. Her sisters thought the house looked tacky, but Kayla thought it looked happy. Her family's house was farthest up the hill. It was beautiful: a large yellow house with white trim, which would fit perfectly on the most expensive street in South or East Hampton. Her pop had built it for Nana because he loved her so much.

Nana had found true love in Bella Cove. Maybe Kayla would find true love here, too, but she doubted it. She had believed Gabe was her soulmate. Was she allowed to find two soulmates? Was there some unwritten rule that you could only find it once? She hoped not, but she suspected there must be some kind of rule.

When they climbed the back porch to her family's house, Kayla stopped to take a deep breath. She looked out at the bay with all the boats bobbing on the water. Pop had found the most perfect view for his love, Nana.

"There you are. I was wondering what kept my new store owner so long." Kayla's mom came out through the French doors holding a big bowl of pasta with vegetables, and kissed Kayla on the head. Her mom was still beautiful with her slim figure, shoulder-length blonde hair, and piercing-blue eyes, and she always wore her hot-pink lipstick. Nana used to say that you should always wear your lipstick, whether you're sitting around the house or not. Kayla thought that was an archaic rule that made no sense. But her nana must have instilled that rule in her mom's head.

"It wasn't me, Mom, I swear," Josh said almost in a panic.

Before her mom put down the bowl, she kissed Josh on the head, too. "I know, dear. You're a good boy."

Kayla rolled her eyes and grabbed the bowl out of her mom's hands, placing it on the long table that ran the length of the back porch. She was grateful they were eating outside tonight. If they ate inside, she wasn't sure she would be able to breathe. She already felt her throat tightening up.

"I'll help you get more stuff," she said as she walked inside and grabbed the water pitcher and salad bowl off the kitchen counter.

"Hey, beautiful, did you sign everything?" Matt, her older brother, asked.

"I did. Thank you." Kayla smiled up at him. She loved her big brother. If he had been a woman, there was a chance Nana would have given him the job of making sure the family was okay and stayed together, but then again, he allowed his wife to tell him what to do all the time. Speaking of her sister-in-law…

"Hey, Matt, is Jessica coming tonight?" Kayla asked.

Jessica was his wife, but she followed her own set of rules. Matt looked down and pretended to rub something off his hand. Kayla knew him well enough to see through the facade.

"Nah, she's really exhausted. She's been working hard."

"I'm sorry to hear that. I'll stop by in the next few days and make sure she's okay. She's an important member of this family. I want you to know that."

Matt smiled, his green eyes twinkling. It made him so happy when the family accepted his wife. After all, everyone knew how much Jessica didn't like the family. No one could figure out why. But Kayla knew. Jessica only loved her own family and apparently didn't have any room left in her heart to love her in-laws. The truth was, she didn't *want* to love them. She could if she tried, but she didn't make the effort. Kayla would make her sister-in-law love them if it was the last thing she did. By marrying Matt, Jessica had become a part of his family, and Kayla was going to make damn sure her sister-in-law knew that.

"Hey, beautiful." Her younger sister Sarah ran into the kitchen and threw her arms around Kayla, smothering her in kisses.

Kayla couldn't help but laugh. She would have thought the moment funnier if she wasn't balancing the water pitcher and salad. "Okay, okay, Mom's going to kill me if I drop this."

Matt quickly grabbed both items out of her hands. "I've got them. Besides, you shouldn't be helping. This is *your* celebratory dinner."

Matt walked outside, and Sarah used that moment to pretty much attack Kayla.

"So! Tell me!" She grabbed Kayla's arms and jumped up and down, using her arms as support. Though she was twenty-seven, she had no interest in a serious relationship yet. She liked to have fun with every man in Bella Cove, in fact. All men loved her. What was not to love? She had straight blonde hair, beautiful brown eyes, and the biggest boobs in the family. Plus, she was tall and thin like a model. At five-foot-nine, she was way taller than Kayla was.

Yet everyone in the family called Kayla *beautiful.*

Sarah looked at Kayla as if she was supposed to be overjoyed at owning the toy store. But Kayla couldn't find much joy in anything these days. She couldn't seem to stop thinking about Gabe.

"I signed on the dotted line, and now I'm the proud owner of Magical Toys." Kayla hugged Sarah, trying to be as believable as possible.

Sarah hugged her back. "It's amazing how life works out. Two years ago, you were on your way to becoming a psychologist, and then the universe changed your direction. Now you own a toy store. Life is so crazy."

"It really is."

Kayla's heart dropped as she grabbed her sister's hand, and together they walked outside. Never in her life did she think she would own a toy store. After Nana died, Kayla had needed to get out of the house as much as possible, especially with her mom yelling all the time. She had thought working with toys would be light and fun, which it was. Melody had been looking to hire someone, so even though Kayla didn't need the money, she applied anyway. However, spending every day looking at the toys and seeing all the happy children made her think of Gabe and what she had given up for her family. She'd made the right decision, and if she had the choice, she would do it again—but Gabe and she had been about to get engaged. They'd talked about the children they would have together, had even picked out names. If they'd had a girl, she would be called Keidi. And if they'd had a boy, they would have called him Noah. They'd hoped to have more than two kids…

Lauren and their dad joined the rest of the family out on the porch a few minutes later. As usual, Lauren looked depressed. Without a man, she felt like a nobody. Kayla needed to figure out a way to help her…to find a man who Lauren would think good enough to be with her.

Kayla's dad winked at her. He was always pretty quiet. On the other hand, her mom was high maintenance. The only reason he hadn't packed his bags was because Nana hadn't let him. Kayla wasn't sure how much longer she could keep her father from leaving. He wouldn't have any trouble finding another wife, either. Women of all ages were always checking him out.

The family dinner was the same as usual. Everyone had congratulated her by that point. Lauren ate in silence, looking miserable. Josh stood by the food, eating as much as he could, but he was clearly in a bad mood. Her dad discussed business with Matt, which was normal for them, and Sarah was texting her friends. Her mom was running in and out of the house, bringing more and more food to the table, as if she were feeding an army of thousands.

And Kayla? Kayla sat in her favorite rocking chair, watching the scene unfold in front of her while she wondered how Gabe would feel about her family. Would he like them? Would he think they were odd? She had told her sisters about him, even though they never had a chance to meet him, but she never told her parents or her brothers. They were always so judgmental about her boyfriends. She didn't want their opinions to touch Gabe, because in Kayla's eyes he was almost perfect.

Still, to this day, Gabe was never far from her mind. Just like tonight. She'd fantasized about him showing up in Bella Cove so many times in the last two years, she was sure she was manifesting it. But tonight, he hadn't shown up, so instead, she'd cherish her family, and put Gabe in the back of her mind with all of her other lost dreams.

Besides, Gabe wanting to see her again was one big illusion. After he'd given her that damn ultimatum, he wanted nothing to do with her. If only he'd understood that she *had* to pick her family over returning to him. And as she looked at her family tonight, she knew she'd made the right decision.

But that didn't stop her from missing him like crazy.

2

WHEN KAYLA OPENED HER SHOP the next morning, she decided to adjust her attitude. The first thing she needed to do was call Mr. Kleiner's office and schedule an appointment to meet with his grandson.

She logged onto her computer and clicked on the contacts list to find Mr. Kleiner's secretary's phone number. Her name was Alice; Kayla had only met the woman a handful of times and didn't know her well, but Melody loved Alice and said she was great. Kayla felt strange, taking these steps without Melody around for guidance. Normally, she would have been in the shop by now, relaying all the gossip in Bella Cove. The store felt empty without her, lonely even. Melody's banter had helped Kayla get out of her head.

She dialed Alice's number, but the call went to voicemail. Instead of leaving a message, Kayla decided to send an email. But she wasn't sure if she should send it from her email address or Melody's. She decided to use Melody's since, first of all, Alice wasn't used to dealing with Kayla, and second of all, Kayla would rather be the one to tell Mr. Kleiner's grandson that she'd taken over the toy store.

To: Alice McMara
From: Melody Fischer
Subject: Magical Toys

Dear Alice,

I'd like to say again how very sorry I am to hear about the passing of Mr. Kleiner. He was such a kind man. I understand his grandson is taking over. I'm sure he's busy, but if possible, I would love to personally introduce myself at his earliest convenience. I also have some very exciting news! Thank you so much as usual. I hope you have a beautiful day.

Best wishes,
Melody

Kayla sighed. She was lying. But at the same time, she didn't want to explain everything to Alice before speaking with the grandson. If Alice told him the news first, there was a chance he wouldn't like the fact Melody had sold the store to her without informing Mr. Kleiner's office first. But Mr. Kleiner had already passed away when she'd signed the contract. Kayla slapped her hand against her forehead. Why couldn't life be easy?

Magical Toys had been hers for less than twenty-four hours, and she had already closed the store early and lied to her landlord's secretary. *Great job,* she thought. A minute later, Kayla's computer dinged. Alice had already responded to Kayla's email. As she clicked on the email and waited for it to open, her heart thudded. She wasn't in the habit of letting others down, and if his grandson discovered she had lied or if he didn't like her when they met, she would feel as if she'd let Melody down. When Kayla scanned Alice's email, what felt like a nervous butterfly flipped in her stomach.

To: Melody Fischer
From: Alice McMara
Subject: Re: Magical Toys

Dear Melody,

Mr. Kleiner's grandson is standing over my shoulder reading your email. He will meet you at your store at noon. He's looking forward to meeting you and hearing your exciting news. His grandfather spoke very highly to him about Magical Toys. Have a beautiful day, too!

Best wishes,
Alice

Noon? Kayla glanced at the time on the computer screen. She had a little less than two hours. If she'd known he'd want to meet today, she would have dressed more appropriately. Instead, she was wearing her favorite pair of skinny jeans and a pink, ribbed tank top with a large, white satin heart in the center. The outfit was fine if she'd be doing nothing more than working at the store all day, but she would have chosen something nicer to meet her current landlord. If she had more time, she would run home and change, but there was still so much to do. Last night, she had left in such a rush, she hadn't taken the time to straighten up. Some of the rows of toys looked messy, and a young boy had spilled the bouncing balls display, so there were balls all over the place.

Kayla ran around the store, picking everything up. Then she ran into her office, reapplied some lip gloss, and ran a brush through her hair. She wished she looked better, but it was the best she could do on such short notice.

At exactly noon, Kayla heard her front door open. She was in the storage room in the back, sorting through a box of children's books that had just arrived. The sound of his heavy footsteps alone made Kayla's heartbeat quicken. It had been a long time since she felt this nervous and oddly vulnerable.

"Hello?" Mr. Kleiner's grandson hit the bell on the counter next to her credit card machine.

His voice was deep and masculine. She thought he sounded familiar, but she couldn't imagine why.

Kayla took a deep breath and brushed away the dust that was clinging to her top and jeans. She couldn't shake this anxious feeling. But she had to get out there and introduce herself. With as much courage and grace as she could find, she stepped out of her storage room and walked down the short hallway toward her new landlord.

At first, he had his back turned toward her as he looked at her selection of dinosaur stuffed animals. One dinosaur in particular seemed to have caught his interest. His preoccupation with the toy gave her a chance to check him out. From the back, he looked to be over six feet tall. He was dressed way more appropriately than she was, in an olive-green, long-sleeved shirt and smart black pants. Normally, she didn't pay much attention to how men dressed, but he looked classy and professional.

He must have heard her approach because he turned around—and froze. He opened his mouth, as if he was about to say something, then closed it. He appeared to be in shock, and Kayla knew why. Her heart knew why. Her entire body knew why.

His green eyes were so familiar that she could barely breathe. She knew this man. She loved this man. And she had thought she was going to marry him.

"Gabe?" Kayla whispered, feeling a little like she was seeing a ghost.

She'd been thinking of him so much lately, he had to be a ghost. Yet, she knew this was real. Because his eyes were blinking, and ghosts didn't blink. Did they even have eyes?

The gorgeous man standing in front of her was definitely Gabe Wademan, except maybe those eyes. She never remembered Gabe's eyes looking so cold. They were always warm. At least, they were warm when they were looking at her. There was no warmth whatsoever in this man's gaze.

"Kayla Conway," he said, his tone short, clipped.

"Yes," she whispered, wanting to step forward. To greet him properly. But it felt as if there were a million walls between the two of them. And the realization that he must be Mr. Kleiner's grandson, which would make him her new landlord, was something she was having trouble swallowing. Or maybe with some luck he just happened to be in town and had stopped by? Maybe she was wrong about him being her new landlord.

"Are you Mr. Kleiner's grandson?" She was proud of herself for sounding stronger than she felt.

"Yes," he said. "You work here?"

"No."

Gabe visibly sighed, seemingly relieved at her answer.

Here we go, thought Kayla. "I own the store," she said.

"Own it?" Gabe's voice raised slightly. He'd rarely raised his voice in graduate school. So he really hadn't forgiven her for never returning. While she was busy missing him, *he* was carrying a grudge over her choice—over the ultimatum *he'd* given *her* in the first place.

"Yes." Kayla lifted her chin.

Gabe took a piece of paper out of his pocket and glanced at it. "I thought Melody Fischer owned this place."

Kayla swallowed hard. "She did, until yesterday when she gave it to me."

"She gave it to you?" Gabe's voice rose even louder.

"Yes," she said softly. "She sold it to me for a cup of coffee."

"And did you think to tell your landlord?" Gabe glanced at the paper again. "According to this email Melody wrote to Alice, she was the one who was going to meet me and tell me some exciting news." He clenched his jaw.

Kayla glanced down at her white sandals before meeting his gaze. "I wrote that email, and *I'm* the exciting news."

Gabe ran his hands through his hair and started pacing back and forth on her newly cleaned wooden floors. After a minute or so, Kayla wasn't sure what she should do. But this didn't feel right at all. They had been separated for two years, and every day, she had imagined what it would be like if she bumped into him. She pictured herself running into his arms. And other days, she begged for his forgiveness. But not once did she picture meeting him because he was her new landlord and nothing more.

"Gabe? Can we start again?"

He instantly stopped pacing. "Start again?"

He looked so flabbergasted, she could have told him she was running for president. Obviously, he thought she meant something else. She could see it in his ice-cold eyes.

"I mean, can we start *this meeting* again?" Unable to stand looking in his eyes for one more moment, she looked at her sandals again and at her pretty, pink toenail polish. She'd gotten a pedicure the other day. So this wasn't a dream. Considering the expression on his face right now, it was more like a nightmare.

"What would you like me to say?"

He spoke softer, and that got Kayla's attention.

"I thought I was meeting Melody Fischer," he went on. "If I'd known I was meeting you, I wouldn't have come."

Kayla's world felt as if it was spinning out of control. She'd woken up this morning wondering how Gabe felt about her. Now she knew. And it made her feel sick. But she couldn't think about all that right now. She had to think about the store she'd been handed.

Having Gabe as her landlord was bad for her. Now that he knew she was the new owner of Magical Toys, would he find a way to break her lease? Melody would be devastated. But Kayla didn't know if he could kick her out—not legally…not unless she couldn't pay the rent anymore. She would have to double check, but she thought she still had ten more months left on the lease.

Kayla sighed. "Look, I understand if you want nothing to do with me. But you're my new landlord, whether you like it or not. So why don't I mail my rent check to Alice every month, so you never have to see me."

Gabe nodded. "That might work. I wish Melody still owned this place and not you."

Kayla bit her bottom lip. "Can we please handle this like adults? This store has been around for years. It's Bella Cove's only toy store, and the folks here love it. You should see all the happy children who come in here. It's nice to watch them pick their favorite toys." Kayla smiled as warmly at him as she could.

Gabe clenched his damn jaw again. She bet he was remembering the times in school when they spoke about their future children playing with their toys and running around in the playground. Kayla blinked back tears that were threatening to fall.

"I would never want to hurt the kind people of Bella Cove."

How did he know they were kind?

"Have you been in Bella Cove long?" Surely, she would have known if he was here. Someone would have told her there was a gorgeous man in town. That was how Bella Cove worked.

"I came here about a month ago when I knew my grandfather was dying."

Kayla cleared her throat. "I'm sorry about your grandfather. I didn't know him as well as Melody did, but he was always nice to me."

Gabe nodded. "I'd been staying at his house in East Hampton since the day he called me. After a week or so, he insisted I visit Bella Cove. So I did."

Kayla's breath caught in her throat. In the two years she had known Gabe, not once had he mentioned that his grandfather owned properties in Bella Cove or anywhere else on Long Island. Yet she had mentioned many times how she'd grown up here and how much she missed it. At any point, he could have mentioned his grandfather, so why hadn't he?

"And what do you think of my small town?"

Gabe ignored her question but continued speaking. "My grandfather said that once he passed on, the house in East Hampton would be mine, along with everything else he owned. But there was a piece of land in Bella Cove that was sacred to him. And after spending a few days here, I decided to check it out. My grandfather was right…it was perfect."

Kayla swallowed hard. "Perfect for what?"

Gabe glared at her. "Perfect to build my house on and settle down."

Kayla was too stunned to speak. When he said settle down, did he mean he had a wife? She didn't see a ring on his finger, but that didn't mean anything. She tried to think of the right response, but there was nothing right about this.

"You look shocked."

"I am." Kayla paused. A million questions were flooding through her mind, but she could only ask the safe ones. "Have you been to Bella Cove before? I mean, when you were growing up?"

Gabe put his hands in his pockets. She should probably ask him to sit in her office, but she still couldn't move.

"I spent a summer or two at my grandfather's house in East Hampton, but he never took me to Bella Cove. He said I wouldn't have appreciated it until now, and he was right."

"I told you I lived in Bella Cove."

Gabe nodded. "I knew there was a chance I'd run into you. But only a small chance. I had no idea I'd be your landlord."

She sighed. "Where's the piece of land?"

Kayla's heart was thudding like crazy. She hoped the land was on the other side of Bella Cove. Far enough away that she wouldn't bump into him too often. The town was small, but as long as he didn't live nearby with whomever he was planning on settling down with, she'd be okay. She wouldn't be happy about it, but she'd survive.

Gabe took his cellphone from his pocket and started scrolling through it. Kayla held her breath the entire time.

"The exact address is 23 Bella View Drive. It's right up there on that hill." Gabe motioned with his head in the direction of the hill.

Kayla knew exactly where it was because she lived on the same street. She briefly closed her eyes. This was not good. To make matters worse, she knew of only one piece of vacant land.

"Do you know where that is?" Gabe asked.

Kayla opened her eyes. "I do." She paused and took a deep breath. "That hill is where I live with my family. Bella View Drive is the street I live on, and the piece of land you own is right above my house. I'm at 21 Bella View Drive, but you must have known this. I gave you my home address when you mailed my clothes back to me." Her face heated up.

Gabe's eyes grew colder, if that were possible. "I didn't remember. I swear."

Kayla looked at her pretty toes again. It didn't matter if he was telling her the truth or not. She couldn't change the situation, although it made her life a hell of a lot more challenging. Her parents didn't even know he existed. Now she'd have to tell them she'd not only dated him but had been planning to spend the rest of her life with him.

And that piece of land had been vacant for generations. Even her nana had wondered who it belonged to. Her pop had tried to find out but couldn't. Her family's house was the highest on the hill. Their property was five acres—second in size only to his, which must be at least six or seven acres. It had the same bay view hers did, except his was slightly higher.

Kayla exhaled a breath she hadn't even known she was holding.

"What are we going to do, Gabe?" she asked, her tone quiet.

He stood up even straighter. "I don't see a problem. We've barely spoken in the last two years. We'll keep it that way. There's no need to speak. You'll mail the rent check to Alice, as you said. I'll be busy building my house, but the land is big enough and private enough that we won't have to see each other."

His words stung painfully hard, but she deserved them.

"Okay. Are you sure you wouldn't feel more comfortable living at the house you inherited in East Hampton?"

Gabe shook his head. "The house I'll be building is perfect to settle down in."

Kayla swallowed. How many times had he used the words *settle down*? She didn't like it one bit.

"Are you married?" She hated asking him, but she needed to know. After all, once the house was built, he would be her new neighbor.

Gabe smirked. "No."

Kayla exhaled. "Fiancée?"

Gabe chuckled. "No."

He might have a girlfriend, but she didn't have the courage to ask that.

"Okay." Kayla wasn't sure what else to say. She had a million more questions, but she could tell from his distant expression he was done answering.

Gabe put his phone back into his pocket. He looked as if he wanted to leave, but she didn't want him to. She wanted to continue talking to him, continue getting to know him again. But she had no right to ask him to stay. If it was up to her, she would ask him every little detail of what he had been up to since she left. She knew he had graduated from checking him out on the internet, but that's all she knew.

She watched Gabe take a deep breath. He hadn't yet asked if she was married or engaged. Did he even want to know? Maybe he didn't even care.

"So you know how to proceed with me from this day forward?" Gabe asked.

Kayla raised her eyebrow.

"You know, mail the rent check to Alice?"

"Yes." Kayla swallowed.

Gabe stared intensely at her, then turned around and started walking toward the front door. Kayla panicked. This felt wrong.

"Gabe?" she said, louder than she'd intended.

It got his attention, though. He stopped walking.

"I was surprised to see you, but I'm glad about it, too." Her heart was beating like crazy.

Gabe smirked. "I wouldn't have seen you if I knew you were here. I told you that."

"I know, but maybe this was fate," she blurted out, then bit her tongue.

"Fate?" Gabe paused. "Our fate was sealed two years ago. You were the one who sealed it." He turned, walked out the door, and slammed it shut.

Kayla leaned against the wall and sank to the floor. She placed her head in her hands. She wanted to cry, felt the tears but they wouldn't flow. In fact, she felt numb. Maybe she was in shock from seeing him again. Or maybe it was the realization that two years ago there was a huge obstacle between them: her family.

During their last phone conversation, he begged her to come back. As difficult as it was, she had to say no. She needed more time to make sure her family could stand on their own two feet again. But it ended up taking them longer than she'd thought. Even though there were so many times she'd wanted to leave them and run back into Gabe's arms, she couldn't. They were her family, and she didn't have the heart to abandon them. She loved them, too. And it hadn't been the time or place for Gabe to meet them, especially since they were all healing over Nana in their own way.

Kayla closed her eyes. Gabe was in Bella Cove. And not only was he her new landlord, he was also building his dream house right next to hers. She knew what his house would look like; they'd discussed it often enough. It would be a white-shingled house with a wraparound porch and windows everywhere. They had both dreamed of a house like that. But she could no longer think that way. Gabe had made it clear he wanted nothing to do with her, and she had to respect that. After all, she was the one who had left him. If only he could understand that she'd had no option.

Kayla sighed. Her first morning as the new owner of Magical Toys had been awful. The love of her life had walked into the store and then right back out. That wasn't how she imagined seeing him again for the first time. But she couldn't dwell on it any longer. Nothing had really changed except her heart. Today, she'd found out he wanted nothing from her. The knowledge hurt, but the only way she'd be able to deal with it was if she threw herself into a project that would get her mind off him. A large project, where she wouldn't have time to obsess about Gabe living here. The only project she could think of was continuing to help her family. She might as well put her almost-a-degree in psychology to good use.

With her newfound determination, Kayla stood and walked to the counter. She picked up the store phone and dialed her sister Lauren. The call went to voicemail.

"Hi, Lauren, I need a little sister time. Would you mind stopping by Magical Toys around four? Love you." Kayla wasn't lying. Even though she lived in the same house as her sisters, she rarely had time to hang out with them alone.

Then she placed a call to her younger sister Sarah, which also went to voicemail. Kayla repeated exactly what she'd said to Lauren.

Kayla felt better. She had a plan. She'd survive Gabe Wademan's unexpected appearance in her life.

"Kayla, Kayla!" The bell rang above her door. Little Ben, a frequent visitor to her store, ran in and gave her a huge hug.

"Hi, honey. How are you?"

The little boy looked up at her, and Kayla's heart clenched. He was four years old, and he had the most beautiful green eyes, just like Gabe's. If she and Gabe had gotten pregnant two years ago like they'd talked about doing, their child would probably look like Ben. The thought brought a lump to her throat. *Huh…*Maybe she wasn't numb after all.

"Mommy said I could get a toy."

Ben's mom, Erica, walked into the store. She was a pretty woman with long, dark hair and blue eyes. Ben's father had joined the military and got shipped out while she was pregnant, and he'd died in combat. Kayla tried to help out by giving Ben free toys, which Melody had completely supported.

"Sorry. I promised Ben I'd buy him chocolate if he cleaned his room, and he did. But instead of chocolate, he wanted a toy."

Kayla smiled, gave Ben a tight squeeze, and walked toward the toys for his age range. "No problem at all."

Erica grabbed Kayla's arm. "I want to pay you this time. I sold some more of my jewelry this month, so I have extra money."

Erica made and sold beaded jewelry, and though her business did well enough to support her and Ben, it normally didn't bring in enough for extras. Her jewelry business also allowed her to raise Ben without having to work a typical nine-to-five job and be away from him all the time. Kayla respected her for that.

"It's my pleasure to help you out in any way I can. Plus, by giving you a free toy, it helps me out, too."

"Really? How?" Erica gave Kayla a skeptical look.

Kayla looked at Ben, who already seemed to have picked a toy he wanted—coincidentally, the same dinosaur stuffed animal Gabe had been checking out.

"Because you're constantly spreading the word about my store. And now, I'm the new owner."

"You are? Congratulations!" Erica gave her a big hug. "I'm so happy for you. This is huge."

Kayla laughed. "Thank you. So how about the next time you work at one of those craft shows in the Hamptons, you take along a stack of my cards?"

Erica seemed visibly relieved. There was no way Kayla would allow her to pay for Ben's toy. This seemed like the best solution. The folks in the Hamptons knew about her store and frequently visited, but she knew the "deal" they'd just worked out would make Erica feel better.

"That's a wonderful idea. I'd love to help you advertise."

Kayla smiled and handed her a bunch of cards from a rack sitting on the register desk. "Great. Then we both win." Kayla turned to Ben. "Hey, honey. Would you like to take that dinosaur home with you?"

Ben started jumping up and down. "Please, Mommy, please, Mommy."

Erica and Kayla laughed together.

"Okay, sweetie."

"Yay!" Ben threw the stuffed animal up into the air.

Kayla kneeled down and met him at eye level. "Ben, do you promise to take care of him?"

"I will," Ben responded.

If Ben hadn't chosen the stuffed animal, Kayla had been thinking of sending it to Alice and asking her to give it to Gabe as a peace offering. But it was probably a silly idea, and now Kayla wouldn't be able to anyway. The little boy loved the stuffed animal, and she wouldn't want to hurt him for anything in the world.

"I'm glad to hear it. Give him a hug every day and tell him you love him."

Ben ran toward the front door. "I will. Thank you, Kayla," he yelled as he ran out the front door.

Erica followed after him, but when she reached the door, she stopped and turned toward Kayla.

"Thank you, Kayla. I really appreciate it."

Kayla smiled as Erica left, closing the door behind her. Kayla used to tell Gabe every day how much she loved him and now she couldn't. She hoped she could remain strong with him living in town, that she wouldn't break down and tell him every thought she'd had about him these last two years. Then again, from the way he'd behaved earlier, he probably wouldn't even care. She'd crushed him by not returning and she was too much of a coward to tell him the full reason why she picked her family over him.

3

AS KAYLA EXPECTED, Lauren was the first to arrive that afternoon. For the last few years, she'd worked at a real estate office part-time in her ongoing search for a rich man. So far, she had only met married men who'd tried to flirt with her, but unless the conversation was business-related, she usually ignored them. It was challenging to meet single, eligible men in Bella Cove. Most were either married, in their early twenties and still trying to find themselves, or artists who hid in Bella Cove to escape the rest of the world. Kayla had spoken to some of the artists a few times, but mostly, they kept to themselves. Every so often, she'd see one of them painting by the bay or taking photos. Most seemed to be extremely interesting people but loners, introverts.

At first, Kayla thought the best solution for Lauren would be to move to Manhattan. Kayla would have given Lauren enough of Nana's money to live there for free for an entire year. Nana would definitely consider this an emergency, and that was one of the rules her grandmother had listed before she died—taking care of family emergencies.

Kayla worked hard alongside their business manager of over twenty years. Mr. Goldstein made sure all their bills were paid and made certain they had enough funds for everyone in her family to survive. The furniture business still brought in a small fortune, so her dad and Matt also got a salary from there. The rest of the money was added to Nana and Pop's money. Her family was all in agreement with the arrangement, as it made everyone prosper.

Everyone except Josh. Kayla refused to give him a dime. Not now, anyway. And even though he worked at the furniture factory, he had to work off the damage he'd done. If he didn't, Kayla would go to the police in a heartbeat and tell them everything.

But when Kayla offered Lauren more of Nana's money to move, she had refused. Lauren loved Bella Cove and had no intention of leaving, which made finding her a husband a difficult task. But Kayla was not giving up hope. She also wanted to teach Lauren that she didn't need a man to be happy. First and foremost, she had to be happy within herself.

Lauren's biggest problem was that she always looked so miserable, but Kayla had an idea to change that…

"Hi, Kayla." Lauren entered the store smiling, which was a good sign.

"Hi, honey." Kayla walked over to her and gave her a huge hug, hoping her plan would work. "So what do you think?" She waved her arm in the air to indicate the store.

She watched Lauren take it all in. First, she walked to the baby section and picked up the rattles and began shaking them. Then she picked up some magic wands and some dolls. She remained silent as she studied all the toys, which made Kayla nervous.

"The store looks exactly how it looked when I visited last week when Melody owned it."

Kayla laughed. "I know, dork, but I wanted your opinion on how I can enhance the place. Since the store is mine now, I'm going to be changing it a little."

"What are you going to do?"

"I thought I'd bring the dollhouse castle from the house and put it here somewhere. You know, the one we played with when we were kids?"

Lauren giggled. "That was the ultimate dollhouse."

"That's what I thought. I figured while the children are here, they can play with it while their parents shop. I also want to paint a yellow border on the ceiling and paint hearts on it, or something, to make the store more charming."

Lauren beamed. "I totally agree. It's a great store, but if you add more of your flair to it, it'll be even better."

Kayla smiled wide. Maybe her plan would work.

"Hello, beautiful ladies." Sarah barged into the store as if she owned the place, then she stopped dead in her tracks. "Oh, my God, I love it here."

Kayla had an urge to jump up and down, but she restrained herself. Unlike Lauren, Sarah rarely visited Kayla here. The last time was probably over a year ago.

"You do?" Kayla asked.

"Yes, but you need to add snowflakes."

"It's summer, Sarah. Where am I going to get snowflakes?"

Sarah dropped her pink purse on the counter and then turned all the way around, taking in the store. "I don't mean real snowflakes, silly. Fake ones."

"Why would customers want to see fake snowflakes in the summertime?" Kayla asked as she walked to the counter and placed Sarah's purse in a drawer.

"Because winter in Bella Cove is beautiful. And it'll remind everyone they need to buy toys for the upcoming holiday season."

"She has a point," Lauren chimed in.

Winter in Bella Cove *was* especially beautiful. Snow covered Main Street, making the small shops stand out. During the holiday season, white and colored lights were everywhere. Unlike in the summer, there were no boats on the bay, which brought an even more peaceful feel to the town.

"I think you're right," Kayla said.

Both of her sisters had the biggest smiles on their faces. But now it was time to put her plan into action.

"So, I have an idea."

"What is it?" Lauren asked.

"Come and sit on the floor with me." Kayla motioned for them to sit. As children, they would always sit on the floor and talk. Those were the times when they spoke from their heart.

"I knew there was a reason you called us both down here," Sarah blurted out.

Kayla responded honestly. "You're right."

"What's wrong?" Lauren asked, sounding genuinely concerned.

"Nothing's wrong. I'm relieved you two love the store."

They both nodded.

"We really do," Sarah said excitedly.

Kayla smiled. "I'm glad to hear it. You see, I'm kind of stressed. When Melody owned this place, I worked for her. With me around, she had time to look for different toys to buy and time for all the accounting that goes into running your own store. But now I need that, too. I need help." Kayla looked at both of her sisters, hoping they would understand what she was saying. She wasn't being completely honest, as she could run the store easily, but she thought this was the perfect solution to help her sisters. If Lauren worked here, she would be happier than she was working at the real estate firm. She wouldn't have the pressure of maybe meeting *the one* every day. And if Sarah worked here, maybe it would teach her to hold onto a job. It would become more of a family business. She flitted from job to job, but she wouldn't do that to Kayla.

"I'd love to work here, but I have a habit of leaving every job I have," Sarah said, playing with the holes in her jeans.

"Maybe you wouldn't leave here. I thought if I brought you both in, it'd be fun."

"What about my real estate job?" Lauren asked.

Kayla placed her hand on Lauren's arm and squeezed. "Are you happy there?"

Lauren sighed. "I hate it, but I thought by working there, I might meet my future husband."

"And has that worked out for you?"

Lauren shook her head. "No."

Kayla smiled softly. "You seem happy here."

"I love the idea of working in a toy store, and I know I have to quit the real estate firm. It's not working for me the way I thought it would," said Lauren. "Besides, it'd be fun, and if we all work together, it'd be incredible." Lauren paused. "What do you think, Sarah?"

"I'm already thinking of different ways to make the store even more successful, but I'm scared I may want to leave anyway."

"You might," Kayla acknowledged. "Or you may love it so much you'll want to stay. Why don't you try it?"

"Okay," she said and sighed dramatically. "I'm in. Lauren?"

"I'm going to give my two weeks notice to the real estate firm, but I think they'll let me leave right away. Once an employee wants to quit, they usually make them leave on the spot."

Kayla clapped her hands. "Woohoo! Group hug."

Her sisters hugged her and laughed. Nana would be proud. But Kayla's good mood only lasted a few moments. She already missed Gabe, and he had only left four hours ago.

"Hey, guys? There's something else I need to tell you."

"Is it something we still need to be sitting on the floor for?" Sarah asked.

Kayla bit her bottom lip—a bad habit when she was anxious, she knew. "Yes."

"Uh-oh," Lauren said.

Kayla sighed. "I don't even know how to say this."

"Okay, now you're making me nervous," Sarah said, sitting forward.

"No, it's not bad." Kayla briefly closed her eyes. "It's just strange saying it out loud."

"What is it? You can tell us anything," Lauren said, putting her arm around Kayla's shoulders.

Kayla smiled softly. "I know, and I always have. Which is why I'm telling you this now."

Sarah grabbed her hand. "Josh drank again. Didn't he?"

"What? No. I mean, I'm sure he will, but today he's sober."

Sarah and Lauren both sighed.

"Gabe is here. In Bella Cove," Kayla admitted.

"Gabe?" Lauren asked.

"Yes, you know, my ex."

"Gabe Wademan?" Sarah shouted. "You mean the guy we never met because we were shitty sisters and never visited you at school?"

Kayla laughed. "Yes, that Gabe. The love of my life." She paused. "I think about him every day. He's constantly in my head. I just haven't said anything to you guys because with everything the family's been through, I try not to burden you with my issues."

"We know, Kayla," Lauren chimed in.

"Yeah, we may not say anything, but we know you miss him." Sarah squeezed Kayla's hand. "So…tell us about Gabe. Why is he here? Does he want you back?"

"Did he come to sweep you off your feet and tell you how he can't live without you?" Lauren added, giggling.

Kayla wished that was the case. "No, those days are done," she said. "He's here as my new landlord."

"Get out," Sarah said, sitting up on her knees. "He's the new landlord here?"

Kayla nodded. "It gets worse. You know that piece of land next to our house?"

"Yes, it's part of our yard now."

"It's not." Kayla paused. "Gabe's grandfather, my old landlord, died. Apparently, he had bought the land next to ours, and now it belongs to Gabe."

"No way," Sarah exclaimed.

Both Sarah and Lauren sat with their mouths hanging open.

"So he's not only my landlord, he's also going to be our neighbor once his house is built."

"Holy crap, Kayla. You either have really bad karma or this is the most beautiful love story I've ever heard." Lauren hugged her sister.

"It's not a love story. Gabe wasn't even happy to see me."

"He's just shocked…unless he knew you were here?" Lauren speculated.

"He knew I lived in Bella Cove, but he had no idea I owned this place or even worked here."

"So what are you going to tell Mom and Dad?" Sarah asked.

Kayla groaned. "I can't tell them about Gabe now. I never told them about him at school. I should have. I know I should have."

Lauren shook her head. "No way should you have told them. They both are always super-judgmental toward the guys we date."

"And Mom would have freaked when you told her he's from California. She wanted you to move back to Bella Cove the second you left."

Kayla closed her eyes again. "And I never told Josh or Matt either."

"But Josh is all screwed up, even though he's trying, and Matt will only want to interrogate Gabe."

Kayla opened her eyes and looked at the floor that needed to be swept again. She'd just swept it this morning. This place accumulated so much dust. "I can't tell any of them now. Mom is finally getting better, and I don't want Dad to worry about this."

"I agree," Sarah said.

Lauren nodded. "Let's just keep it between us for the time being."

"Is that what Nana would have done?" Kayla asked.

"Nana was married when she was eighteen. She didn't have problems like we do."

Kayla smiled softly. Her sisters always made her feel better. "Thanks, guys."

"For what? You're always here for us. Let us at least keep your secret for you." Lauren kissed Kayla on the cheek.

"We better meet him this time," Sarah joked.

"Since he's my new landlord and our soon-to-be neighbor, I'm sure you will," Kayla said, already dreading that moment. It wasn't as if she didn't want her sisters to meet him. But he used to be her almost fiancé, and now he wasn't. How would she introduce him? *"Lauren and Sarah, this is the man I planned to spend the rest of my life with"*? Talk about awkward! Well, there was nothing she could do about the situation. Sooner or later, Gabe and her sisters would run into each other. Her parents were her real issue.

"Come here." Kayla pulled Lauren and Sarah close and hugged them tightly. Talking to her sisters made her feel much better. Knowing they had her back helped her believe everything would be okay. And as long as she kept her distance from Gabe, it would be.

Once her sisters left, Kayla logged onto her computer and wrote out her to-do list for the next day. First thing, she would go over her accounting and figure out a way to pay her sisters fairly. The only way she could think of was to give herself a lesser salary, but that was okay. Nana provided enough that she didn't need extra money.

Her sisters had left feeling so excited about the store. Sarah had great ideas to draw in more customers, and Lauren wanted to rearrange some of the toys to highlight ones that were more popular.

Kayla sighed. Today had been an especially long day. Not only was it her first day as the owner of the toy store, but she had also seen Gabe. She couldn't believe it. The entire situation felt surreal. After leaving graduate school early, she'd thought she'd never see him again. She'd wanted to…desperately… but she'd known the odds were against her.

And he was angry. She would never forget the look on his face when he came home from class that day, and she told him she was leaving the next morning and didn't know when she'd return. He'd already been looking for a ring, and they'd been planning to meet each other's families when the time was right. But for her, the time had never been right.

On the phone one night, not that much later, she wasn't surprised when he asked her to return to him either now or never. In his eyes, she broke up with him. But she had to be honest with Gabe; she owed him that much. From the cold way he had looked at her earlier, it was obvious he hadn't forgiven her. And she hadn't forgiven herself either.

Kayla stared at the empty space where the dinosaur stuffed animals sat, where Gabe had been looking earlier. Suddenly, she remembered…she'd seen another stuffed dinosaur in the storage room earlier, one just like the toy he'd been looking at so warmly. Immediately, she ran back there and found the dinosaur in one of the newly opened boxes. She held it to her chest. This stuffed animal would soon be in the arms of Gabe, which was where she wished she was…where she would have been if the circumstances were different.

She walked into her office and grabbed a piece of stationary that read Magical Toys, plus an envelope and a pen. On the envelope, she wrote:

> *Alice,*
> *Please give this to Mr. Wademan.*
> *Thank you so much,*
> *Kayla*

Inside the card, she wrote:

> *Gabe,*
> *A peace offering.*
> *Kayla*

She wanted to write *Love, Kayla,* but that seemed wrong.

Besides, she hoped she was doing the right thing by even sending him the darn thing. But she had to do something. Anything to lighten the tension. After all, he was her new landlord and her soon-to-be neighbor.

Kayla sighed. She was lying to herself. That wasn't the real reason she was sending him the dinosaur. She missed him, and she hated how he'd looked at her, as if she was someone he didn't know. Someone he had never been intimate with. Someone who hadn't made love to every inch of his body.

Kayla would ask Sarah to drop the package off to Alice tomorrow. She was sure her sister would love to finally meet Gabe. Tonight, she needed to get home, take a long bath, and somehow, prepare herself for Gabe Wademan living in her town and maybe being back in her life.

4

THE NEXT MORNING, Kayla arrived at work bright and early. The bath last night had done wonders. She gave the dinosaur stuffed animal to Sarah to give to Alice. Her sister should have been back at the shop thirty minutes ago, so Kayla hoped everything had gone okay. It would have been smarter to ask Lauren to do it, but the real estate firm had wanted her to work one more day. Whether Lauren realized it or not, she was ending one chapter in her life and starting another.

Kayla knew that feeling well. She missed her dream of becoming a top psychologist. Was Gabe working as a psychologist? She wished she had asked him yesterday. Obviously, he had taken over his grandfather's properties and responsibilities, but he would have made an amazing therapist. In school, he had told her that after graduating, he planned to work for his dad and then eventually open his own private practice like his dad had. By now, that dream might have been a reality. She wondered if his name was Dr. Gabe Wademan. If that was the case, she had addressed the envelope to Alice incorrectly.

Her main concern was Alice finding out about her and Gabe's past and telling everyone. Even though their office was in East Hampton, word spread quickly around here. She also imagined Alice would be attracted to Gabe. Alice was older, but she was attractive. And he was gorgeous, after all. Thinking along those lines, though, wasn't helping Kayla's mental state. It would be smarter not to imagine things like that at all.

In the bath last night, she'd contemplated telling her parents about their soon-to-be new neighbor, but she thought it would be best if they ran into Gabe on their own. What was the point in telling them, anyway, when there was nothing to tell? She had no future with Gabe. He'd made that pretty clear yesterday. Nana always taught Kayla there was no point in living in the past, as it would only bring you down. Her grandmother had been right, of course. Nana was always right.

"Hi, beautiful, I'm here," Sarah called as she ran into the store.

"Did you have any problem finding the office?" Kayla asked, relieved to see her sister.

Sarah ran to Kayla and gave her a huge hug.

"Whoa, what was that for?" Kayla laughed.

"Because I love my new job already." She was beaming.

"I'm so glad, but why?"

"Because I just met our sexy new landlord who used to date my beautiful sister." Sarah giggled.

Kayla made herself busy by dusting the books and restacking them. Cleaning always made her feel better. "You met Gabe? Or maybe I should call him Mr. Wademan since he's my landlord?"

Her sister went behind the cash register counter and sat on the stool.

"You can call him Gabe. He let me call him by his first name. Besides, he may be your landlord, but he was once your boyfriend," Sarah said. "Oh my God, Kayla. You sent me pictures of him when you were at school, but they did not do him justice. He's fucking gorgeous. Major eye candy. I introduced myself and told him I'd be working here, in case he wanted to pop by for a visit." Sarah giggled again.

Kayla's heart clenched. "Remember, Sarah, you said it yourself: he's our new landlord and my ex. He's still upset with me for the way I left. We don't want him to raise our rent."

As Kayla dusted the books, she noticed her hands were shaking. If her back wasn't facing Sarah, her sister would have definitely noticed. Having Gabe in town was too much, especially since there was no way Kayla could avoid him.

"I know. You don't have to tell me that. And I didn't tell him that I know you guys dated."

Kayla briefly turned toward her sister and smiled. "Thank you. I appreciate that."

"Anyway, there were boxes all over the office, and Alice was running around packing everything up. He told me he's moving offices. Do you want to know where he's moving to?"

Kayla's heartbeat faster. "Where?"

"Across the street. Right next to the art supply store. So there'll be no need for him to pop by and see us. We could randomly leave the store at the same time he's leaving his office."

Sarah giggled again, which was getting on Kayla's nerves.

"Please don't," she said sternly.

Sarah stopped laughing. "What?"

"You know. Flirt with Gabe. You can flirt with anyone in the entire world, but please don't flirt with him."

Sarah raised her eyebrows. "Do you want to get back together with him?"

"I only saw him one time. I can't make that decision, especially since he wasn't being warm. But I do want him to respect us." Kayla didn't want Gabe to think badly of her sister. She loved Sarah, but she tended to flirt shamelessly with anyone and everyone in Bella Cove. Unfortunately, she had that reputation.

"Are you mad at me?"

"No."

"Are you telling me the truth? Because I promise, I'd never go for Gabe. He was your boyfriend. I hope you don't think I'm *that* kind of girl."

Tears welled up in Sarah's eyes. She had worked at the store only an hour, and already, Kayla was messing things up.

"Of course I know you wouldn't." Kayla exhaled. "I'm sorry. Gabe being here is really messing with my head. Plus, I'm stressed about taking over this place. You know, all the new responsibilities." She tried to smile.

"But you love responsibilities. In fact, you thrive on them."

Several customers walked in, so Kayla and Sarah couldn't talk anymore. She meant to ask Sarah if Gabe had liked the dinosaur. One of the customers was Meredith, an adorable nine-year-old, who was accompanied by her mom. Meredith was intelligent for her age and became bored easily. Sometimes, after coming into the toy store, they'd leave empty-handed and instead go to the bookstore farther down on Main Street.

Sarah jumped off the stool eagerly to see if she could help them. Kayla was grateful, but she knew Sarah's real reason for welcoming the interruption. She was afraid Kayla might try to start a heart-to-heart talk about Sarah's flirting and her view on marriage. One day, they would have that talk, but now was definitely not the right time. Sarah's flirting habits weren't as much of a problem as were her views on love. Every time Kayla tried to find out why, her sister refused to speak.

It was nice watching Sarah with Meredith, though.

"So most toys bore you. I understand; most toys bore me, too," Sarah said to Meredith.

That's a lie, Kayla thought. Sarah loved toys.

"You get bored, too?" Meredith asked.

"Yes. If I was to get any toy in the store, I'd get a journal."

"But journals are just empty notebooks."

Sarah smiled and moved a piece of dark hair out of Meredith's eye. Her mom stood there, stunned. Sarah didn't know it, but Meredith didn't like anyone touching her.

"You're right, Meredith. But look at this one." Sarah grabbed a large box with a journal inside. "This journal is my favorite. You see, there are different-colored rhinestones inside. First you decorate the journal however you like, and then inside on these blank pages, you write all your thoughts. It's fun."

"Mom said sometimes my thoughts aren't nice."

"I have thoughts like those, too. Do you want to know what I do when that happens?"

"What?"

"I write them in my journal, and then I don't think about them anymore, and I feel better."

Meredith looked as if she was considering Sarah's words.

"If I did that, maybe Mom wouldn't punish me for saying my thoughts out loud. And then when I talk, I'll only say happy things."

Sarah knelt down and looked Meredith directly in the eyes. "It's okay to not always feel happy, but I think the journal will help you get your feelings on paper. And it'll be your own, so you can make it look as pretty as you'd like."

Meredith turned toward her mom. "Can you please buy me this journal, Mom? I promise to take care of it."

Her mom agreed. Kayla took the journal from them and rang it up, showing Sarah how to add the information into the computer and run the customer's credit card through. Melody had put a lot of money into accounting software specifically for retail businesses and Kayla was grateful. Sarah seemed to be grasping it quickly.

Once Meredith and her mom left, Kayla grabbed Sarah's hand.

"I'm proud of you," Kayla said.

"You are?"

"Yes, you gained the respect of two people in Bella Cove. And you didn't have to flirt to do it. If you acted like your brilliant self to everyone in this town, can you imagine how many more people will love and respect you as much as I do?"

Sarah kissed Kayla on the cheek. "Point taken." Then she straightened up the shelf with the journals.

The rest of the day passed in a blur. Tons of customers came in, which kept the sisters busy. Sarah was doing great though. Better than Kayla had anticipated. And she seemed really happy, which made Kayla happy, too.

Every so often, Kayla glanced out the window at the storefront where Gabe was moving his office to. About an hour earlier, a moving truck had arrived filled with boxes. Shortly afterward, Alice showed up and began instructing the movers as they unloaded the truck. Alice's long, dark hair flowed down her back. Usually, she wore it in a stark bun. Kayla couldn't help but speculate if Alice had worn it differently to impress Gabe. Not for the first time, Kayla wondered if he already had a girlfriend. But thinking that way only made her crazy. She'd have to stop.

Finally, briefly, she saw Gabe. He was wearing jeans and a red polo shirt. He used to wear jeans all the time at school.

He must have sensed her looking because he turned toward her. Then he ran to the moving truck and took out the dinosaur. He held it up and nodded. Then he smiled softly. What did that nod mean? Something else she'd probably analyze to death.

Sarah left at five to go to the gym, while Kayla looked over their sales for the day until closing at six. On her way out, she glanced over at Gabe's office, but the lights were off and the place appeared closed.

She wasn't ready to go home quite yet. Instead, she walked along Main Street, checking out all the pretty storefront windows. Some nights when she'd walk here, she'd pretend she was living in the 1800s. That was how Bella Cove felt to her. And the way her family was structured made her feel as if she really was living way back then. Once her family was a little more stable, she'd feel as if she'd honored Nana's wishes. Kayla would still make sure the family stayed close, and she'd continue guarding her grandmother's money, but other than that, she'd be free to make different choices for herself, and she craved that.

Kayla walked past the bay. Instead of going to her house up the hill, she made a right and headed toward Matt's place. He lived in a pretty brick colonial overlooking the bay. Matt brought in a mid-six-figure income from the family's furniture business, so it wasn't imperative that Jessica continue to work, but she was a third-grade teacher at Bella Cove Elementary, and she seemed to like her job.

As Kayla walked up their brick path, she felt like butterflies were doing somersaults in her stomach. Matt was working late, so she'd have time alone to talk with Jessica. She wondered if Nana had ever gotten nervous when she had to deal with a family issue. Kayla doubted it.

She rang the doorbell and waited for what felt like an eternity before Jessica opened the door. She looked surprised to see Kayla, and also a little angry.

"Hi, Kayla. Is everything okay?"

"Everything's great. I didn't see you at my celebratory dinner the other night, so I came to see how you're doing."

That annoyed look appeared in Jessica's eyes again. "Oh, yes. Congratulations. Matt said the dinner was nice. I'm usually wiped out when I come home from work. If I came to dinner, I would have fallen asleep."

Kayla sighed inwardly. Whenever Jessica's family had an important dinner, Jessica would go—work night or not—and most of the time, she'd cook for them, too. Kayla understood Jessica loved her family and put them first, but she rarely spent time with Matt's family. And Kayla could tell it was beginning to bother her big brother.

Kayla took a deep breath. This wasn't going to be easy, and from the way Jessica was holding the screen door only slightly open, she clearly didn't want Kayla to come inside. But this was too important to ignore.

"May I come in?" Kayla asked, her tone sweet as sugar.

The annoyed look in Jessica's eyes intensified, but Kayla wasn't about to back down. She had to say her piece. Matt was too important to her.

"Of course."

Jessica moved away from the door so Kayla could step inside. She sat on the couch, pretending to make herself at home. After all, this was her brother's house, too. She should feel at home.

Jessica swallowed hard. "Would you like a drink?" It was obvious she didn't want to offer Kayla anything.

"No, I'd like you to sit, so I can say what I have to say and then leave you to your alone time."

Jessica sat on the chair, facing the couch but barely looking Kayla in the eye.

Kayla inhaled deeply. "Do you love Matt?"

Jessica sat up straighter. "Of course I do. He's my husband."

"A lot of women don't love their husbands. Let me rephrase the question: Are you in love with my brother?"

"Of course," she said softly.

Kayla smiled. "I'm relieved to hear that."

Jessica shifted in her chair. "Why would you think I don't love him?"

Kayla knew Jessica loved Matt. Whenever she looked at him, her expression told everyone how she felt. That wasn't the issue.

"I thought you loved him, but I've been concerned. Matt comes with a family he loves, and we love him back. I know you're close to your family, just like we're all close." Kayla paused. "And I love that you and Matt have that and a million other things in common. But from what Matt tells me, he goes to all your family dinners and special events, and he does so willingly because he loves you. And I know my brother. If he didn't want to see your family, he wouldn't. He can be pretty stubborn when he wants to be."

Jessica laughed. "That's true."

"Yet you haven't seen us in months. I understand the pressure of having a tight-knit family. But sometimes, Matt wants you on his arm. He's proud of you. And because Matt loves you, we love you, too. I miss seeing you." Kayla paused and looked Jessica directly in the eyes. "I guess what I'm asking is if you'll give us a chance. If you get to know us and you hate us, you never have to see us. But maybe you'll like us in a different way than you like your family."

Jessica sighed loudly. Maybe this was a bad idea after all.

"Kayla, it's not that I don't like you guys; it's just…my family can be pretty overwhelming. Between them and work, I don't have time to cultivate any other relationships."

Kayla stood. "All I'm asking is that you try. And in turn, if you have to miss an event here and there because you're too tired, we'll be more understanding."

Jessica nodded. "Okay."

Kayla smiled gently. "I'd like to be your friend if you'd let me."

Jessica smiled back. "I'll do my best."

Kayla gave her a brief hug. "It was good seeing you, Jessica. Have a good rest of the night."

Jessica walked Kayla out and closed the door behind her. When Kayla heard her sister-in-law click the lock, she laughed to herself.

The sun hadn't set yet, thankfully. Kayla liked walking up the hill to her house in the daylight. Bella Cove wasn't a dangerous area. In fact, she couldn't even remember the last time there had been any kind of major crime here. Everyone knew each other and watched over each other. But there was something slightly different in the air tonight. Bella Cove smelled the same and looked the same. Birds were gliding in the air as they always did at this time of the year. But something was different…

As she continued climbing the hill to reach her house, she knew what—or rather, who—it was. Gabe was here in Bella Cove. She stopped walking and stood there as reality hit. Gabe Wademan was in town. Here. In Bella Cove. She repeated it in her head again. *Gabe's in town.* The shock of seeing him here must be wearing off finally. And for all she knew, right now, he was checking out the piece of land he was planning to build his house on. Life was strange.

When Kayla reached her house, she walked to the back porch, trying to ignore the piece of land next to hers. How many times had she stared at it and not paid any attention? How many times had she played hide and go seek over there as a little girl? There had never been a fence around it. In fact, the property blended into their backyard so perfectly, they felt as if it was theirs.

Kayla inhaled the sea air before opening her back door. Her mom was yelling at her dad again. It was getting increasingly hard to keep them together.

"Mom, why are you yelling?" she asked.

"Because your father put mustard all over the turkey dinner I made him."

Her mom was cleaning a pot and her dad appeared to be eating his dinner as quickly as he could.

"Mom, Dad has always put mustard on his food. Ever since I was a kid."

"Well, I'm sick and tired of it. It takes me a long time to make dinner for the family, and it's bad enough we don't all get to eat together. But when I see your father sneak into the fridge and grab mustard, I get irate." Her mom scrubbed furiously.

"I wasn't sneaking. I never sneak. Kayla, have you ever known me to sneak into the fridge? I'm a grown man who works hard all day long. If I want to put mustard on my dinner, then I will."

Kayla ran her hands through her hair. It had been a long day. All she wanted to do was run to her room and take off the blue sundress she had worn in case Gabe stopped by her store.

"Every time you slather mustard on my food, I want to pour it over your head," her mom shouted.

"Enough, both of you." Kayla placed her hands on her hips and faced her dad. "Dad, did you like the meal Mom made for you tonight?"

Her dad stopped eating and looked up at her. "It was delicious."

"Then why did you put mustard on it?"

"He slathered it on," Kayla's mom chimed in.

"Mom, stop. We're going to get to the bottom of this. You've had the same argument for years, but tonight, this issue will be resolved." Kayla exhaled in frustration. "Okay, Dad. Why do you add mustard to Mom's food?"

"My dad used to do it when I was growing up. I took on the habit. I sort of became addicted to mustard, I guess."

Her dad seemed to be taking the conversation seriously. She'd known he would, and she also knew he would answer honestly. Her dad didn't have a mean bone in his entire body.

"Thank you. Could you try to add less mustard, so you can taste Mom's food better?" Kayla asked.

"Are you capable of that?" Kayla's mom butted in again.

Her dad put his silverware on his plate and sat farther back in his chair.

"I love the food you make, Lynne. I always brag to our friends about how great of a cook you are. I admit, I'm addicted to mustard. I'm sorry. I'll try to lessen it."

Her mom's expression turned to shock. Kayla gazed at her dad, trying to remember the last time she'd heard him compliment her mom. It had been a long time... too long. She was about to thank her dad for his honesty, but her mom spoke first.

"Thank you. That's nice to hear." Her mom put the pot on the counter and ran her hands down her apron. "I understand addiction. I used to be addicted to diet soda. Remember, Kayla?"

"Yes, I remember." Kayla thought it ironic they could talk about their mustard and diet soda addictions so easily, but they struggled to find a way to talk about their son Josh's addiction.

"Thank you for trying to reduce the amount you put on your dinner, Paul."

Kayla's dad continued eating, and her mom went back to cleaning the pot. With another family disaster averted, Kayla grabbed a plate and opened the fridge. She placed some turkey on it with some mashed potatoes.

"Do you want me to heat that up for you?" her mom asked.

"No, thank you. I think I'm going to take this outside." Without another glance at her parents, she opened the back door and stepped onto the porch. She put her plate on the table and stepped close to the railing, filling her lungs with the fresh air. The wind gently touched her face, soothing her like it always did. Then she felt a prickly sensation, as if she wasn't alone.

She looked to her right. Standing on his property and staring directly at her was Gabe. He was far enough away they wouldn't be able to hear each other if they spoke, yet it felt as if he was standing on her back porch with her. She wasn't sure what she should do, but staring at him like this didn't feel right. Two years ago, she would have run to him and shared her dinner, but everything was different now…especially the cold look on Gabe's face as he continued to stare at her.

Kayla picked up her plate of food. Maybe she'd go eat in her room instead. As she turned to go back inside, she gave in to the urge to glance at Gabe once more. As she watched, he kept looking back and forth between her and the bay, as if he couldn't stop himself from turning her way. But he was standing there stiff and unwelcoming. And he wasn't smiling.

Kayla groaned and was about to go over and talk to him, but unfortunately, her mom barged through the back door.

"Why aren't you eating? You don't like my food, either?"

With her back to her mom, Kayla rolled her eyes and sat down at the table. "I love it, Mom."

"You have a funny way of showing it." Her mother grabbed the plate from Kayla's hands and then stopped. "Who's that man on the property over there? Do you think he's a trespasser? Is that why you're staring? Should I call the police?"

Kayla inhaled. This conversation was bound to happen sooner or later. She was trying to think of the best way to answer when Sarah ran up the back steps.

"Hi, guys." She smiled.

Her mom turned around. "We're not guys. I'm your mother, and this is your sister."

"Okay, fine. What's my mother and sister looking at?"

Kayla closed her eyes. This was getting worse by the second. She wished Gabe would leave.

"There's a stranger on the land next door," her mom said.

Kayla tried to speak but nothing came out of her mouth. It didn't matter anyway. Sarah ran to the railing to see who they were looking at.

"Oh, that's Gabe Wademan."

Kayla's heart fell. Would Sarah keep her secret? Did it even matter anymore?

"Who's that? Should I call the police?" her mom asked again.

"No. He owns that land. Hey, Gabe!" Sarah yelled. "Gabe!"

There was about an acre between them, and the land curved, hugging the bay. It was hard to hear but not impossible.

Gabe waved and then turned and walked away. How funny. Kayla already felt the loss of him.

"What do you mean he owns the property?" her mom asked.

"Who owns what property?" Her dad picked that moment of all moments to come outside.

Kayla had no choice but to explain who Gabe was, but she didn't want to tell them everything. Right now, she couldn't handle the questions that would definitely come. Maybe once she got used to him being here she would.

Again, Sarah spoke before Kayla figured out what to say.

"Gabe Wademan is his name, and he's also Kayla's new landlord," Sarah said.

Kayla wanted to run up and hug her sister for not divulging any more than that.

"What?" Kayla's mom asked.

"Mr. Kleiner was the landlord of the building where Magical Toys is located. He passed away a few weeks ago and left everything to his grandson, Gabe Wademan. Mr. Kleiner owned the property, too. His grandson wants to build a house on it," Kayla said, making sure to keep her tone neutral.

"Do you know this Gabe fellow, Kayla?" her dad asked.

Kayla swallowed. Three pairs of eyes were staring directly at her.

"He came into the store yesterday and told me about building the house." She didn't have the heart to blatantly lie to her parents. What she said wasn't the whole truth, but at least it was true.

"He also moved his office from East Hampton to right across the street from her store," Sarah added.

"You'll be running into him a lot then. Maybe he's nice," her dad replied.

"Dad, I have a lot on my plate right now. I have no time to date." She was still telling him the truth, at least that part, but he was smart and no doubt sensed there was more to the story. She could see it in his eyes. But he was wrong. Her and Gabe's story had ended.

"He's super nice, Dad, and he's gorgeous," Sarah said.

If Kayla didn't feel so bad that she and Sarah were lying, she'd laugh. She could tell from the twinkle in Sarah's eye that she was having fun playing the lying game. But Sarah shouldn't have told their dad Gabe was gorgeous. That went a little too far.

"He's also your sister's landlord, so be careful, Sarah," her dad said.

"Well, if he's your new landlord and our soon-to-be neighbor, do you think it'd be appropriate for me to cook him a meal?" her mom asked, looking at Kayla.

If it was any other man, it would be the right thing to do. And if she refused, they would be surprised. Kayla always did the right thing. Her stomach felt sick; good thing she still hadn't eaten.

"I think that's a good idea. Maybe we should wait until he starts building his house, though. We don't want to scare the poor man away yet."

Everyone laughed, apart from her dad.

"Is he married, Kayla?" he asked.

Kayla opened her mouth, but her sister answered for her.

"Nope, and according to Alice, he doesn't have a girlfriend, either."

Kayla's heartbeat quickened. Why hadn't Sarah told her that today? That was huge news. If they were alone, Kayla would wring her sister's neck.

Her father seemed to perk up. "Great, well, whenever you think it's appropriate to have him to dinner, we will. And I'll make sure we're all on our best behavior."

Kayla sighed. Sometimes, life felt as if it was slipping through her fingers and there was no way to stop it or control it.

She also wondered if Alice was hoping to be Gabe's girlfriend.

5

ON THE WAY to her family's furniture factory and showroom the next morning, Kayla felt exhausted. Last night, she went to sleep without eating more than a few bites and threw away a large portion of her mom's turkey dinner.

The conversation she'd had with her parents about Gabe was making her sick. Kayla could have told them the whole truth. But she'd kept it from them for the last two years—four, if you counted the two years she and Gabe had been dating. How would she even begin to tell her parents the truth now?

"Mom and Dad, your new neighbor was my almost-fiancé. We were a few months away from being engaged. He was saving up money for a ring, and I loved him more than anything in the entire world."

She could tell them that. But she wasn't ready to expose her heart to them just yet. Some days, she felt as if *she* was the unstable one in the family.

When she arrived at the factory, she opened the heavy door and inhaled. She loved the smell because it reminded her of her Pop. She walked toward the back, where she knew Matt would be. Sure enough, he was lying on the floor with goggles on, sanding down the wood on the bottom of a couch. Pop had taught the men in the family how to make furniture by hand. He used to say his furniture sold well because of the craftsmanship put into every piece. Not all the furniture was handmade, but many of the pieces still were.

Matt saw her standing there but continued to sand the wood. "What's up, beautiful?"

Kayla smiled softly. "Are you mad at me?"

He stopped sanding, looked at her, and continued. "For talking to Jessica?"

Kayla nodded.

"I was when I heard, but I understand why you did it."

"You do?" Kayla leaned against a desk he had recently made.

Matt stopped what he was doing and sat up. He took off his goggles and ran his hands through his hair.

"You want me to be happy."

"I do."

"She makes me happy, Kayla."

Kayla swallowed. "I know she does, but the family wants to get to know her, Matt. You've been married for over a year, and we've barely met her. We want to love her like you do. She's automatically a part of us because she's a part of you."

"She works hard and her family is high maintenance."

"I'm not asking for her to be with us constantly. Once a month would be nice. She needs to make the effort."

Something didn't feel right to Kayla. She paused, then asked, "Is everything okay with your marriage, Matt?"

He inhaled. "We can't get pregnant."

Kayla sighed. That was the last thing she'd thought he'd say. "How long have you been trying?"

"Since we got married. A little over a year."

"Have you gone to see a doctor?"

"Yes. He said nothing was wrong. We even went to a fertility specialist to consider IVF, but Jessica wants to get pregnant naturally or not at all. But it's killing her. I can see it."

"It's not killing her, Matt. It's making her sad."

He ran his hands through his hair again. "Yeah."

Neither of them said anything for a few minutes.

"I'd like to help," Kayla whispered.

"I know Nana made you the matriarch, but there's nothing you can do to fix this."

"I don't consider myself the matriarch. I don't even like that term—you know that. But Nana wanted me to help the family. Please, Matt. Let me keep my word. Let me try."

Matt didn't say anything, and Kayla thought he'd decline her offer. Tell her it was none of her business.

But finally, he nodded. "Okay."

Kayla stood and walked over to him. She knelt down and kissed the top of his head.

"That still doesn't excuse her absence from the family. If anything, we'd add to her support system. We'd be your biggest cheerleaders."

Tears welled up in his eyes. "I know," he said. "Thanks, Kayla."

Kayla left the factory, determined to help Matt and Jessica. There had to be a solution to their fertility issues. At least it would get her mind off Gabe.

She felt a sudden need to rush back to her store. She had allowed Sarah to open herself this morning to give her some extra confidence, but it was time Kayla went to see if everything was okay.

She pulled into her reserved parking spot, grabbed her oversized white Coach purse, and opened the back door of her shop. She stepped inside and froze. Gabe was standing on a ladder, his blue jeans and white t-shirt spattered with paint, apparently because he'd been painting a yellow border along the top of her walls. Kayla stood there and stared.

"Hey, beautiful." Sarah walked out of the storage room with Lauren.

"What's going on?" Kayla directed the question to her sisters, as Gabe completely ignored her.

"You told me you wanted a yellow border around the top of the walls, so I thought it'd be a great idea to surprise you and have it done while you were gone. Then I thought I'd start training Lauren, starting with the storage room. Gabe said he'd let me know if any customers came in."

Kayla's purse dropped to the floor, but she couldn't move to pick it up. Her sisters were staring at her, smiling. Sarah meant well, so Kayla shouldn't be angry, but she was. Unless Sarah had asked Gabe to paint for other reasons. Kayla needed to make it clear to her sisters that having her ex here made her seriously uncomfortable.

"Why did you ask our landlord to paint for us? I was planning on doing it myself." She took a much-needed deep breath, struggling for control as her face heated up.

Sarah put her hands on her hips and glared at Kayla. "Calm down, Kayla. It wasn't like that. When I dropped off the dinosaur for Gabe yesterday at his office, Alice told me that Mr. Kleiner used to paint their office every few years, which left them with a ton of extra paint. She asked if she thought we could use some. I told her I'd ask you, but then I forgot all about it until this morning. So, I called her and asked if they had yellow paint. But I couldn't leave the store to pick it up, so Gabe said he'd drop it off. When he came here, I asked if he had a ladder since I didn't see one. I wanted to surprise you when you got back. He said he did, but he didn't feel comfortable with us using it. He was worried we'd fall, so he asked what we wanted to paint, and I told him. He said he'd do it for us, and then he left to get his ladder. And now here he is, painting the border you wanted."

Sarah whispered the entire story, thank God. Kayla wouldn't have wanted Gabe to hear all that. But when she glanced at him, he was chuckling under his breath. She hated that Gabe was painting for her—why was he doing it, anyway?

"It wasn't a big deal. He's really nice, Kayla," Lauren chimed in, winking at her.

Kayla wanted to scream. Having her sisters spend time alone with him made her feel edgy. Never would she have allowed that. At least, not until after Kayla had a real conversation with Gabe. To clear the air. Now she had to wonder if they'd mentioned her name and what they'd talked about while she'd been gone all morning. Dealing with Gabe as her landlord and not her boyfriend had her all screwed up. She hated it.

Both of her sisters looked upset. Kayla sighed through a wave of guilt. It wasn't Sarah and Lauren's fault. This entire situation was extremely awkward.

She smiled softly. "It's okay. It was nice of you to think of me. I feel awkward about it because he's our landlord...and my ex." She mouthed the last part silently. "But if he volunteered to do it..." Kayla took a deep breath. She didn't want to upset her sisters. But she would need to talk about Gabe again with them. Maybe they thought she was over him. She *was* over him, she supposed, but a part of her couldn't stop thinking about him. And a part of her still loved him.

To her relief, they both returned her smile. Kayla decided to change the subject—or, better yet, maybe get them out of there for a little while until she could find out what Gabe was up to…

"Why don't you both take a break and go get some iced coffees." Bella Coffee Café was a few stores away. They made the best iced coffee drinks and pastries.

"That sounds amazing! I even promise not to flirt with the cutie behind the counter." Sarah clapped her hands.

Kayla laughed as she reached down, picked up her purse, and rummaged through it to find some cash.

"Only if you bring me back a large iced coffee with milk and two packages of raw sugar." Kayla paused. "Gabe, would you like an iced or hot coffee?"

Gabe stopped what he was doing and looked at her. The feeling of panic she'd been trying to stuff down consumed her. She briefly closed her eyes to calm herself. This had been a difficult morning, to say the least.

Gabe nodded. "I'll have the same as you."

He resumed painting, while Kayla had the strongest urge to roll her eyes at him. He'd been listening to every word they'd said. *Figures.* Did he realize the effect he was having on her by being here? Was that his purpose for agreeing to paint her border? He probably liked to torture her. The old Gabe wouldn't, but this was a brand-new Gabe.

She glanced back at her sisters, who were both watching her. Kayla hated feeling as if she was in the spotlight. Her role was to help everyone else out with their problems. She was the one who usually kept her problems to herself.

She put her purse back down on the floor. She'd forgotten she was holding cash to give her sisters. "Do you need money?"

"No, we're good, but are you?" Lauren asked.

Kayla smiled wide. Lauren and Sarah were pretty perceptive, but she wasn't ready to talk about her feelings. Not until she sorted them out for herself. "I'm relieved that both of you are here to help me make this place more successful."

Lauren raised her eyebrow, but Sarah was already grabbing Lauren's hand and pulling her out the door.

"Bye—take your time and enjoy the beautiful day. You've both earned it. Let me know exactly how much it is, and I'll pay you later," Kayla yelled, making sure they heard her before they slammed the door behind them. Unfortunately, she now had to deal with the obvious.

She walked toward him slowly and then cleared her throat. "Hi, Gabe."

He continued painting, completely ignoring her.

"You know you didn't have to do this."

Still, he didn't say anything.

"Gabe," she whispered.

Silence filled the room for what felt like an eternity. Maybe she should have left him alone.

"I'm not doing this for you," Gabe said, continuing to paint and not looking at her.

Kayla sighed with relief that at least he had acknowledged her, even though his words felt like a knife slicing through her heart.

"I understand," she said.

"I don't think you do," Gabe said. "I'm doing it for your sister."

He might as well have punched her in the stomach. Unable to look at him, she looked at her sandals.

"Why? Are you attracted to her?" Her sister was beautiful.

"Both of your sisters are gorgeous, but that's not why I offered to paint."

"Then why?"

She looked up as she felt his eyes on her. He had stopped painting and was staring at her. She felt as if he were staring into her soul with the coldest eyes she'd ever seen.

"I wanted them to get to know me, even if we'll never be family. And I wanted to know them because I never had a chance to do that two years ago."

Kayla clenched her hands into tight fists. "My sisters know about you. About us. I told them when you and I started dating. But I never told my brothers or my parents. And I lied to them last night when they saw you standing on your property."

Gabe gripped the side of the ladder. His knuckles turned white. "I'd like to know why, but it's none of my damn business anymore."

As he looked at her with hatred, shivers ran up her spine.

"Gabe," she whispered. "It feels so weird with you being here like this. I've always envisioned you here as my boyfriend." Kayla cleared her voice. "My fiancé."

He clenched his jaw. "It is what it is," he began. "You never thought I understood why you had to leave. You never thought I understood how Nana passed on the role of rescuing your family." He put the paintbrush down and wiped his forehead with the back of his arm.

When he looked at her again, she saw regret and sorrow. Tears welled up in her eyes. She took a step back so she could breathe.

"Gabe, I swear, I didn't realize it would take so long."

"So, what you're trying to tell me is that your family is still messed up." He huffed, shaking his head. "Your sisters seem fine to me."

"They still have their issues, but then again, you made it clear I didn't have anything in California to return to. You'd given me an ultimatum."

Gabe chuckled, but not because anything was funny. "Because you handled it all wrong. I would have left school with you. I would have been by your side when your nana died. We were a team. We were partners. Or so I thought."

"I couldn't let you do that. I'd have felt awful if I'd stopped you from getting your degree."

Gabe took a deep breath. "But did it even cross your mind to ask me? Because to me, it looked like you just ran."

Kayla's heart was tied up in knots. She had made some terrible mistakes.

"I couldn't let you see my family the way they were. It was the wrong time to introduce you. You heard my mom screaming and sobbing when you called. And her constant screaming fits only scratched the surface. My family was a mess," she admitted, even though she hated bringing up that awful time.

"Well then, tell me, Kayla. Tell me the truth of what happened. Tell me once and for all what kept you from the man you planned to marry."

As Kayla was debating confessing all this to Gabe, her sisters came barging back into the store with their hands filled with coffees. The minute they saw Kayla, they stopped.

"What's going on?" Sarah asked, concern etched all over her face.

She and Lauren looked at Kayla and then at Gabe.

Kayla swiped at the tears that were clearly present in her eyes. They didn't know how she'd ended things with Gabe. With all the chaos in the family, she'd never sat down and told them details. Now wasn't the time, either.

"I was telling Kayla how much my grandfather liked her and the store. Whenever he came in, Kayla made him feel right at home," Gabe said.

Kayla smiled softly. He'd saved her. Now *that* was something the old Gabe would have done. She closed her eyes briefly as beautiful memories flooded her mind.

"When he was on his deathbed, he told me he wanted me to take over all his properties. At first, I rejected the idea. I've never owned properties like these, but then he told me to visit Bella Cove because I'd change my mind. So I came here for a few days. I even visited the store, but someone else was working here," Gabe continued.

Kayla stood there in stunned silence. She knew exactly what he was doing. He had made up a lie to appease her sisters and then ended the lie with some truth.

She wished she had been there that day. Kristina must have been working. She was one of Melody's friends' daughters. Kayla had the flu for a week, and Melody had been on vacation. They'd been desperate for help and grateful when Kristina had agreed to work for a few days.

"I'm glad you agreed to take over your grandfather's properties, even though I'm sure you're sad about him," Sarah said as she smiled at Gabe.

"I appreciate that, Sarah."

She handed him his iced coffee and then gave Kayla hers.

Lauren kept looking at Gabe and Kayla. "We had something similar happen to our family," she finally said.

"Oh, yeah?" Gabe climbed down the ladder and leaned against it while sipping his coffee.

His full attention was on Lauren and what she was about to say.

"Our nana passed away two years ago and gave Kayla the thankless job of acting as the new family matriarch. And let me tell you, our family has a huge amount of issues."

"I may have been given the title, but I don't really believe in it. I like to think of myself as the family helper. That's how I'm honoring Nana. Besides, everyone pitches in and does their share in keeping the family together," Kayla added.

"No," Sarah said. "You're the one who keeps us on the straight and narrow."

"Thank you, but that's not true. We're all in charge of making our own choices."

"We love you." Sarah threw her arms around Kayla's waist.

For a moment, Kayla forgot Gabe was in the room. But then she heard him shift his feet. She glanced over and found him looking at them with an intensity that had been missing in his eyes up until that point.

Kayla stepped away from Sarah. "Look, I want to clear the air for a second," she said, glancing at all of them. "I told Gabe that you both know he and I were together."

"Oh, thank God," Lauren said. "This was starting to feel awkward."

"And you suck at lying," Sarah said, laughing.

Kayla grabbed her sisters' hands. "Thank you for not blurting out to Gabe that you knew about us. Thank you for protecting me."

Lauren threw her arms around Kayla and Sarah. "Sisterly love."

"Sisterly love," Kayla and Sarah said in unison.

"Okay, enough. You guys are making me nauseous," Gabe said as he continued painting.

The sisters laughed.

"Get used it, Gabe," Sarah said.

Kayla's heart clenched. She wasn't sure what Gabe was thinking. He wasn't her boyfriend. Only her landlord. He didn't have to get used to anything when it came to her and her family.

Gabe didn't look at them when he responded. "I could get used to way worse things."

Sarah and Lauren laughed, but Kayla didn't. His response made her heart flutter, but what did it mean? He'd barely been back in her life for two days. Was he thinking he wanted more? Did *she* want more? Well, as he'd said, there could be worse things.

A few minutes later, it was back to work as usual. Gabe finished painting half the wall and said he'd be back to finish another day. Kayla reiterated that she could do it herself, but he said he enjoyed painting. Customers started rolling in, but once business died down a little, she sent Lauren and Sarah home. They'd opened the shop early. They deserved to leave before closing.

As Kayla was about to flip over the shabby-white sign to indicate the store was closed, Ben and his mom, Erica, walked in.

"Kayla!" Ben grabbed her leg and gave her a huge hug.

"Hi, cutie." She hugged him back.

"Sorry, I'm in a bit of a rush. I'm taking classes in acupuncture, and they allow Ben to stay on the side and play. He's very quiet. The only problem is, I need to find something to keep him busy. Do you have a coloring book, by any chance?" Erica asked.

"Of course." Kayla went to grab one of the coloring books with pirates on it when a thought occurred to her. "How do you like acupuncture?"

"I love it. My grandmother taught me when I was young, but I need a proper certification so I can make money with it. I love my jewelry business, but acupuncturists seem to be doing well these days. I thought I could do both."

Kayla handed over the coloring book with crayons and then gently squeezed Erica's hand.

"Can I ask you something? And you'll keep it confidential?" Kayla asked.

"Anything for you. Kayla, you've helped Ben and me more than you know."

Kayla smiled. "My sister-in-law has been trying to get pregnant, but she's struggling. I've heard that acupuncture does wonders for fertility issues."

"You're right. My grandma taught me a lot about fertility. Does she live in Bella Cove?"

Kayla nodded.

"How about I stop by her house tomorrow evening and see what's going on with her?"

"I'd love that, but let me make sure it's okay with Jessica first." Kayla gave her a hug. "I know you're in a rush, so I'll text you her address and confirmation that she's available. Her name is Jessica Conway."

Kayla was so excited that the second they left, she called Jessica and left a message on her voicemail.

"Hi, Jessica. It's Kayla. I have a dear friend who's a customer at my store. She's also an acupuncturist who knows a lot about fertility, and she wants to help you and Matt. If you're open to it, she could stop by your house tomorrow. Please let me know, so I can give her a heads up. Thanks."

Then she texted Matt and told him the same thing. She grabbed her purse, but before she went out the back door to get into her car, she looked out her front window toward Gabe's new office. She had liked seeing him today in her store. Gabe being there felt right but wrong at the same time.

Just as Kayla was about to turn away from the window, Gabe came out of his office door and locked it. He glanced across the street at her store, and she wondered if he sensed her looking at him.

When he was at the store earlier, she'd had such an urge to throw her arms around him. She missed his hugs. He had strong arms, and when he used to hug her, he'd envelop her in his warm embrace. She'd always felt so safe when Gabe had his arms around her. No one else ever made her feel that way. But she didn't know if Gabe still hugged the same way. She didn't know much about him at all now.

Kayla was the first one to look away. Not because she wanted to. She had to exert every ounce of effort to look somewhere other than at him. But she had made a mess of things by leaving him. She'd destroyed them. When the time was right, she would speak her truth. Not that it would make a difference, but she didn't want him to hate her. He was her only true love. Always had been and always would be, no matter what.

KAYLA PULLED INTO THE GARAGE and leaned against the steering wheel with her head in her arms. Today had been an exceptionally difficult day…another one in what was starting to seem like a stretch of them. At the same time, it hadn't been all bad. She was hopeful about helping Matt and Jessica. And her sisters were doing a wonderful job at the shop. They loved working there even more than Kayla did. Not that she didn't enjoy owning her own store…but the heartache she experienced every time she looked at a child's smiling face was killing her. Deep down, Kayla had given up all hope of ever having children. How could she take care of a child when her family sucked up so much of her time? But what she'd noticed and found incredibly odd was that when Gabe had been in the store today, she hadn't felt sad…not even once.

She grabbed her purse and was about to exit her car when the passenger door flew open. Josh sat down, and Kayla screamed.

"Josh, don't ever do that again. Are you trying to give me a heart attack?" She glared at him. He looked terrible. *Now what…?*

"I know, I'm sorry. I'm going crazy, Kayla," he said as he ran his hands through his hair and then down his face, which looked as if it hadn't been shaved in days.

"Maybe you should try showering and shaving. That'll make you feel better."

He slammed his hand on the dashboard, making Kayla jump.

"Nothing will make me feel better except a car. But Dad refuses to buy me one."

Kayla had had enough. She placed her hand on his arm.

"Josh, what's going on with you?" she asked, keeping her tone soft, unthreatening.

He was breathing loudly through his nose. "Nothing."

"Are you struggling to remain sober?"

He glanced at her, then looked straight ahead. One second passed. Then two. "Yeah, I am."

Kayla kept her hand on his arm. "Why are you choosing to be sober, then?"

His eyes remained straight ahead. "For a car."

Kayla shook her head. "I don't believe that."

"It's the truth."

"It may be part of the truth, but that's not the only thing keeping you sober. You don't need a car. You can always take a train or bus out of town. There are solutions, and you know it."

He looked at her. "I work at our furniture factory every single day. I should be able to buy my own car."

"You're right, and I'm sorry. But I personally added up how much the furniture business lost when you gave away our secrets. There are consequences to your actions."

"I understand that, but according to your calculations, I won't be earning money for another two years and three months."

Kayla sighed. "But you have a place to live, I make sure you have new clothes, you have food to eat, and when you want to go out with your friends or on a date, I make sure you have money. As long as you're in Bella Cove, you have to pay off your debt. It's not fair to the family. You harmed us, Josh."

Josh hit the dashboard again. "I can't leave Bella Cove unless I have a car."

"I told you, if you really want to leave, you can take a bus or train." Kayla paused. "I know what's really going on here, Josh. You can't fool me. By staying sober you think that either the family will cave in and start paying you a salary again, or you think I'll cave in and give you some of Nana's money. You know Dad won't give you money because if it was up to him, you wouldn't have been able to even step foot in the furniture factory."

Josh groaned. "I know."

"Yet you keep on trying to push him to give you money. You know he won't, but maybe I will. Because you think I'm weaker than Dad is."

Josh looked at her directly. There was a meanness in his eyes that unnerved her.

"You're not weaker than Dad is, but Nana said on her deathbed that you're in charge of her money. If there was any type of a family emergency, you're to use it. *This* is a family emergency, Kayla. I'm dying here."

Kayla looked at him, stunned. "So you're staying sober so I'll give you some of Nana's money to buy a car." Her heart dived into her stomach. "I don't think you've changed, Josh. You may have fooled everyone in the family, but you haven't fooled me. Even Dad thinks you're calmer now, but I know differently."

"I've been sober for a year. Two months ago, I screwed up and had a few drinks, but I told the family."

"You had no choice. You came home drunk and smelling like alcohol."

"But you were the only one who saw me."

"But I would have told everyone if you hadn't, and you knew that. Still, the only reason you told everyone was so they'd think you were really sorry." Kayla dropped her hand, inhaled, closed her eyes, and leaned back in the seat. "How can I give you Nana's money when you stole her jewelry?"

"But you found it in my room. So maybe I took it, but I didn't sell it."

Kayla glared at him. "This conversation is over, Josh." She grabbed her purse, opened the car door, climbed out, and then slammed the door shut. She knew how to solve so many of her family's problems, but she had no idea what to do with Josh. He was so different when they were growing up. They used to laugh together, and he'd follow her and her sisters around the house. Whenever they had a play date with one of their friends, Josh would come, right up until they became teenagers. Even then, Kayla would go to him if she had a question about a boy. It was too hard to talk to Matt about that stuff. He was the oldest, and extremely protective over her and her sisters, but they could go to Josh. Now she couldn't remember the last time she had gone to him for anything.

She walked into the house and heard Josh following, stomping his feet as if the world had wronged him.

Kayla was about to grab some leftover turkey from the fridge when she saw her parents out on the back porch, talking with Gabe. He seemed to be showing them a blueprint an architect must have drawn for him. He rolled it out on the back table and was pointing to a few things. Kayla had just finished dealing with Josh, and now she had to deal with this. How long had Gabe been here? Maybe he had told them about the two of them. Years ago, he wouldn't have betrayed her like that, but who knew what he might do now?

Kayla inhaled deeply and opened the back door.

"Hi, Mom, Dad, Mr. Wademan." She smiled at all of them, even though she wasn't feeling very pleasant on the inside.

"I'm your landlord and new neighbor. Please, call me Gabe," he said.

He was looking at her in that distant way she disliked, but he also made it clear he hadn't revealed their secret. She was grateful for that at least.

"Gabe is building a spectacular house," her dad said.

Kayla didn't want to look at the blueprint, but she was tempted all the same. She stepped forward and took a peek, then immediately regretted it.

"So the house will be white?" her mom asked.

"Yes. I've always dreamed of living in a large white house."

Kayla's heart clenched. Her first instinct was to run or scream, but she couldn't leave Gabe alone with her parents or make a scene. Gabe was well aware of that.

From what she could tell, the drawing depicted the exact house he had described to her when they were at school. *Their* house. God, this was so unfair. If he had even mentioned he knew of Bella Cove and that his grandfather lived a few miles away, things could have been different, *would* be different now. All she'd known was that he grew up in Los Angeles, and his parents still lived there. In order to marry Gabe, she'd have to live there, too. Gabe made it clear that they'd be working for his dad after graduation.

And she would have done that. She would have remained in California, married him, and worked for his dad, who was some big psychologist, even though her heart had been split. Half of it had been in Bella Cove and half had been with him. But everything changed when Nana died.

"We're so lucky to have a nice new neighbor," her mom said, beaming. "Would you like to stay for dinner?"

Kayla's heart dropped into her stomach. She looked at Gabe, begging him with her eyes to say no. Luckily, he was shaking his head.

"I already ate at my office. I just came here to introduce myself and show you my plans. And also to tell you in advance that I'm sorry for all the noise. They're starting to build tomorrow, and it's going to get really loud."

"Not a problem. It'll be a beautiful house when it's finished," her mom said.

"Thank you."

"But, please, you have to stay for cake at least. I made my favorite crumb cake. You love that cake, don't you, Kayla?"

Kayla swallowed hard. "I do."

"Well then, I can't refuse crumb cake, especially if it's your daughter's favorite."

"I'll get the cake." Kayla's heartbeat sped up. She practically ran inside the house and found the cake on the counter. She took a slightly shaky deep breath and turned around, only to find Gabe standing a few feet away.

"You didn't need to come in. I have the cake."

"It's the gentlemanly thing to do, to help."

She scooted around Gabe and glanced outside. Her parents were still there, looking over his blueprint.

"You didn't need to come here," she whispered.

"I did. Tomorrow, they're going to start building my house, and I wanted to warn your family. I know it'll be disruptive, and I wanted to apologize and introduce myself at the same time. It's called having good manners, Kayla."

Kayla moved to his side, so she could face him and still see her parents out of the corner of her eye. Her dad was already looking back, a suspicious expression on his face.

"It wasn't necessary." Kayla kept her voice down.

"It was the right thing to do." Gabe's jaw was clenched.

Kayla couldn't take this anymore. Gabe being around her family was too much.

"Why didn't you tell me at school that your grandfather lived in the Hamptons near Bella Cove?"

"I didn't know. I knew he lived in the Hamptons, but I had no idea that was near Bella Cove."

"But it was on Long Island." She raised her voice, then quickly looked at her parents to make sure they hadn't heard.

Luckily, her mom was talking to her dad, no doubt discussing Gabe's new, "beautiful" house.

"First of all, I wasn't familiar with Long Island, and second, I hadn't spoken to my grandfather in a long time, not until two years ago. My parents stopped speaking with him when I was seven. It was one of those ridiculous family squabbles. My grandmother passed away, and a year later, my grandfather started dating someone else. No one liked her or the idea he was dating so quickly, so everyone stopped talking to one another. My grandfather tried a few times, but my parents wanted nothing to do with him. I contacted him two years ago because it was the right thing to do, and I needed him. We spoke a few times. Then three months ago, he called me out of the blue and told me he was sick. He wanted to see me before he died. Of course, I agreed. He tried to reach out to my parents again, but they're stubborn. I'm telling you the whole truth, Kayla."

Kayla swallowed. What was it about this man that made her body pulse and her heartbeat quicken? That made her question every decision she had made in the last two years?

Gabe ran his hands through that thick, dark hair that she loved. She turned to go back outside.

"The problem wasn't me, Kayla. The real problem was that you didn't fight for us. You abandoned me and everything you and I had built, which was trust. You killed that, and that's on your head, not mine."

Kayla froze mid-step. "I checked up on you, on the internet. When I missed you so much it hurt. By the way, congratulations on graduating. Your name was listed as a graduate on the campus website. Did you end up working for your dad?"

"I had my own practice, about twenty patients. My dad supervised me while I was getting my doctorate and until I got my license. When Grandpa gave me his properties, I informed all my patients. I haven't lost a single one. We Skype and have phone sessions daily. With Alice being such good help and with the buildings being in great condition, I have a lot of time on my hands. But I think I like running my grandfather's properties more than being a psychologist. I think my grandfather knew I would."

Kayla gripped the cake plate in her hands tighter. So Alice was such a wonderful helper, huh? Did the secretary have some kind of an ulterior motive? "So…you're still blaming me for leaving?" she whispered.

"Absolutely," he said.

Kayla hadn't thought her heart could sink any further. She closed her eyes and sighed.

"But I'm not blaming you for this."

Without warning, Gabe grabbed Kayla and pressed his lips against hers. She opened her mouth in shock. The moment she did, Gabe slipped his tongue inside. Her heart thudded. God, what if her parents looked this way? With all her strength, she pushed Gabe away with her elbow, making sure not to drop the cake.

"Gabe, my parents are right outside."

His breathing was just as fast as hers was. "I know. I was watching. But they're preoccupied with my house plans."

Her lips were still tingling from his kiss. "Why did you kiss me? Especially now, with my parents right outside the door!"

Gabe's eyes grew distant. "I wanted to see if your kiss was the same, because nothing else about you is."

Kayla was about to open her mouth and tell him off, but her mom opened the back door.

"What's keeping you two? And grab some plates, forks, and knives while you're in there."

Kayla nodded and grabbed what her mom wanted, but she couldn't look Gabe in the eye anymore. He held the plates while she held everything else, but they were both silent. There wasn't much left to say. Regardless of the kiss, he blamed their failure on her, and he was right to a certain extent. Besides, he had finished his degree and had a whole bunch of patients. If he didn't want to continue with his practice, he had his grandfather's properties to run, which he enjoyed doing. He was living his dream while she'd turned her back on hers.

Right before they stepped outside she forced herself to look at him. "That kiss. Was it the same or different?"

Gabe grunted. "Way different. Your passion is gone, Kayla. You're a shell of yourself. And the funny thing is, Bella Cove is one of the most inspiring, beautiful towns I've ever been to—and yet, your soul has died here. How ironic, huh?" He stepped out and held the door for her, acting all gentlemanly.

Her mom came to take the cake from Kayla's hands, so she didn't get a chance to respond, but what did it matter? Two years ago, he could read her so well, and apparently, he still could. But her soul hadn't died because she was in Bella Cove or because she had all these responsibilities to her family... she loved it here. He was right; the little town was beautiful and inspiring. But the emptiness, the dead space inside her had appeared the moment she'd lost *him*. And she had no one to blame but herself...

When she sat at the table, her dad eyed her suspiciously. She was too devastated to hide how she felt. If her nana was here, she would have helped Kayla feel better. She would have thought of some solution for the situation between Kayla and Gabe. But grandmother was dead and had left the problem-solving to Kayla.

Her dad sat next to her and squeezed her hand under the table. She was grateful for that, but the kind gesture made her want to cry. She was stronger than that, though; at least, she needed to be. Thank goodness Gabe had made sure her parents hadn't seen him kiss her.

Her mom seemed oblivious as usual. Mom sat at the head, and Gabe sat across from Kayla. Needing to do something, she took a small piece of cake, but then she realized she hadn't eaten any dinner. Her mom started asking Gabe more questions about his house, and her dad added his opinion, which Kayla found odd. Usually, her dad was so quiet.

Gabe ignored her. He hadn't even glanced her way once. She looked at him a few times, mostly out of disbelief that he was sitting on her back porch. The times she'd allowed herself to envision him here had been nothing like this. For one thing, in her fantasies, Gabe never ignored her.

Unable to tolerate the situation a moment longer, she stood. "I haven't eaten dinner yet," she said. "I'm going inside and getting some real food."

"Oh, absolutely," her mom said. "There are leftovers in the refrigerator, dear."

Gabe didn't even say goodbye. He simply nodded at her. She hoped the kiss hadn't turned him off completely. They may not have a future, but she did have her pride. Her dad blew her a kiss. At least *he* made her feel loved. It wasn't Gabe's job to make her feel that way anymore, but she wished he didn't have to act like a detached asshole toward her.

When she got back inside the house, she grabbed some leftover pasta salad and a glass of water and went upstairs to her bedroom. Both her sisters were at a yoga class, so, thankfully, she wouldn't be disturbed for the rest of the night. And Josh wouldn't be speaking to her for a while. When she reached her bedroom, she kicked the door closed behind her.

She liked her room…her only sanctuary. She sat on her queen-sized, canopy bed. Her room was decorated in shades of lavender, her favorite color. The walls were painted a light shade of lavender. Her canopy bed was also lavender, as was her bedspread. Her floors were dark wood like the rest of the house, but she had a white and lavender area rug. She put her drink on the floor and took a forkful of pasta, but she wasn't hungry. Her window had been left open from this morning. She liked feeling the breeze from outside. But tonight, she wanted to shut it. Hearing Gabe outside her window charming her parents was killing her.

She put her barely eaten food on the floor, debating whether she should go back downstairs and put it in the fridge, but her tiredness won out. Gabe's words from earlier were playing in her mind like background noise. That, and the memory of that short-lived kiss. He was right…the kiss hadn't been so great, but what did he expect? She'd been scared to death her parents would see.

She shook her head. She had to stop replaying those moments in the kitchen with him. This wasn't any way to live. The only way to stop her swirling thoughts was to sleep. She lay back on the bed and closed her eyes. With Gabe back in her life, she was forced to look back on all the mistakes she'd made in the last two years, and she couldn't take the pain anymore. So she did what she always did when life became too much. She fell asleep.

An hour later, Kayla woke up with a completely different mindset. She was pissed. How dare Gabe kiss her? And how dare he accuse her of being different? Her family had been through hell and back when her grandmother passed. Between Josh's addiction, and her mom acting hysterical and telling everyone she should have died instead of Nana, of course she'd be different. And that didn't include Sarah and Lauren running amok or Matt being sick in the hospital. Nor did it include her dad's depression.

But they'd come out the other end stronger. Not perfect. But stronger. *She'd* come out the other end stronger. So, no, she wasn't the same naïve girl he'd fallen in love with. In her mind, she was tougher. She was a fighter. And if Gabe didn't like it, maybe he shouldn't have kissed her, maybe he shouldn't have moved his office across from her store, and maybe he shouldn't be building a house where she could see it from her bedroom window.

THE NEXT MORNING, Kayla awoke to the sounds of bulldozers and construction workers speaking loudly. From what Gabe had said last night, he had obtained all the proper permits and approvals to start building. There was no way she could stop him from being her neighbor now. She could wish it, though.

After only sleeping a few hours, she felt utterly exhausted and depleted. If Nana was looking down at her, she'd be so disappointed. More than that, Kayla was disappointed in herself. No man was worth sleepless nights. That was something her grandmother would say. She glanced at her clock on her night table. Six o'clock. Last night, she'd overheard Gabe ask her parents if it was okay if they started at six the first day, and from then on, he'd honor some noise ordinance rule of starting at eight. He'd been so charming; of course, they had agreed.

With the loud noise outside, there was no use trying to go back to sleep. That was okay. She'd get to work early. She had given Sarah the day off since she had been working so hard. Plus, Kayla wanted to train Lauren alone. After taking a much-needed deep breath, she leaped out of bed and decided to change her attitude. And her attitude could only improve. If it was any lower, she'd be immobilized in bed. She needed to find the anger she'd felt when she'd woken up in the middle of the night.

When Kayla arrived at the store, she opened the door and screamed. Gabe was leaning against her cash register counter with his arms crossed.

"What are you doing here? How did you get in?" Her heart thudded like crazy.

"I was waiting for you, and I have a key. I'm your landlord, remember?"

Unfortunately, she did remember. "It's seven-thirty in the morning. If you're here for a good-morning kiss, you can forget it."

Gabe chuckled. Kayla had always liked the sound, but today, it grated on her nerves. He looked way too wide awake and perfect for this early in the morning. In his jeans and a red button-down shirt, at least he didn't look stuffy like he had the day he'd stormed into her store. And yeah, that's how it had felt—like a storm had hit her.

He continued staring at her with his arms crossed. "I couldn't sleep." His stare was intense, as if he were trying to penetrate her soul.

"So you came here instead?" It gave her some satisfaction, knowing he'd had trouble sleeping, too. Must've been the kiss. Their lips hadn't touched in two long years. No matter how bad he thought it was, that had to have affected him.

"I was awake all night, waiting to talk to you." Gabe paused and glanced at the front door. "Why don't you close the door, so we can have an adult conversation?"

She didn't like his choice of words, but at the same time, the sight of him being there had surprised her so much, she'd forgotten to close the front door. Once she closed it, she regretted it. Now, she was trapped with Gabe and with the intense energy he was exuding. She shifted beneath his steady gaze. Needing to do something other than stand there waiting for him to tell her whatever it was that haunted him enough to disrupt his sleep, she walked through the store as if she had a purpose and pushed open her office door. Gabe followed and leaned against the doorframe in the same way he'd been leaning against her register when she'd first come in.

"Shouldn't you be at your property, overseeing the construction of your house?"

Gabe clenched his jaw. "I should be, but I needed to get some things off my chest first."

Kayla swallowed and sat down. She couldn't sit still with him being this angry at her. Being this close to him made her forget everything except how much she missed him when he wasn't around.

So she logged onto her computer and opened her desk drawer to take out her to-do list.

"Kayla, stop."

Gabe's stern tone caused her to freeze.

Without looking at him, she spoke. "Just say it, Gabe. Say whatever it is you need to say to hurt me."

"I'm not planning on hurting you."

She did look at him then, her face heated up. "Aren't you? Two years ago, I hurt you, and now it's your turn. And you're going to give it back to me tenfold." Relief flooded her as the anger she'd felt last night came back full force.

"That wouldn't be possible."

Kayla sighed dramatically. "What happened to us not seeing each other? We planned on me mailing my rent check to Alice, remember? You would stay on your property and I'd stay on mine."

"That's not possible either."

This time, Kayla clenched her jaw.

"Gabe, say what's on your mind." She was so frustrated, she could barely draw a full breath. One minute, she wanted to scream and tell him to go back to California, and the next, she wanted to run to him and throw her arms around him and kiss him in the way he'd remember.

He was about to speak when the sound of the door opening and closing came from the front of the store.

"Hi, Kayla."

Kayla's heart sank. Lauren had walked in and was on her way to the office.

"I'm sorry," she mouthed to Gabe. What she really wanted to tell him was that their second kiss would have to wait.

Gabe looked as if he was ready to explode. He turned and leaned out into the hall. "Hey, Lauren, can you give Kayla and me a minute? We're talking about the building. Would you mind getting us the same delicious iced coffee you got me the other day?"

He spoke before Lauren had a chance to reach the office, so Kayla couldn't see her sister's expression. No doubt, Lauren must be shocked to see Gabe here so early. Gabe took some cash out of his pocket and handed it to Lauren. Kayla heard her sister thank him, and then Lauren left the store again.

When Gabe returned, he appeared even angrier if that was possible.

"Let me get this off my chest before your sister comes back," he said, running his hands through his hair again. "I hate that your parents don't know about us. You were wrong to lie to them when we were in school, and you're wrong for lying to them now."

"You're right," she admitted.

Gabe's eyes grew wide. "Are you thinking of changing that?"

Kayla looked down at her hands gripping her desk. She hadn't even realized she'd been doing that.

She nodded. "I'll come clean. I'm not sure when, but I promise I will. You deserve that. We both deserve that."

He glared at her for a moment. "Tell them soon, Kayla. Because by you not telling them, I feel like I'm lying, too."

He walked out of her store as Lauren came back in. That was fast. There must not have been a long line. Kayla heard Lauren offer him the iced coffee. He must have said something charming to her because she laughed. Then Kayla heard the front door close. She had to figure out a way to put her happy face back on. She didn't feel like breaking down in front of her sister. That would raise all sorts of questions she wasn't ready to answer. He'd never even mentioned their kiss. It may not have meant anything to him, but it meant everything to her.

Lauren's heels click-clacked down the small hallway that led to the office. "Hey, beautiful." Lauren stood in the doorway, looking lovely in a black cotton sundress with white flowers on the bottom. But it wasn't the outfit that made her look pretty; the smile on her face made her glow.

When was the last time Kayla had seen a genuine smile on her sister's face? She had made the right decision by hiring Lauren.

Kayla smiled back as Lauren handed over the iced coffee. Immediately, Kayla took a large sip, which made her feel a whole lot better.

"Thank you. I feel ready to attack the day now."

Lauren laughed. "How come Gabe was here so early? It seemed odd, don't you think?"

"The construction on his house started today. He stopped here before going to check it out."

"Oh, I know; they were so loud. I guess we'll have to get used to the noise for a while."

"If it gets too bad, we can always sleep here." Kayla laughed, but inside, nothing felt funny.

"Hey, Kayla?" Lauren asked softly. "Are you okay with Gabe being back in your life? I mean, I know he's not your boyfriend anymore, but he seems to be around you a lot."

Kayla exhaled. "It feels weird. I have these moments when I forget he's *not* my boyfriend, but then I see how he looks at me. All detached and standoffish. And my first instinct is to throw my arms around him. To cling to him. Anything to get that look off his face. But he's not open toward me anymore. The best thing I can do for myself is to keep busy and to throw myself into the store. So come on...let me show you a few things."

Lauren gave Kayla a compassionate look before following her out of the office.

They spent the remainder of the morning learning how to use the computer at the register. Melody had bought an intricate system, top of the line but not always easy to work out. Sarah had learned the basics, but Kayla wanted to show Lauren a little more detail. She'd been smiling and laughing all morning. Tomorrow, they would bring over the castle they used to play with growing up and make paper snowflakes to hang. Lauren asked if she could go through the catalogs and check out some toys she thought they should buy. Lauren was trying. For her, that was a huge step in the right direction.

After lunch, customers came in and out. When there was a lull, Lauren played with a ball, throwing it in the air and catching it, until a customer came in.

Lauren became quiet, so Kayla looked up to see what or who had caused the change in her sister's mood. A gorgeous man with dark blond hair and blue eyes had walked into the store and was looking around.

Kayla nudged Lauren. "Go and help him," she whispered.

If he happened to be single and they hit it off, Kayla would do a happy dance and not care who saw her do it.

"Come with me."

Lauren grabbed Kayla's arm and practically dragged her over to the man. Kayla would have preferred Lauren meet him alone, but if Kayla's presence made her sister feel better, then so be it.

They walked over to the blond god, who was scratching his jaw while staring at the section of toys for seven-to-ten-year-old boys. Kayla was about to ask him if he needed help, but surprisingly, her sister beat her to it.

"You look like you could use some help," Lauren said, giggling.

He must not have heard them approach because he jumped a little when Lauren spoke to him. Then he stared at her.

"Did you just come out of the princess section? Are you a live doll?"

Lauren burst out laughing, but it took all Kayla's strength not to roll her eyes at him. Her sister was beautiful, no doubt, but he was laying it on a little thick. If a guy spoke to her like that, she would have ignored him and given him the cold shoulder. Lauren, on the other hand, appeared to be eating it up.

"You busted me," Lauren said. "I escaped the other dolls by the skin of my teeth."

Lauren giggled again, and the blond hottie joined in. Kayla looked at her sister in disbelief. Never in her life had she heard Lauren flirt.

"So…can I help you, for real?" Lauren asked.

"Not unless you give me your name," he responded.

"Only if you tell me if you're married, engaged, or have a girlfriend."

Wow, Kayla thought. *Gutsy.* She was starting to feel like the third wheel.

"I'm single. What about you?" he asked.

"I'm single, too," Lauren said, still smiling.

"So…? Will you give me your name?"

"Lauren." She put her hand out for him to shake. "Lauren Conway."

The man grabbed her hand and then lifted it and kissed the back of it. "Jordan Wolf."

"Like the animal." Lauren giggled.

He held her hand a little longer than necessary then, finally, he dropped it.

"Everyone asks me if I'm a veterinarian. I assure you, I'm not. Not that there's anything wrong with being a vet. But I paid my way through law school, and I wouldn't give that up for anything in the world."

Lauren playfully hit his arm. "Oh, come on. You know you'd rather help animals."

"I love animals. I grew up with two dogs and a cat. But I faint when I see blood, so that would be a problem."

"Just a small problem," Kayla chimed in.

"This is my sister, Kayla. She owns the store."

Jordan put his hand out to shake Kayla's, but no kiss for her…thank goodness. The last man who had kissed her hand was Gabe. In fact, the last man who had kissed her at all was Gabe. She hadn't even been on a date since she'd left California. She wondered whether Gabe had, but then she put the thought out of her mind. Too painful.

Lauren and Jordan were laughing at some of the toys while Kayla had been obsessing over thoughts of Gabe.

She walked away without Lauren or Jordan noticing. At least she had a few minutes to be by herself. Gabe showing up this morning was messing with her head. One day, she wanted to explain everything that happened in the last two years, assuming he'd let her. She had abandoned him, and she couldn't change that fact, but maybe they could be friends.

Kayla escaped to her office when she saw that Jordan had picked a toy, and Lauren was about to ring him up. Could Lauren have finally met her future husband? How awesome would that be? The second Kayla heard the front door close, she came out of her office.

"Well?" Kayla asked.

Lauren jumped up and down, laughing. "He asked for my number." She kept jumping.

"Okay, calm down for one second and give me the details." Kayla pulled her down to the floor, where they could talk easier.

"I worked at that stupid real estate firm for seven years, and not once did I meet a single man who asked for my phone number. Thank you for asking me to work here."

Kayla smiled. "My pleasure."

She smiled back. "When Jordan walked in, I thought he was the most beautiful man I'd ever seen. Apparently, he has a business associate who has a house in the Hamptons, and he needed to buy a toy for the man's son. Jordan Googled toy stores on the way to the Hamptons and found us. He was really interesting. He said he's about to be a partner at a real estate law firm in Manhattan. I asked him if he'd heard about the firm I used to work for, and he hadn't. Anyway, I helped him pick out a toy, and he asked for my number. Of course, I gave it to him. Do you think he'll call?"

Kayla gave her sister a big hug. "I do."

They continued talking about him and guessing what he liked to do. Lauren wondered if he liked going to the movies and what his apartment in Manhattan looked like. But the entire time Lauren talked, Kayla kept thinking about how she would describe first meeting Gabe. Lauren said Jordan was the most beautiful man she'd ever seen. That was exactly how Kayla had felt when she had met Gabe for the first time. And to be honest, she still felt that way. In fact, he hadn't aged at all, but at the same time, he seemed manlier. When she fell in love with him, he'd been a boy, regardless of his age. Now he was a man.

By the time Kayla arrived home, it was late and she was exhausted. Lauren had left an hour early to get her hair done. Kayla had stayed past closing time to go through the recent shipments of toys. With Melody gone, she could buy more creative toys for the shop. Melody preferred popular toys that sold well at the bigger toy stores. Kayla thought those toys were important to stock, but she liked more unique toys, which the bigger stores wouldn't necessarily shelve. Melody also didn't like a lot of children's books, whereas Kayla loved them.

As she was climbing the stairs to her bedroom, she heard her mother crying. Kayla sighed. She wanted to crawl into bed and fall asleep. The only time she had for herself these days was in her bed. Then she could finally allow her mask to fall and be herself.

But her mom needed her.

Kayla walked back downstairs and found her mom sobbing on the living room couch.

"Mom, are you okay?" Kayla sat next to her mother but refrained from hugging her. If she touched her, she would only sob more. Kayla had learned that the hard way. Her mom tended to break down and cry at least four times a week. She *could* ignore her and let her deal with her pain on her own, but if Kayla knew that if she didn't help with whatever was going on, Mom would stay in bed and refuse to leave for days. At least her mom wasn't threatening to kill herself anymore.

When Nana had passed away, Kayla had been mourning the loss of two major people in her life—her grandmother and Gabe. She hadn't been mourning one more than the other, although she couldn't speak to Nana again, and she could, technically, speak to Gabe. For the first week after Nana passed, Gabe and Kayla spoke every day—even if only to say a quick "hello" or "good night." After about a week, Gabe had asked when she'd be coming home.

And that's when she was honest with him and told him she didn't know. She wanted to return to him very badly, but she hadn't expected her family to go off the deep end, which they had. He'd heard her mom screaming in the background, crying her head off, so he knew she was telling the truth. But it wasn't enough for him. She even told him about her dad's depression, her sisters moving out, and Matt going to the hospital for pneumonia. But she didn't tell him about Josh. She'd mentioned he was drinking, but she didn't have the courage to tell him everything else. Gabe had told her that her family should take care of themselves, and it would all work out the way it should, but she needed to return to him. She'd heard panic in his voice, when normally he sounded strong and steady. So she'd asked him to give her three months, and then she'd return to him. But after three months, she wasn't ready. If she'd left, she didn't think her family would have survived Nana's death.

When she told him at three months to give her another three months, he'd insisted on flying to her house. But the timing had been wrong, so she told him not to. He'd begged her to return to him anyway. When she said no, he gave her an ultimatum: Return now or never. Her family was in such a state, she'd said never. Yet she still called him at the six-month mark. And at six months, he didn't pick up his phone, so she'd left him a voicemail and told him she was sorry. But she needed another three months and then she was sure her family would be able to stand on their own two feet again. There had been no word from Gabe for a week after she'd left that message. She'd called a dozen more times. Finally, a week later, she'd received a text that had read: *Too Late.*

That had been one of the worst days in Kayla's life. The only other day that had been as bad was the day Nana died. Truth was, Kayla couldn't return to Gabe until she knew her family would somewhat be okay. They were functional at the year mark. But since the only other time she'd heard from him was when he texted her saying he needed her home address because he'd packed up her stuff and it would be on its way to her soon, she'd been scared to tell him she could finally return to him, but she did anyway. She texted him and told him she was willing to get on the plane the next day and be with him. That night, she'd received her last text from him. Gabe had written, *No, thank you. Take care, Kayla.*

When Gabe had given her the ultimatum, she'd thought maybe he was bluffing. At the same time, she'd understood that in his eyes, she'd betrayed his trust and their love. Unfortunately, if she had to do it all over again, she'd do the same thing. As much as she loved Gabe, she couldn't abandon her family until they were somewhat back on their feet. And that had nothing to do with Nana asking her to take care of everyone. Kayla's conscience wouldn't have allowed her to do anything less.

She glanced at her mom, who continued to sob, but Kayla knew the drill. She had to ask her mom three times if she was okay before she'd respond.

"Mom, are you okay?" Kayla sighed. She knew what this was about. It was always the same thing. Mom didn't think Dad loved her anymore.

Kayla always consoled her when her mom was in this state or she'd get a lot worse. Her mother had been known to wake up Dad in the middle of the night, screaming that she wanted his love. Those were the times when he'd threaten to leave. Kayla believed he *did* love her or he would have been long gone by now.

Once Nana died, Kayla had sat her father down and told him directly that if he wanted to leave her mom, Kayla would make sure Mom was okay. Kayla had felt she needed to give her dad the option. There was nothing worse than feeling trapped. Her hope was that if he felt he had the choice and decided to stay, any feelings of resentment and bitterness would disappear. He had looked Kayla directly in the eye and told her he was staying. He didn't give her a reason, but he didn't have to.

Kayla cleared her throat, took a deep breath, and repeated, "Mom, are you okay?"

Her mom let out a loud sob. "No. I tried to give your father a hug before he left to go to a meeting and he pushed me away." She sobbed even louder.

Before Kayla left for work that morning, she had heard her mom criticizing her dad, telling him he wasn't wearing the right clothes, his hair was messy, he wasn't sitting up straight when eating breakfast, he'd gotten crumbs on the floor, and so on.

"Mom, when you're mean to Dad, he doesn't want to touch you. At least, not for a few days."

"I see you're on your father's side. I'm never mean to him, Kayla."

Kayla sighed. "I heard you this morning. You were criticizing him left and right. You might as well have told him he's a disappointment as a husband."

Her mom stopped crying, which Kayla knew would happen, but her sadness switched quickly to anger.

"I love your father. He doesn't love me. I try to be a good wife." And then the anger switched to self-pity.

In about five or ten minutes, she could go back upstairs.

"Mom, you have to stop criticizing Dad. It makes him feel bad. I'm not saying there aren't certain aspects of him that don't annoy you, but that's normal in any marriage."

"How do you know? You've never been married."

Ouch. "Mom, when you're mean to Dad, you hurt him, so he shuts down. When you hurt him, he doesn't want to touch you. You have to earn his love and affection."

"After all these years, I still have to earn his love and affection?"

"And after all these years, you're still constantly criticizing him. Try not to do that, even for a few days, and see what happens. I bet he'll be warmer toward you."

"I criticize him so he'll be better," her mom snapped back.

Kayla smiled softly. "I think he's doing pretty okay for a sixty-five-year-old man. He works hard. He maintained the furniture business even after Pop passed. And he loves his family, whether you believe it or not."

Her mom became quiet, which was exactly how Kayla wanted her to be.

"I believe he loves the family, but I'm not sure if he loves me."

"Mom," Kayla said through clenched teeth.

Her mom sighed dramatically. "Okay, I'll try not to criticize him. It won't be easy, though."

Kayla smiled. "I didn't say it would be." She felt safe enough to give her mom a hug without her breaking down again.

Her mom hugged her back tightly and then pulled back, looking at her straight in the eyes.

"Nana made the right decision by making you the matriarch of the family." She smiled a bit.

Kayla groaned. "Mom, I am not the matriarch. Even using that word makes me cringe. In Nana's generation, there were matriarchs. She asked me to look after the family, so that's what I've been doing, except now much less. You're all pretty much on your feet. We don't have a matriarch in our family anymore. That was healthy at one time, but now it isn't. The world is a very different place from when Nana was born."

Her mom sighed. "I know. It's just some days, I really miss her."

Kayla gave her mom a kiss on the cheek. "Some days, I do, too."

She needed to get up to her room. Suddenly, she felt edgy. She smiled and then escaped upstairs. Her life had been going fine until a few days ago when Gabe showed up. Since then, she had been forced to reflect on a life she had left behind. And it hurt so badly, she'd had a constant ache in her stomach and heart. Then he'd kissed her. She wished she could have it all. And she had never felt so alone in her entire life. The only other time she had felt that way was the day Nana had died, when all hell broke loose.

WHEN KAYLA OPENED HER STORE the next morning, she wasn't surprised to see Gabe painting the other side of her wall.

"You don't have to do this, you know." Kayla's intuition had told her he would be there, so she'd stopped on her way in and bought two iced coffees—one for him and one for herself. "I brought you something."

Gabe stopped painting and looked down. The second their eyes met, the tension in the room increased. His eyes weren't as cold as they had been. They weren't exactly warm, but at least when she looked at him, shivers didn't run through her body.

He climbed down the ladder and took the iced coffee out of her hand. "Thanks."

He didn't smile, but he wasn't looking at her with daggers, either. Something had shifted inside him, but she wasn't sure what it was.

"Good morning," she said softly.

He nodded while sipping his coffee. "Good morning."

He was being civil with her. She could do civil. Maybe they could call a truce and move on from the past and all their drama.

"I mean it, Gabe. I can paint. You don't have to."

"I don't mind. I promised your sister I'd do it. I always keep my word."

"Can I help you, then?" she asked, wanting to be near him.

Gabe raised his eyebrow. "Help me?"

"Yes, I have a paintbrush in the back."

"But I'm only painting the border. It wouldn't make sense."

"I could hold the paint."

Gabe chuckled. "The paint rests fine on the top of the ladder."

Kayla had to do something to get closer to him. "Come on, we did that in our apartment, remember? You'd paint a wall, and I'd either hold the paint or paint with you."

"That was then, and this is now," Gabe said. He took a drink of his coffee.

"Then I'll sit on the ladder while you work."

"Suit yourself, but when I have to move it, are you going to get up?"

Kayla smiled. She couldn't help herself. The vision of him moving the ladder with her on it almost made her laugh. If there wasn't so much tension between them, she would have.

"Of course I'll get up. I've gained a little weight since graduate school. I wouldn't want you to pick up both me and the ladder." She had to bite her bottom lip to stop herself from laughing.

"You look perfect. You didn't gain any weight. Looks like you lost some. With the constant pressure of making your family happy, I'm not surprised."

Kayla looked at her iced coffee and took a sip. What could she say to that?

Gabe shook his head, put his drink on the ground, and started to climb the ladder again. Kayla was about to sit on the other side of the ladder like she said she would when Gabe looked back at her.

"Are you happy, Kayla? You spend so much time thinking of ways to make your family happy, but are *you* happy?"

"How do you know I'm making them happy?" she snapped.

"I've watched you with them. You don't need your sisters working here. You're doing it to help them for different reasons. If anything, them being here is more work for you. I think you'd prefer it if you were running this place alone. You always liked to have time by yourself. Instead, you thought them working here would be best for them."

Kayla exhaled and sat on the ladder.

"You didn't answer my question. Are you happy?"

She paused before she spoke. "That's a hard question to answer. I think everyone has good and bad days."

"They do; I agree. But even though I have days like that, overall, I'm happy."

Kayla's heart clenched. It wasn't that she didn't want him to be happy; she did, but once upon a time, he'd been happy with her. Maybe her pride and ego were bruised. She wished he had said he was happy, but that he'd been happier with her. But as far as she was concerned? Yes, she did feel happy. She loved her family deeply, and she liked owning her own store, but she felt happier with him. There was no two ways about it. She felt more complete with Gabe by her side.

"I'm happy," she said, reaching out and touching his bare leg. He was wearing gray shorts today. She'd always loved his legs, and she couldn't help touching them.

"You could have fooled me."

Gabe picked up the paintbrush and resumed painting. He took a step further up the ladder, forcing her hand to fall.

She missed touching him. In just that one moment, her whole body felt alive. That's what she remembered most about the time she'd been with him: He always made her feel alive. Kayla sat there feeling like an idiot with nothing to do, but she was determined not to leave. She had millions of things she could do to keep herself occupied, yet nothing held her interest like the man painting her wall.

"Gabe?"

He immediately stopped painting, but he didn't put the brush down or look at her.

"Yes?"

"I felt happier when I was with you," she said softly. "And I'm sorry I couldn't return to California earlier, like I thought I would. It took me longer than I thought to handle things here. My family really struggled for a long time after Nana passed. But I had every intention of returning to you once they got back on their feet, and they pretty much had. They're not perfect, but no one is. But they were on their feet enough that I could have been with you. Like I said in that text I sent you."

He still didn't look at her. "I didn't believe you." He paused and got really quiet for a few seconds before continuing. "Are you saying all this because you think it'll make me feel better? Because you think it's the right thing to say?"

"No," Kayla admitted. "I mean every word." Tears welled up in her eyes, but she blinked them away.

"It's too bad I didn't believe you then, and I don't believe you now."

"Why?" she asked, raising her voice. She'd finally spoken her truth, and he'd responded with a verbal slap to her face.

Gabe continued painting. "Because I no longer trust you. I no longer trust what you have to say. My trust for you ended two years ago," he said. "And I never should have kissed you the other night. I can't get your damn lips off my mind."

"Oh, really?" she asked, her tone sarcastic. "You mean we can't kiss again? I'd like a retry—*without* my parents a few feet away."

Gabe chuckled under his breath, shaking his head. "Not a chance."

"Can we at least try to get along?" Kayla was sick of his…his *shit*. There was no other word for it. She was trying to be nice, and she was sick of him acting like an asshole toward her. She may not have handled leaving him the right way, but she didn't deserve him acting like a dick.

"We have to. Bella Cove is a small town, and we'll both be living here. I'm also your landlord."

Kayla groaned. "Please don't shut down my store. People in this town love it."

Gabe kept on painting. "I told you I won't."

"Thank you. And while we're at it, let's try to be friends."

Gabe paused with the brush hanging midair in his hand. "That's asking too much. We can be civil. I'd prefer it, actually. I don't want to look at you or be around your family and think all these negative thoughts."

"Is that what you do?" Kayla stood, her mouth hanging open. There was no point in being close to him.

Gabe resumed painting. "That's exactly what I do."

"Don't do that." She raised her voice again. "I'm sorry, Gabe. I'm so sorry for what happened to us. I'm sorry I left you. I'm sorry I left us. But you're the one who gave me an ultimatum on the phone. I texted you anyway and you told me I was too late. So you had a part in our breakup, too." Kayla had had enough. If only she could control the tears that were falling. "I'm sorry my family was so fucked up. And I'm sorry I didn't return on your timeline. But I can't redo the past, Gabe. And neither can you." She glanced out the window.

Sarah was walking toward the store. She couldn't let her sister see her like this. That would make everything worse than it already was. She glanced up at Gabe and saw he was still painting. Clearly, she wasted her vocal cords on him. He was done with her.

"I have to go. Please, tell Sarah I had something to do." Kayla grabbed her bag.

"I'm not going to lie for you," he said, still not bothering to look her in the eye.

Kayla groaned. "Fine. Just tell her I'll be back a little later, then."

She wasn't sure if he nodded or agreed, but once she left, she would text Sarah.

Unfortunately, Kayla had walked to the store today, so she didn't have her car. Today, of all days, she wished she could drive far away. Even though Nana had always told Kayla to face her problems, right now, she had to get out of there before her sister came in.

Without another look at Gabe, she practically ran out the back door. If she continued to run, someone would see her. It was hard to hide here. Right now, she didn't want to see anyone. But if she continued walking behind all the stores on Main Street, she'd be okay.

Her plan worked. When she reached the spot where she always sat when life became too much—a large rock on the far left side of the bay—she sighed with relief. She loved this part of Bella Cove. It was away from the homes that overlooked the bay, and, usually, folks didn't come here.

Kayla texted her sister and told her she'd been at the store super early and needed to get something to eat. That wasn't a complete lie, but there was no way she could eat anything. Her stomach wouldn't allow it, but she *had* been at the store early. She hoped Gabe would at least verify that part. Sarah texted back, telling Kayla to bring back some kind of treat for her. Kayla sighed. Her sister believed her, which meant she had at least thirty minutes to herself. She couldn't remember the last time she'd had thirty minutes to herself during the day. So she inhaled the sea air, relishing the few minutes of freedom, and briefly closed her eyes.

Gabe's earlier statements ran through her mind. He'd pretty much nailed it. She *would* have loved to have run the store by herself. The only reason she'd hired her sisters was to help them, but, hey, her plan seemed to be working. Better than she'd even imagined. And who knew what the future held for Lauren and Jordan? This morning, Lauren had gotten up early to go to the gym and had caught Kayla on her way to the store. Jordan had already called, and they'd made plans to see each other. On his way back from the Hamptons, he would meet her for coffee. So Kayla had given Lauren the day off. She'd wanted to shop for a new outfit... and how could Kayla say no?

Kayla laughed under her breath. Finally, she had thirty minutes to herself, and all she could think about was her family. Did she even know what she wanted out of life anymore? Was she so consumed with worrying about her family's happiness that she had forgotten all about her own? She had goals to accomplish, too. But she was having trouble remembering her dreams. She'd known what they were before Nana died—Kayla had planned to marry Gabe and live happily ever after. Now, she wasn't sure she had any dreams of her own.

For a brief moment, Kayla closed her eyes and allowed herself to fantasize. Her ultimate vision was to marry the man of her dreams and be a top psychologist while living in Bella Cove—but not in her family's house. She would have her own home that overlooked the bay. And since she was daring to dream, the man she would like to marry was still Gabe Wademan. Kayla took in her newfound revelation and repeated it in her head a few more times. She would marry Gabe, even though he was acting like a complete asshole. But he wasn't really an asshole. He just had a million walls up around his heart. She needed to break down those walls. She needed to help him release all that bitterness he had from their past.

Kayla groaned. She was handling him all wrong. Gabe was in Bella Cove, and she was in Bella Cove. If she could get him to trust her again and to stop acting like an asshole, maybe there was the slightest glimmer of hope for them. Of course, there were other obstacles. They'd have to get to know each other again. Fall in love with each other again. But Kayla was open. She was still extremely attracted to him. And her family was in a better place. Maybe she *could* have it all. Maybe she could find a way to win her true love back. Maybe she could finally stop mourning over Gabe, and instead, get a second chance at being with him. It was time she found the courage to fight for the man who was a part of her soul.

9

WITH HER RECENT EPIPHANY, Kayla stayed at her sacred spot a little longer than thirty minutes. By the time she made it back to the store, she had her sister's favorite cookies in her hand and a smile on her face. If she had returned any other way, Sarah would know something was up. With Kayla's longer-than-usual absence, her sister probably already suspected something.

"Hi, Sarah," Kayla said, glancing around the store.

"You brought me my favorite cookies." Sarah ran over and grabbed the bag out of Kayla's hand.

Kayla laughed. "When did Gabe leave?" She tried to sound as nonchalant as possible, even as her heart sank.

With a cookie stuffed in her mouth, Sarah responded. "A few minutes ago. Didn't he do a great job?"

Kayla looked at her walls. Gabe *had* done a great job. Not that she'd expected anything less. The yellow borders looked amazing. But since he had finished painting, did that mean he wouldn't visit her shop anymore? She liked opening her store in the mornings and seeing his handsome face, even if he was still angry and hurt. Especially with her recent revelation.

"It looks amazing. I love it," Kayla said, her tone quiet.

Her sister continued to stare. "You've been different lately. What's wrong with you?"

Kayla sighed. "Gabe painting the walls made me think of when he painted our apartment."

Sarah put down the cookies. "Do you miss him? I mean, I know you just saw him, but do you miss him as your boyfriend?"

Kayla paused and thought about that for a second. "I miss him, but the Gabe from today is not the same man I dated. I miss who he was at school. I miss how he made me feel. But this Gabe only makes me feel guilty for staying after Nana passed." Kayla didn't want to add that she was ready to fight for what they'd had, and might still have, together.

Sarah crinkled her forehead. "Kayla, you had to stay. We were all fucked up. If you didn't stay, we would have died."

Kayla laughed. "No one would have died. You're so dramatic."

Sarah shrugged. "Maybe, but we needed you," she said, biting her bottom lip. "What are you going to do?"

Kayla looked at her pedicure that needed redoing. "I don't know. I'd like him to trust me again. Then maybe I could see if the Gabe I used to know still exists." That was the truth. She only had to figure out how to accomplish her goal.

Sarah threw her arms around her. "You'll find a way to get him to trust you again. And if he doesn't, then he's stupid. You're like an angel to anyone who crosses your path."

Kayla smiled warmly. "Thank you. Do you know how much I love you?" She squeezed Sarah tight.

Sarah burst out laughing. She had a great laugh…the kind that made everyone around her want to laugh, too.

"If I didn't know before, I do now." Sarah squeezed Kayla back hard. "I love you, too."

Kayla broke the hug. "Thank you, but enough sisterly love. We've got a store to run."

"Oh, I have good news," Sarah said, jumping up and down. Even though she was twenty-seven, sometimes she acted like a little girl. She was also fun and intelligent. If only she'd stop flirting with every man who crossed her path.

Sarah opened one of the drawers in the register desk and took out a huge stack of paper snowflakes. "While Gabe was working away, I thought I'd make the snowflakes I told you about. It was so quiet in here, I didn't know what else to do."

Kayla checked out the snowflakes, but she was more concerned with why Gabe had been quiet. When she was with him, he couldn't seem to stop talking. Kayla assumed he'd be all light and fun with Sarah.

"I love them," she told her sister.

Sarah was beaming from ear to ear. "Thanks. I had a blast making them. Where would you like me to hang them?"

"Since this was your vision, why don't you hang them wherever you want?"

"Perfect. I'll get right on it." Sarah grabbed some tape out of the drawer and walked to the corner of the store that led to the hallway.

Her sister had chosen the exact spot Kayla would have suggested, but she wanted Sarah to feel good about herself and be in charge of something. She never had any visions or goals. But first, there was something Kayla had to find out or it would continue to drive her crazy.

"Hey, Sarah?"

"Yeah?" she asked, holding one snowflake under her chin while hanging another one on the wall.

"Since I've been spilling my guts to you about Gabe, what's happening in your love life? I haven't heard you talk about any guy lately."

"Because I don't have anyone. Nor do I want one." Sarah continued putting up the snowflakes, but she must not have liked how one of them looked because she took it down and put it up again a few inches over.

Kayla leaned against the wall, watching Sarah work.

"Do you ever think of getting married?"

Sarah looked over at Kayla and rolled her eyes. "Kayla, stop. I don't want to get married. At least, not for a very long time. I like my freedom, and from what I've seen and heard, marriage makes most people feel trapped."

"That's not true. You're around Mom and Dad too much. They may have their issues, but neither of them feels trapped."

Sarah sighed and went back to putting up the snowflakes. "Dad sure does."

Kayla crossed her arms. "I don't think so. If that was the case, I think he'd have left by now. I believe he loves Mom, but she drives him crazy sometimes. Even in those times, he doesn't leave."

"Because of us."

Sarah was avoiding looking at Kayla. *Interesting…* Apparently, their parents' marital problems were affecting Sarah more than Kayla had thought.

"I think he stays for Mom, also," Kayla said. "You know, Matt and Jessica have a good marriage, and so did Nana and Pop."

"Matt puts up with a lot of garbage from Jessica. He wants her to be a part of our family, and she refuses."

"I'm working on that," Kayla responded.

"Nana and Pop had a nice marriage from what we saw. But I think they had their moments. We just weren't aware of them."

They both grew silent. Why did Sarah think Nana and Pop had their moments? Everyone else thought they'd had a perfect marriage. They were always holding hands and looking adoringly at each other. Kayla would have to ask her sister what made her think there'd been trouble behind the scenes but not today. Today, she needed to discuss something else.

"Hey, Sarah, Mom and Dad think we should have Gabe over for dinner. Do you think that's a good idea? I thought it'd be a good start to him getting to know me again." She didn't want to tell Sarah that deep down, Kayla hoped she could marry him. Not until she had time to let it sink in.

Sarah laughed. "Yeah, it's a good idea. Then he'll see what nutjobs we all are, and he'll understand why you had to help us."

Kayla grinned. "He won't think that. You know Mom and Dad will be on their best behavior. I know there's only a slim chance of us getting back together, but I'd like to at least be friends."

"I agree." Sarah hung another snowflake. "Besides, whether we like it or not, he's going to be a part of our lives."

Kayla nodded. "I'll have Mom ask him."

"Are you going to tell Mom and Dad the truth about him? And Matt and Josh?"

Kayla sighed. "I will. I'm just not ready yet."

"I understand. I'd wait, too."

An hour later, Kayla's mom had already called all the siblings in the family and told them to show up at dinner the next evening. Then she called Gabe, who, according to her mom, had accepted the invitation right away and seemed pleased with the idea. After that, Kayla and her mom planned the menu. They decided to barbecue hamburgers, hot dogs, and salmon with mashed potatoes or French fries and grilled vegetables on the side. At least Kayla's mom was excited. Maybe she'd lay off Dad for five minutes.

Kayla was dying to know what Gabe had thought when her mom called with the invitation. Had he been surprised? Was he glad she'd asked or dreading having dinner with them? Kayla regretted not introducing him back at school, and she was tired of living with regret. They may not be together, but she could fix that mistake at least.

Or maybe the dinner was a terrible idea, and it would only make things worse between them. Either way, she would have her answer tomorrow night.

10

BY DINNERTIME the next night, Kayla was ready to jump out of her skin. She must have changed outfits a million times, which was unlike her. Finally, she settled on a pink and white sleeveless maxi dress, which made her feel feminine and pretty. She wore her hair loose, and thanks to her flattening iron, it hung straight and smooth down her back. She added a smidgen of pink gloss to her lips and some eyeliner to the bottom of her eyes. She thought she looked good, but she wasn't sure if that mattered. When she was with Gabe at school, he had always complimented her, telling her she was beautiful, but she didn't know if he still felt the same way. Maybe his disappointment in her made her appear unattractive. After all, he'd only kissed her that one time and had pretty much told her it was awful.

She'd left the store early, so she could help her mom prepare dinner and then change. By the time she made it downstairs, everyone was outside, including Gabe, who was laughing with Sarah.

"There you are, beautiful. Your father just put the burgers on the grill," her mom said as she grabbed the potato chips from the kitchen counter and went back outside.

Standing at the kitchen window, Kayla watched her dad barbecue. He had recently purchased a large gas grill, which he loved using. He appeared happy and relaxed, which was nice to see for a change.

Kayla took one more deep breath to calm her nerves before she opened the back door and stepped out. The moment she did, all eyes were on her. Even Josh stopped stuffing his face with potato chips long enough to stare her way.

"Hi." She didn't address anyone specifically, but instinctively, she turned her head and locked eyes with Gabe.

The warmth that had filled his eyes while he'd been talking with Sarah faded away.

"If my family hasn't already told you, thank you for coming to dinner." She held her smile. She couldn't even count how many times she had envisioned Gabe at one of her family dinners. Just not like this.

"I appreciate that. Thank you."

Kayla looked around at her family, but she didn't hold eye contact with any of them for long.

"So what did I miss?"

"Your family was welcoming me," Gabe said, grabbing a potato chip.

"Great. Then the party has started."

"Absolutely, beautiful," her dad said, flipping the burgers.

As she glanced over at her father, Matt and Jessica came up the back stairs. Kayla's heart skipped a beat as she went to greet them.

"Hi, Matt." She gave him a big hug.

He kissed her on the forehead. "Hi, beautiful." He took a step back and winked at her.

When Kayla hugged Jessica, she whispered in her sister-in-law's ear so no one else would hear. "Thank you so much for coming. You have no idea how much it means to all of us."

Jessica smiled. "Thank you for sending us Erica. We started acupuncture at my house. She's wonderful. I can't tell you how much better she's helped me feel. Normal, and even a bit hopeful."

Kayla gave Jessica a warm smile. "I'm glad. And if acupuncture doesn't work, we'll think of something else."

Jessica and Matt then introduced themselves to Gabe, who seemed completely at ease. She would love to know what he thought of her family.

"Let's make a toast," Kayla said, grabbing a bottle of water. To help out Josh, the women in the family only drank water or soda around him. Her dad and Matt each had a beer, but only because Josh hated beer and would never touch it. "To friendly neighbors, but most of all, Gabe. I hope Bella Cove gives you everything you're looking for. It's a magical town, where miracles happen every day." Kayla raised her bottle of water, hoping Gabe understood what she was trying to say.

"Thank you. And thank you, Lynne and Paul, for inviting me here. You have a lovely family, and I'm looking forward to being your neighbor."

"As your new neighbor, is it okay if I go skinny dipping in the bay some night?" Sarah blurted out. She was such a tease.

"Only if you warn me. If I look outside, my eyes may hurt from the awful view." Gabe laughed, and Sarah threw her napkin at him.

"Sarah, there'll be no skinny dipping," her mom said sternly, taking a sip of her ginger ale.

"Is it okay if I grab a microphone at two o'clock in the morning and start reciting the Constitution?" Lauren asked, batting her eyelashes.

"Do you even know the words to the Constitution?" Josh asked.

"I'll learn it once Gabe's house is built and he moves in," Lauren said.

Her entire family laughed hysterically, including her parents.

"I know Matt and I aren't your neighbors, but would you mind if we brought our karaoke machine here to sing at the top of our lungs late at night?" Jessica asked sweetly.

"Jessica forgot to add that we're both completely tone deaf," Matt added.

Everyone was laughing so hard. Kayla was beaming inside. Her family had touched her with how natural they were being and how Jessica was embracing them all. She was proud of them.

"All of you can do whatever you'd like; just warn me ahead of time, so I can stay at my grandfather's old house in the Hamptons," Gabe said with a twinkle in his eye.

"The Hamptons? We're so much better than the Hamptons. In fact, we're the way the Hamptons should be. They should rename the Hamptons *Bella Cove Wannabe*. West Hampton would be renamed *West Bella Cove Wannabe*. Southampton would be renamed, *South Bella Cove Wannabe*, and East Hampton would be *East Bella Cove Wannabe*," Sarah said.

"What about all the other towns there like Amagansett and Sag Harbor?" her dad asked, placing the hamburgers on the table.

"Just Bella Cove Wannabe."

"I like it, sis. I think it could work," Matt said.

"I like Bella Cove better than the Hamptons, too." Gabe grabbed a burger and put it onto his plate. "Everyone's been really warm and inviting to me here. It's much better than I expected. I'm pleasantly surprised."

"Why do you think that, Gabe?" Mom asked, as she threw some salmon and hot dogs on the grill for Dad to cook.

"I found something here I thought I had lost two years ago, and I didn't expect that to happen."

Kayla looked at her empty plate as her heartbeat quickened.

"What did you find?" Matt grabbed a burger and added ketchup to it.

Gabe paused, his expression turning deadly serious. "I found a part of me I'd been missing, a part of me I once loved."

Kayla inhaled as she glanced at Gabe, who was looking directly at her. She turned toward her dad, who was still busy grilling, so she was safe from anyone noticing the tears that had formed in her eyes, but her dad chose that exact moment to look at her. He didn't say anything. He simply looked her directly in the eye and winked. He suspected something, but there was nothing she could do. So far, he hadn't confronted her, but it was only a matter of time.

The rest of the meal went smoothly. Everyone continued to laugh and joke. Jessica grew tired, so she and Matt were the first to leave the party. Gabe said goodnight and thanked everyone again. But before he left, he looked at Kayla and took a deep breath. This night had been one of the best nights of her life because Gabe had met her entire family, and it had gone so well. But it had also been one of the worst because he came as her neighbor, not as her fiancé or husband. Still, she didn't regret tonight. She only hoped her plan was starting to work, and he'd leave there feeling less bitter and resentful. She hoped maybe the hurt he felt toward her was starting to go away. If that was the case, then tonight may be the start to a friendship at least.

Without considering the ramifications of her actions, she followed him. "I'll be right back," she told her family, not giving a crap what they thought. "I want to personally thank him for coming."

"That's a good idea, honey," her dad said.

She glanced at him. Was he being sarcastic? Didn't matter…she had to speak with Gabe alone for a moment. She dashed down the back steps and around to the front of the house.

"Gabe," she shouted.

He was getting into his SUV. Right before he was about to close the door, he must have seen or heard her because he paused. He had parked up by his property, so she had to run up the hill to reach him. By the time she got to his truck, she was out of breath.

"Thank you," she said as she grabbed onto his car door and caught her breath. "For coming to dinner with my family."

Gabe clenched his jaw. "I don't want to talk about it."

"Then what do you want to talk about?"

Gabe grabbed the back of her neck and kissed her. But this kiss was different than the last one. This time, *she* reacted differently. She opened her mouth, craving his tongue, and when she felt it against hers, she moaned. She kissed him back with everything she had, enjoying the feel of his lips, the feel of his tongue, the feel of his stubble that was rubbing against her cheeks.

Gabe dug his hands into her hair, stopped kissing her, looked into her eyes with such intensity it burned, and then resumed the kiss. He kissed her as if he couldn't get enough of her, as if she'd disappear.

They were breathing each other in, and Kayla couldn't tell if her lips were leading or his were. All she knew was she didn't want the kiss to end. But when she touched his chest over his shirt, Gabe pulled away. Maybe the touching part was too much.

Gabe released her and looked up toward her family. They couldn't see. There were too many trees separating them.

"What was that for?" she asked, hoping he'd say something like he had in front of her family. That he'd missed her and loved her. Even though that wouldn't solve their problems, she still wanted—*needed*—to hear him say the words.

But he didn't say anything like that. "I saw a drop of the old Kayla. I wanted to see if it showed in the kiss."

"Did it?" she asked quietly.

"It did."

That's a start at least. "I'd like to spend more time with you, Gabe. I'd like you to get to know me again. And I'd like to get to know you again, too."

"Why?"

Kayla smiled softly. "Because I miss my best friend."

"Baby steps, Kayla."

Kayla didn't have a chance to respond because Gabe started his engine and closed the door, forcing her to step back. Then he drove away, leaving her standing there feeling as if he'd stolen her heart and had taken it with him.

Kayla briefly closed her eyes. She could work with baby steps. It was a beginning. This dinner had been a success, after all.

WHEN KAYLA WALKED into Magical Toys the next morning, her heart sank. Deep down inside, she'd been hoping to see Gabe. But he had finished painting, so there was no reason for him to be there. In the past, seeing her would have been a good enough reason for him to come by, but those days were clearly gone. She already missed him like crazy. That kiss had really jarred her. She'd swear she could still feel her lips tingling.

Aside from his kiss, last night's dinner had been special. Throughout the whole meal, she'd felt his eyes on her. There were moments when she'd look back, and he'd glance away. Knowing he was looking at her—and not ignoring her as he usually did—had helped her make it through the meal. Her family had behaved. In fact, everyone had been in a good mood, including Josh. Everyone had acted as if Gabe had been a member of their family for years, which was both difficult and beautiful at the same time. But his eyes had soothed and calmed her. And made her body pulse. She felt alive for the first time since Nana became ill.

Kayla had tossed and turned all night long, wishing Gabe was lying next to her, craving him like there was no tomorrow. He'd told her he was willing to take things slowly. Baby steps, he'd said. So when she couldn't sleep, she'd been obsessing over what her next baby step should be. If she had his cellphone number, she'd call him and ask to go for an iced coffee. To sit and talk. But she'd have to call his office, and Alice would probably answer. She could do that, but she'd rather not have to go through Alice first.

Last night, after Gabe had driven away, Kayla had walked back to her house and helped her mom clean up. Lauren had tried to talk to Kayla about her date with Jordan, but everyone in the family was still around, so Kayla was hoping she and Lauren would get a chance to chat today.

"Hey, beautiful." Lauren walked into the shop beaming. "I can't believe how early you get here."

*Speak of the devil...*Kayla didn't want to tell her sister she arrived early only because she'd been hoping to find Gabe here, too.

Instead, she said, "I own this place. I want to make sure we're ready for the day."

"Are we ready?" Lauren threw her purse inside the office and then leaned over the register desk, balancing her upper body while her legs were dangling slightly in the air.

"Someone's happy this morning and bursting with news," Kayla said, smiling at her sister.

"I had the best time ever with Jordan. He was on his way home from his friend's place in the Hamptons, so we only had time for coffee. But we sat at the coffeeshop for three hours yesterday afternoon."

"Wow," Kayla said.

"I know. And he's charming, funny, and handsome." Lauren smiled dreamily, zoning off into space.

At one point in Kayla's life, she remembered feeling that same way.

"So what happened at the end? What did he say?" Kayla asked. The last fifteen minutes were always the most important part of the date because that was when the woman found out where she stood and what the guy's intentions were.

When Kayla went on her first date with Gabe, at the end of the evening, he'd said she was the most beautiful and spectacular woman he'd ever met. Although he hadn't really given marriage any thought, he'd known she was meant to be his wife. Kayla had wanted him to explain how he knew, and he'd said he couldn't. He just knew.

In a sense, she'd known, too. On their first date, she had never been so drawn to a man as she had been to him. He was good looking, but his intelligence captured her heart. She would bring up any topic, and he'd flow with her. He would challenge her, and he forced her to think outside of her normal box. The topics of their conversations were far from mundane, and their discussions ran deep. Deeper than any other conversations she'd ever had. On their first date alone, he had inspired her and made her feel alive.

And maybe that was why everything about his return to her life felt wrong. Their kiss last night had been amazing, but still, they were both being careful with each other. There were walls around them, thick walls that had never existed before. She had to destroy those walls or they'd never have a chance for a future. And Kayla wanted that. She'd settle for friendship, but her heart wanted more. She wanted all of him.

"Kayla? Hello, Kayla? I've been trying to tell you about my date, and you look like you're in la-la land."

Kayla blinked. "I'm sorry. I guess I'm a little tired."

"Uh-huh. I don't buy it."

"What do you mean?"

"I saw the way Gabe was checking you out at dinner. He couldn't stop looking at you. Sarah noticed, too."

"No, he wasn't, silly." Kayla kept her tone light despite the emotional turmoil going on inside her.

"I think he's still in love with you."

Kayla rolled her eyes, even as her heartbeat sped up. "He sure doesn't act like it. I think he's still mad at me, but last night, he said he's willing to take baby steps with me."

"Oh, my God," Lauren said, throwing her arms around Kayla. "That's amazing. It's a step. A baby step but still a step. Kayla, he could be your future husband like you always imagined."

Kayla laughed as she squeezed her sister and then stepped back. "You're such a romantic. I'd settle for friendship."

Lauren grabbed a ball from the floor, picked it up, and put it back in its proper place. "Don't settle for anything. That's what you've always told me. Take your own advice. Besides, there's no way he can resist you. He may be putting up a good fight, but you're gorgeous, intelligent, and you have a great heart. He'd be an idiot not to give you a second chance."

Kayla put her finger on her nose, pushing it up, like they did as a kid when they were trying to see who could make a funnier face, while batting her eyelashes. "That's the nicest thing anyone's ever said to me."

Lauren busted up laughing. "You're also a dork," she said in between chuckles.

"And that's why you love me." Kayla reached out and messed up Lauren's hair, knocking the ball over where her sister had just placed it, causing it to go flying through the store.

Lauren ran after it. "That and the fact that if it wasn't for you, I wouldn't have met Jordan," she said, catching her breath.

There was one major thing about Jordan that disturbed Kayla.

"Lauren, he works in the city. Are you willing to move to Manhattan if things become serious? I know you've only gone on one date with him, but he's the first guy in a long time who's managed to catch your interest."

Lauren looked at the ball as she twirled it in her hands. "I've thought about that. I don't think I could leave our family, Kayla. I know you did when you went to graduate school, but you're so much braver than me. And stronger, too."

Kayla smiled warmly. "Manhattan is a lot closer than California. We could see you all the time. You could come here every weekend if you wanted to."

Lauren groaned. "Let's not think about that now. I already told him how much I love Bella Cove and that I never saw myself moving."

"What did he say?"

"He said he wasn't attached to Manhattan, and that wasn't where he saw himself raising his children. Right before he left, he told me he really likes me, and if things continue to progress between us, he could definitely see us in a relationship."

"Did you think that was too much to say on the first date?" Kayla asked. Gabe had said more, but her sister had certain views on how men should behave on each date.

Lauren paused. "Normally, I would have thought so, but with Jordan it's different. I agree with what he said. We clicked."

Kayla understood more than her sister would ever know. "Then I think you should keep an open mind and see what happens."

Lauren nodded. "I will, but I won't leave Bella Cove. That's a deal-breaker for me."

A customer came in, interrupting their conversation, and Lauren helped her. Lauren's spirits had drastically lifted in the few days she'd been working there. Meeting Jordan had helped. Kayla hoped her sister and Jordan worked out. It would be nice if her older sister was happily married. Lauren deserved it.

The next three days passed in a busy routine, but not once did Kayla see Gabe. She kept hoping he'd at least pop into her store to say hello. Maybe even steal another kiss. But nothing. He wanted to take baby steps, but they were standing still.

Her mom had said she'd seen him talking to his builders, and he'd stopped by to thank her for dinner. How insane was it for Kayla to feel jealous of her mom because she had spoken with him? She hated how much she missed him. And she couldn't stop looking for him. When she was in the coffee shop, she looked for him. When she was in the local bakery, she looked for him. She stared at his office door all day long to catch a glimpse of him leaving. She saw Alice coming and going, but not him. Was he okay? Her mom had invited him to come again to dinner whenever he wanted, and he told her he'd definitely take her up on that. So that gave Kayla a bit of hope at least.

She was going crazy. She hadn't seen the man in two years, and she had survived. Now, three days had passed without her catching sight of him, and she was losing it. Things had gotten so bad, she'd started counting the days until it was time to pay her rent. How insane was that? Originally, Gabe had wanted her to mail the rent check, but since he'd moved his office across the street, that wouldn't make sense. Even if he still wanted her to put the check in the mail, she wouldn't do it. If that was the only way she'd get to see him, then she would use it. Luckily for her and her sanity, the rent was due today.

Lauren hadn't pestered Kayla about him again or mentioned the fact she thought he had the hots for Kayla. Her sister was too consumed with seeing Jordan over the weekend. And Sarah was busy thinking of different ways to improve the store. First, she'd created the snowflake corner, where she also placed the castle. Kids loved playing there. Her next goal was to add a superhero section. She had been setting up a small table with superhero figures on it. For the first time in her life, she seemed to have found a purpose and a passion.

Kayla hoped her sister's enthusiasm for working in the store lasted. Sarah's other issue—her habit of flirting with every man who crossed her path—still worried Kayla. Two boys who'd just graduated from college had come into the store looking for Sarah, but she'd been out to lunch. Kayla had shooed them off, and she hadn't been too nice about it, either. She'd have to help Sarah with that, but not today. Today, she was paying her rent and, hopefully, seeing Gabe.

Kayla held the check in her trembling hands. The last time her hands shook this badly, she'd been signing the contract to take over the store from Melody.

She inhaled and closed her eyes. It was six o'clock. Her plan was to close the store and walk across the street to hand Gabe the check. Sarah and Lauren had left a half hour ago. Kayla had pretty much kicked them out so she could deal with this on her own.

Heck, Gabe might not even be over there, so all this stress and drama could be for nothing. But the light was on in his office, and she had seen Alice walk out a little while earlier. Handing the check to him could also be a really bad idea. The encounter could go either way. Clearly, he hadn't come to see her for a reason.

Kayla glanced in the mirror one more time. She had dressed this morning with him in mind. Opting for a casual look, she'd chosen her skinny jeans and a black, ribbed tank top with a small white peace sign in the corner. The peace sign seemed appropriate.

Kayla groaned. It was now or never. And the idea of never seeing him again was no longer an option. She had to give him the rent check anyway.

Taking one more deep breath, she grabbed her purse, raised her chin slightly, and left her store, making sure to lock the door behind her. Looking across the street, she saw the light still on. She could do this. Handing her rent check to Gabe shouldn't be such a big deal, but if he took it and didn't say anything, she would leave feeling hurt. She was a little bit more sensitive than usual as she'd suffered through way too many disappointments in the last two years. This would add to them, and she didn't want that.

When she got to his office door and knocked, no one answered. Then she saw the little sign to the side of the door: *Please ring the bell.* So she did.

Finally, after what felt like an eternity, the door opened. Standing there in a green t-shirt to match his gorgeous eyes, and wearing a pair of black jeans that hugged him just right, was the man she had almost married.

"Hey." Gabe raised both his eyebrows.

Then she caught him checking her out.

"Hi, I have the rent for you," she said, holding out the check and speaking a little louder than normal, so he could hear her over the noise from the passing cars.

He took it from her. "Thanks." He folded the check and stuck it in the pocket of his jeans. "I didn't charge for the paint job." Gabe smiled warmly, revealing his perfectly white teeth.

She smiled back. "I appreciate that." Her heart was thudding like crazy. He was being nice, but he hadn't invited her inside.

"You should thank my grandfather." Gabe turned his gaze toward heaven. "He told me to look out for Magical Toys. He wanted me to take good care of you."

"I'm grateful, but he probably meant Melody. They were friends."

Gabe shook his head. "No, he said there was a short, dark-haired woman who always made him laugh, and a beautiful blonde who looked and acted like an angel."

Kayla looked at the street, regaining her composure, then back at him. "I really liked your grandfather. He was always so kind."

"He was. It's funny how he never gave me your name before I came here."

"If you'd known it was me, would it have changed anything?" She tilted her head slightly.

"I told you that first day, I wouldn't have come. Now, I'm glad I did."

Hope burst through Kayla's chest. "You mean it?"

Gabe nodded. "It's been interesting, seeing you in your element, especially at dinner the other night. And I'm not talking about what happened right afterward."

Kayla's cheeks heated as she turned toward a car behind her. It stopped short and then continued. It was rush hour and Main Street's busiest time. She wished Gabe would ask her to come in already, so she could hear him better.

"Did you learn anything?" she asked.

Gabe's eyes changed. They became more intense, as if they were zooming in on her soul. "I did."

"What did you learn?"

Gabe chuckled. "That you belong here. With your family."

Kayla swallowed hard. "I once belonged with you."

"You did, but your family needs you."

"You needed me, too."

"I didn't need you, but I wanted you badly. I wanted you around me. I wanted you as a lover. And I wanted you as my best friend."

"I was your best friend." Another car drove by fast. She had to step forward, so she could hear him better.

"People don't leave their best friend the way you did."

So he still hadn't forgiven her. Neither the dinner nor the kiss had changed anything.

"But after watching you with your family, I pitied you," he added.

"Why?" She wouldn't be able to stand it if he felt sorry for her. That was the last thing she wanted.

"I could see how you're torn. They need you too much. I saw how they rely on you. You're their comfort and safety. But you had to give up all your dreams in order to take on that role."

"It's not a role," she shot back. "They were really screwed up when Nana passed. I was screwed up, too, because I had to figure out how to deal with all them. I never expected them to go off the deep end. But they all pretty much have their act together now."

Gabe shook his head. "You're the most loving, loyal, generous, and caring person I know. I've never met anyone like you. But that other side to you, the side I witnessed every day for two years, is buried deep. At dinner, I saw glimpses of the real you, and it drove me crazy. That's the woman I chose to kiss. At the same time, every time the real you came out, you'd stuff it down. I don't think I've ever felt so frustrated in my entire life."

Kayla huffed. "You're right. I have changed. Having the weight of your family on you can do that. I've also seen a side to life I never thought I'd experience when you and I were together. I was pretty sheltered from all the bad stuff. But I'm not a sheltered girl anymore. I'm a woman who has seen the darker aspects to life. So if you're frustrated with me, then that sucks for you. But you had said after that kiss that we could take things in baby steps. I'd still like you to know the woman I am today, and maybe, just maybe, we could put the past behind us and move forward."

Even though Kayla was spilling her guts to him, her heart felt split in two. Part of her wanted to throttle him, and the other wanted to beg him to let her inside, so she wouldn't have to juggle the noise from the cars, and they could sit down and talk. Like two adults. Her adult side won. "May I come in?" she asked.

Gabe's jaw clenched. "No. I'm locking up in a few minutes and then leaving."

Kayla sighed. "All right, I'm going to go then."

She turned to leave, but Gabe's voice stopped her.

"I'm thinking of putting my grandfather's house in East Hampton on the market soon. How long does it take for houses to sell around here?"

"That depends. How long will it take for your house next to mine to be finished?"

"Nine months."

A couple strolled by, walking hand in hand. Kayla stared after them.

"I'd put your grandfather's house on the market in about six months. From what Lauren used to say when she worked at the real estate firm, houses in the Hamptons usually sold pretty fast."

"Okay, I'll tell my real estate agent."

Kayla swallowed. "My family really liked you. They're happy you'll be our neighbor."

Gabe chuckled. "I really liked them. All of them. But that was the hardest meal I've ever sat through."

Her heart sank. "Then why did you come?"

"Your mom invited me, and it was the right thing to do. The neighborly thing to do. But looking around at your family, knowing they were also supposed to be my family, was really hard for me."

"I'm sorry," she whispered, meaning it. "I would have loved nothing more than to introduce you as my boyfriend or fiancé or even husband." Gabe's eyes darkened, but he didn't respond. "Well, it was good seeing you. I hope to see you again soon."

Gabe nodded. She took a step back, and he was already closing the door. She never should have handed him the rent check. She should have called Alice and asked her to come over and get it.

Without looking back toward his office, Kayla began walking home. Even though she was walking away from Gabe yet again, she was heading toward her family who needed her.

By the time she arrived at the house, she was so exhausted she could barely stand up. The walk home had been good for her, though. The fresh air and exercise had given her a chance to clear her head, but it hadn't lifted her spirits. Somehow, she had to think of a way to get through this, especially with him living as her neighbor. Sooner or later, he'd start dating, if he wasn't already. Alice sure was pretty. Kayla had always prided herself on coming up with solutions to help others, but she couldn't think of a way to help herself.

She opened the door, hoping no one was in the kitchen to ask her about her day. Instead, she walked into a normal evening, where her mom was throwing dishes at her dad and screaming her head off. But unlike other nights, tonight, she couldn't take it.

"Enough, both of you!" Kayla never raised her voice, so when she did, everyone listened. "What's the fight about now?"

"Your father has to go back to the factory for the third night in a row."

Kayla looked at her dad. "Dad, are you going to the factory because you have furniture that needs to be finished soon or are you trying to avoid Mom?"

Her dad ran his hands through his hair. "I have a huge shipment going out in three days. I still have to finish the bed and the custom-designed night tables that have been challenging to make. They're good, loyal customers. I don't want to let them down."

Kayla sighed. "Okay, Dad, go."

Her dad immediately stood from the kitchen table and left out of the back door.

"You see, Mom? This isn't about you or an indication he doesn't love you. But I can tell you one thing—he's not going to love you if you continue treating him this way. I've had enough, and the whole family has had enough of you screaming at Dad. This needs to stop."

Kayla didn't wait for her mom's response. She was already climbing the stairs. She knew what was going to happen. Her mom was going to sit at the kitchen table and cry her eyes out. This time, she was going to let her mother cry all by herself. She was tired of her mother acting this way. If her dad didn't love his wife, he would have been gone by now.

Before she even made it to the top step, there was a knock on the back door. And only friends of the family knocked on the back door. Kayla sighed and looked back downstairs. Her mom got up from the kitchen table, sobbing like Kayla had predicted. As the person at the door knocked again, her mom ran down the hallway, leaving Kayla to go to the door. Her sisters were usually at the gym at this time of night or she would have let them answer it, and who knew where Josh was. Even if Josh was home, he was too lazy to answer the door.

Whoever was there was being persistent. How important could this be? They kept knocking. When Kayla reached the bottom of the stairs, she walked to the back door and paused when she realized it was Gabe. Of all people, she didn't think it would be him. What was he doing here? He saw her through the glass door and nodded. After their confrontation, she couldn't imagine why he'd be here, unless he wanted to torture her some more. He probably came here to point out more mistakes she had made. Or maybe he wasn't here for her at all. Still, she felt her heart speed up and a nervousness she couldn't seem to get rid of whenever she saw him.

Kayla opened the door and debated asking him to come in since he had made her stand outside earlier. But she refused to be rude like he was.

"Is everything okay? I assumed you were on your way to your grandfather's."

Gabe handed her an empty plastic container. "I wanted to talk to my builder and return this. Tell your mom thank you. I ate every single one of her delicious brownies."

Kayla had forgotten that her mom had given Gabe brownies to take home with him after the dinner. "I will. I'd let you tell her yourself, but she's busy right now," she said, placing the empty container on the counter behind her.

"I know. I could hear her yelling from my property."

Kayla cringed inside. She would have to tell her mom she was embarrassing herself in front of the neighbors. "Sorry about that." She wondered how long he had been listening to her mom yell at her dad like that. She had left Gabe at his office, but she'd walked home, so he must have beaten her home by driving.

"No problem. I see she's no longer yelling, so you must have solved another one of your family's problems."

Kayla grinded her teeth. "I didn't solve her problem, Gabe. I only stopped her from yelling." She was in no mood for him to be an asshole. She was about to close the door, but he got that cute twinkle in his eyes and leaned against the door, so she couldn't close it on him.

"That's all you *can* do," he said and smirked.

Kayla stared into his eyes. He was the most confusing man she'd ever met.

"Don't you judge me. I'm doing the best I can," she said, her tone sharp.

He crinkled his forehead. "I'm not judging you."

"Nana would have done a better job with my mom. Part of the reason my mom is like this is because when she lost her mom, when Nana died, Mom lost a huge part of her life. You used to hear her yelling in the background of our phone conversations. Nana was Mom's world. Even more than my dad and her children." She was tired of having to defend her family.

"I'm not judging you, Kayla."

Her entire body grew tense. "Nana would have known what to do, Gabe. She always did. When my mom fought with my dad, Nana knew the right thing to say."

Gabe placed his hand on her shoulder. Kayla froze.

"I'm not judging."

Kayla looked at his hand. She couldn't handle him looking into her eyes in that knowing way while touching her at the same time. She wanted more than his hand. She wanted more than his kiss. She wanted his heart.

"Kayla, look at me." With his other hand, Gabe raised her chin slightly, forcing her to look into his mesmerizing green eyes. "After school, my parents got a divorce. And even though I'm older, it was hard for me and hard for the whole family. If I hadn't been in graduate school, maybe things would have been different. Maybe they could have worked through their problems."

Kayla's heart fell as she instinctively placed her hand over his and squeezed. "What happened with them? I remember them being close, from what you said." She had never met them, but she had heard Gabe talking to them on many occasions.

Gabe shrugged but he didn't pull his hand away. "They grew apart. Fell out of love. That's what they told me."

"I'm sorry," she whispered, and she truly was. Gabe loved his parents very much.

He nodded and finally removed his hand, forcing hers to fall by her side.

"I appreciate that, but what I'm trying to say is that I wish I could have been there to help them."

"Gabe, even if you were, there's not much you could have done. You could have guided them, offered advice, but at the end of the day, it was their decision whether they want to stay in their marriage."

Gabe raised his eyebrow. "I could say the same for you."

So this had been a lesson all along. Gabe was trying to help her. Maybe this was his way of calling a truce. Maybe it was a better way than having him come to dinner with her family.

"Are you forgiving me?" she asked.

Gabe looked at her, and at first, he didn't answer. And she wanted him to, badly. More than anything, she needed to hear that he had forgiven everything she had done to them. Not knowing what else to do, she placed both her hands on his cheeks. He gently brushed them away and took a small step back.

"No," he said. "I wanted you by my side while they were divorcing. I was without my partner."

Kayla's heart sank. Her family had wanted her here, too.

He shook his head. "But we were also friends. And as an old friend, I'm concerned about you. Maybe you can guide your family, but you can't solve their problems. Only they can do that. But you can work on solving your own."

"I know," she said defensively.

They stared at each other for another moment, and then Gabe turned, walked down her porch steps, and headed back to his property. They didn't say goodbye, and Kayla never even had a chance to ask him to come inside. Even if she had, she was certain he wouldn't have accepted the invitation. He'd admitted he hadn't forgiven her. Maybe he had no intention of ever forgiving her. In one of her psych classes, she'd learned it was healthier to forgive the other person, as the issue would only eat away at your insides and not the other person's. But she'd have to disagree. Gabe not forgiving her was definitely eating her up inside and was probably bothering her more than it bothered him.

Kayla locked the door and then turned around. She could have sworn she heard footsteps, but maybe she was wrong. She would have known if it was one of her sisters. They would have run up to Gabe. And her mom wouldn't be leaving the guest suite until tomorrow. That left Josh. Even if he had heard her and Gabe talking, he wouldn't care. All he wanted was a car. He didn't seem to care about anything else.

Quickly, Kayla climbed the stairs before something else happened that required her attention. She passed Josh's door on the way to hers and saw it was open. He'd probably been on his way into the kitchen to grab some dinner when he'd heard them talking. She should talk to her brother to see what he'd heard and to ask him to keep it quiet. But it didn't matter. Out of all her siblings, she cared the least about Josh knowing her history with Gabe. He was too preoccupied with his own problems to stick his nose into hers.

Kayla went into her room and closed the door behind her. She walked to her window to close the curtains and froze. Gabe was standing on his property staring out into the bay. What was he thinking? Did he miss the two of them? Was he even thinking about her? She wished she could read his mind.

Kayla smiled to herself. The moon was making him glow. He ran his hands through his hair, and her smile slipped. He only did that when he was frustrated. She was sure she was the cause. But if he wasn't ready or open to forgive her, her hands were tied. There wasn't anything else she could do.

A deep urge to touch him consumed her, so she raised her arm, as if by doing so, she could reach him. And that was the moment he turned and looked toward her window. She was sure he saw her. He didn't wave, and neither did she. Although they were separated by a great distance, the intensity between them felt so strong he might as well have been standing in her room. If only she could see the expression in his eyes. Then she would have a better idea of what was going on in his head. But even with him so far away, her body heated up and tingled. He always did have that effect on her.

Gabe turned around and walked away. Probably a good thing because Kayla had been seconds away from running back down the stairs, out the door, and across the grass so she could throw her arms around him and beg him to try to at least give them another chance. But it was too late now.

She wasn't even sure when she'd see him again—the rent wasn't due for another month, but she'd try to think of an excuse. He may be able to ignore her, but she sure couldn't stop thinking about him. Tomorrow was a new day in Bella Cove, and anything could happen. Miracles happened here every day, just as she'd toasted the other night at dinner. She and Gabe were a miracle. She'd never thought she'd see him again and look what had happened.

Tonight, she'd learned something valuable. Although he said he'd wanted her to be there for him when his parents were getting divorced, he'd also needed her. And she hadn't been there for him. She'd abandoned him because she'd chosen not to abandon her family. This explained why he gave her that damn ultimatum. If Kayla had only known what he was dealing with, she would have made a different choice. Maybe she would have stayed a week with him and then a week with her family. She wasn't sure, but she would have done something.

Well, this changed everything. He had said baby steps. Kayla wasn't going to give him baby steps. Nope. She was going all in. Two years ago, she'd abandoned him, but there was no way she'd ever do that to him again. Unfortunately, she couldn't change the past, but she could make up for the hurt she'd caused him. While her family went through hell, she'd learned she was stronger than she'd thought. As of tonight, with the moon as her witness, she decided not to give up and to fight for the man she loved.

12

WHEN KAYLA ARRIVED at the shop early the next morning, she was on a new mission—making Gabe understand that she didn't plan to abandon him ever again. After obsessing over it all night, she'd come to the conclusion she had to show Gabe she was still fun to be around. That would be the first step.

She glanced out the window about a hundred times, watching for him to arrive at his office. Around seven, Kayla saw him parking his black SUV in front. As he stepped out of his car, Kayla grabbed her purse, ran out of the store, locked the door quickly, and shouted his name. "Gabe?"

As he was putting the key in the door, Kayla ran across the street, careful not to be hit by a car.

"Gabe," she shouted again.

Finally, she got his attention.

"Hey," he said right before stepping inside. "Is everything okay?"

She loved how concerned he sounded. "Everything's okay. Do you have a meeting within the next hour or something you need to be doing?"

Gabe chuckled. "There's always something I need to be doing."

Kayla smiled. "Let me ask this differently. Gabe Wademan, would you like to spend the next hour with me?"

Gabe raised his eyebrow. "Just you and me? Alone?"

She laughed. "Just us. There's a special place in Bella Cove I'd like to show you. It's a sacred spot, and even if you paid to go on the East End tour bus, they wouldn't stop there."

Kayla could tell he was checking her out. His gaze roamed down her body. She'd chosen a navy-blue sundress with spaghetti straps, an outfit that showed off her cleavage, just for him. He'd told her at school that he loved her in navy because it brought out the depth in her eyes.

Gabe sighed. "I think you're up to something, but you also have me intrigued. Come on. Let's go. I have a free hour, but then I have a meeting with the manager of an apartment building my grandfather owned. He's coming all the way out from the city—I don't want to be late for him." He locked his door and put his keys into his pocket.

Kayla smiled wider. "Deal. I'll show you the spot, and I'll make sure I return you in exactly an hour." Without thinking, she grabbed his hand. "I'll lead."

She hadn't realized they were still holding hands until they were crossing the street. Instead of removing her hand, she gripped his tighter, waiting for him to say something negative or to pull away. But he didn't.

She led him through an alleyway, a shortcut to the bay. Neither spoke—Kayla wasn't sure what to say. She'd figure she'd wing it when they reached the spot. All she knew was that she refused to have a serious conversation. They'd had enough of those.

When they reached the bay, she went left.

"You're taking me to the bay? I've been here before," he said.

Kayla noted a drop of disappointment in his voice. "Don't worry. I promise you'll love where I'm taking you." She wasn't lying. This was her favorite spot.

The bay took a sharp turn, and the path came to an end, but Kayla kept going. They walked through a small field, which ended by a forest.

"We're walking through here," she said, glancing back at Gabe.

He looked wary. Kayla couldn't help but laugh.

"Don't worry. We may run into a deer, but other than that, we're pretty safe."

"You said *pretty* safe. You didn't say very safe or even just safe. What if we run into a bear?"

She laughed harder. "Don't be a pussy," she said, pulling him along.

"Did you just call me a pussy?"

Kayla turned and looked at him. His eyes twinkled.

"Yes, I believe I did."

"You'll pay for that, Kayla Conway."

She smiled wide. "I look forward to it."

The trees ended, and the bay sat right in front of them. Several medium-sized rocks by the water led to a larger rock.

"We're here," she said, releasing his hand and climbing the smaller rocks until she reached her favorite. "I'd like to introduce you to Kayla's Rock."

"Kayla's Rock," he echoed, smirking.

"Yes. It's my rock. If you don't believe me, look." She pointed to the side of the rock that faced away from the water.

Gabe bent down, squinting. "You carved your name?"

"I did," she said proudly. "When I was a little girl, my brothers and sisters and I used to play hide and seek around Bella Cove. We played until my mom found out and yelled at us. You see, playing hide and seek around your yard isn't as much fun when you can play it all over town."

"You'd be much harder to find."

Kayla smiled. "Exactly. I'm glad you understand."

He nodded, and his eyes twinkled again.

Kayla continued. "So one day, while we were playing, I found this rock. I fell in love with it instantly. Not because it was a rock, but because it was large enough for me to sit on and even take a nap if I wanted to."

"Were you into naps?"

"Considering my brothers and sisters would sneak into my room at all hours of the night, playing practical jokes on me, I was tired. So, yes, I was into naps."

Gabe chuckled as she made room on the rock for him.

"Would you like to sit?" she asked.

There was more than enough room for both of them, but she could see his trepidation. She watched him checking out where they were, looking at the trees, the rocks, the boats, and the houses in the distance.

"It's private here."

Kayla put her hands on her hips. "Are you afraid to be alone with me, Gabe Wademan?"

Gabe chuckled as he shook his head. "Maybe." He sat down next to her anyway.

There really was enough room for both of them, but suddenly, Kayla thought the rock felt smaller. "Was that so hard?" she asked.

"Yes. You may have changed on the inside, but you're more gorgeous than ever on the outside."

Kayla had no idea how to respond. If she did, it could lead to another serious conversation, and she hadn't brought him out here for that. She looked down at her dress, which had ridden up. Only her thigh was exposed, but she didn't want Gabe to think she purposely sat that way.

"Sorry," she said, pushing down the dress. "This is how I sat when I was a little girl."

Gabe was staring at her thigh. He swallowed hard. It was good to know he was as attracted to her as she was to him. That part hadn't seemed to have died. If anything, their attraction was stronger than ever.

He cleared his throat. "So…when did you carve your name?"

"I was about ten when I found the rock. I was so proud. We started hide and seek on the other side of the bay. When I saw the trees, I ran through them, not knowing what to expect. I remember how excited I felt. As the trees ended, I saw all this. It was the most beautiful spot I'd ever seen. And I felt like it was my discovery. I walked over to this rock and sat down. I sat here for at least an hour, or at least it felt that long. It was so peaceful that I decided I didn't want my siblings to find me here. I didn't want them to take this sacred spot away from me. When you live with two sisters and two brothers, there's always chaos. That was the first time I felt utterly at peace.

"So I left this spot and let them find me on the other side of the trees. I've come here ever since. Especially when I need to think. One day, when I was visiting my dad at the furniture factory, I found a small knife. I knew exactly how to put it to good use. So I told my dad I was going to the library—but came here instead and carved *Kayla's Rock*, claiming it officially as my own. Out of every place in Bella Cove, this one spot feels like mine."

He nodded as he grabbed her hand and squeezed. "Did you come here a few weeks ago when we were having a conversation at your store and you saw Sarah about to come in?"

She smiled softly. "I did."

He stroked her inner palm with his thumb. "I wondered where you went."

Gabe stared at her while continuing to massage her palm. Kayla shifted a little on the rock. Why did it feel as if his eyes were penetrating her soul?

With his free hand, he reached into his pocket and took out a pocket knife.

"I found this in my grandfather's desk drawer. I was bringing it to the office to fix a cabinet that seems to be stuck." He released Kayla's hand and bent down to where she'd carved her name. Slowly, he used the knife to carve something, too.

"What are you writing?" she asked.

"Come look for yourself."

Kayla scooted forward and then bent down next to him. She gasped. Underneath her name, he'd carved the word "and," then underneath that, "Gabe's Rock." It now read, "Kayla's Rock and Gabe's Rock."

Her heartbeat quickened, and she felt as if a butterfly jumped in her stomach. "I didn't say you could claim part of my rock." She smiled wide.

He smiled back. "Kayla Conway, may I claim part of your rock?"

She laughed. "Yes, Gabe Wademan. You may." She wanted to tell him he could claim anything he wanted of hers because he'd already claimed what mattered most — her heart.

Kayla walked Gabe back to Main Street exactly an hour later as promised. She couldn't remember the last time she had such a great morning. The only part she didn't like was when he'd dropped her off at her store and gave her a kiss on the cheek. She didn't expect him to give her a kiss like he had outside his car, but a peck on the lips would have sufficed.

Apparently, he knew she was upset because he chuckled. "Remember, Kayla. Baby steps."

She rolled her eyes before opening the door. But she turned before he walked away. "If it weren't for your damn sexy lips, that wouldn't be a problem."

Gabe didn't say anything back. He just laughed and shook his head.

Kayla could hear him laughing all the way back to his office. She wasn't sure exactly what he felt was so funny. She was telling the truth. He had the sexiest lips she'd ever seen. But she couldn't think about them right now. She had to catch up on her morning routine of straightening the toys and responding to her email. Late last night, she'd gotten an email from one of her vendors who had sent her a toy shipment late, which meant there was an empty space on the girls' shelf, ages nine through twelve. She would have to think of a way to fix that.

Melody would have freaked out over something like that, but Kayla worked differently. She never sweated the small stuff. After watching her mom freak out over every little thing, Kayla had decided to roll with life and take certain things in stride.

Her first task was dusting off the toys, so she grabbed a rag and started on the little animal figures. When she reached down to the second shelf filled with horses and cows, the front door opened. At first, she thought it was Sarah, arriving early, but it was Jessica.

"Hi!" Kayla put down the dust rag and ran to give her sister-in-law a huge hug.

"Hi." Jessica hugged her back. "I hope you don't mind me coming here so early, but I don't have to be at work for another twenty minutes."

Kayla was surprised to see Jessica but was more concerned with how nervous she appeared.

"No problem. What's going on? Is everything okay?"

Jessica inhaled. "This may sound strange, but your friend Erica—who's the best acupuncturist ever, by the way—recommended I buy a small baby toy and place it under my pillow at night. She believes it'll help me to manifest a baby."

"And do you believe it will?" Kayla asked.

Jessica laughed. "I'm open to anything. I really want to get pregnant."

Kayla smiled. "Well, *I* believe it."

"You do?" Jessica grinned.

"Erica knows what she's talking about. If she suggests you do it, I think it's a great idea."

Jessica looked visibly relieved. "Okay, I felt funny telling you."

Kayla rolled her eyes. "Oh, honey, I've heard it all. Whatever gives you hope is what I believe in. If I wanted to have a baby, I'd do the exact same thing."

"Erica said when I look at it, I should visualize my baby."

"I think that's a great idea, too. Let's go to the baby section and you can pick out a toy."

Jessica grabbed her arm. "Thank you, Kayla. Your help means a lot to me. And I wanted you to know I told Matt about this, and he thought it was a fantastic idea, too."

Kayla smiled. "Then let's have some fun picking out the perfect toy."

Kayla spent the next fifteen minutes with Jessica. After her sister-in-law had chosen a toy and left the store, Kayla imagined herself buying a toy for her own baby. At one time, she had wanted four children. Now, she didn't think she'd have any. She heard someone say that either you were meant to take care of adults or you were meant to take care of children. Kayla must have been meant to take care of adults because her family was a huge amount of work. Still, it would be nice if she could have both.

Sarah barged through the front door, ran to Kayla, and wrapped her in a hug.

Kayla laughed. "Hey, hey, hey, good morning to you, too."

"You're going to love me after I tell you what I've come up with." Sarah released Kayla and started jumping up and down. She'd always jumped, even as a kid.

"I love you already. I couldn't imagine loving you anymore than I already do." There had been many times in the past when Kayla had acted as Sarah's mother. In fact, when anyone asked who her mom was, Sarah told them Kayla, and that had gone on since elementary school. Kayla always corrected Sarah, saying she was her sister, but Sarah disagreed.

It wasn't as if they had a bad mom, but Mom was so consumed with herself and her problems, she didn't have time to think of her children unless it involved planning meals and cooking. Her mom should have been a baker or chef. When Kayla took over monitoring Nana's money, she had asked her mom if she'd like to open a bakery or a restaurant. She would have even used the funds to make it happen, but Mom wasn't interested, which was such a shame.

"Kayla, your mind's wandering. I want to tell you my idea."

"Sorry. Yes, please, tell me." Kayla had to admit, her mind had been wandering a lot lately.

"I figured out a way for the store to generate more income."

"Okay." Kayla hoped it was an idea she could support.

"I think we should have classes here, like Mommy and Me classes, and art classes for kids. The storage room is huge, and there's so much empty space in there. We can divide the room in half, make the other side look pretty, and hold the classes there. And I could run them."

Kayla smiled. "I absolutely love the idea. Let's do it."

"Really?" Sarah clapped her hands.

"Yup—when there are no customers, we can start cleaning the room. I'll even pay you according to how many kids show. So let's say we charge ten dollars for the Mommy and Me class; you'll get five for each Mommy and Me pair, and the store gets the other half. How about you call our insurance company, too, and see if we need to add more coverage to the plan?"

"You don't need to pay me, Kayla. You already pay me more than enough. I want the store to benefit."

"The store *will* benefit. Oh, and call the fire department, and see how many people we can have in the room."

Sarah threw her arms around Kayla again and gave her an even tighter hug. "Thank you, thank you, thank you."

Kayla laughed. Between Sarah and Jessica, the day was already a success. Not to mention her dream morning with Gabe. Kayla would have time to obsess over how amazing it was when she had time alone.

Sarah also had another idea. She thought they should hang paper hearts above the girls' toy section, since the snowflakes were such a hit with the kids. So they cut out paper hearts until Sarah decided to go to the fire station to ask how many people were allowed in the updated storage room. Kayla tried to convince her it wouldn't matter if she flirted all day with the men at the firehouse. Rules were rules, and they wouldn't change them because Sarah was beautiful and great at flirting. But Sarah was convinced going in person would help their case.

Kayla was left by herself to stand on her stepstool and attempt to hang the hearts. If only she had Gabe's ladder, the task would be so much easier. Sarah had suggested she call him and ask if they could borrow it, but Kayla didn't think bothering Gabe was such a great idea right now, especially since they'd spent the morning together. Kayla could have told her sister that but wanted to keep thoughts of that special time to herself.

Her stepstool was pretty high. It had three tiers, so Kayla stood on the highest one. She was petite, so she had to stand on her tiptoes. Sarah's vision was to punch a hole in the top of the heart, tie a string in the hole, and use an adhesive sticker so it would stick to the ceiling. But that method made Kayla's job harder. She had tried to convince Sarah to ditch the string and just tape the hearts on the ceiling, but Sarah didn't think that would look as nice. And since Kayla was trying to give Sarah extra confidence, she had agreed—much to her chagrin now.

The stickers were especially hard to stick on the ceiling. If she was taller, the job would have been a whole lot easier. She groaned, stretching as high as she could, as she tried to attach the sticker onto the ceiling. At least there was no one else in the store besides her. Anyone who passed by could see under her dress. As long as no one walked by and stopped to look through her window, she'd be okay. Today of all days, she'd just had to wear the damn navy sundress to impress Gabe. The higher she stood on her tiptoes, the higher her dress rose.

Finally, she managed to adhere one of the stickers on the ceiling, but when she pulled her hand away, she almost fell over. She grabbed the top of the stepstool just in time. With any luck, Sarah would bring back a firefighter who could help her. That could be one benefit to Sarah flirting. A tall man could finish hanging these stupid hearts in five minutes. Kayla had managed to hang one in thirty.

"What do you think you're doing?" Gabe stormed into her store, looking less than pleased.

"Hanging up some beautiful artwork Sarah and I made." Kayla pushed down her dress to cover up her thighs. Not that it mattered. He'd seen them this morning.

He rushed over to her and grabbed the hearts out of her hands.

"They look like paper hearts to me."

"You don't think I could hang them in a gallery in Manhattan?"

Gabe didn't even crack a smile. "No, I don't. I also don't think you should be standing on that rickety stepstool. You're too short to hang those."

Kayla rolled her eyes. "Thanks."

"Why didn't you ask me to do it?"

Kayla frowned. "I don't feel comfortable asking my landlord to hang hearts on my ceiling."

"Ah, so now I'm back to being your landlord. Don't forget, I'm also your neighbor, and helping out now and then is the neighborly thing to do."

Kayla groaned. "That's not what I meant. I wasn't going to ask you to hang them for me because you may be many things, but you're not my handyman," she said, her tone sharp. "But could I please borrow your ladder?"

He clenched his jaw. There went the easygoing attitude from this morning.

"No, you may not. But I'll bring the ladder here and hang your hearts. There's no way I'm going to let you climb the ladder. You could fall," he said, his voice stern.

"You could, too, and I'm strong. I'm way more physically fit than I was at school."

Gabe gave her a no-nonsense look, which she remembered from two years ago when he'd been determined to have his own way. His expression made her laugh.

"What's so funny?" Clearly, nothing about this situation was funny to him.

"I haven't seen that look on your face since school." Kayla paused and smiled. "I've missed it, even though you're being an arrogant asshole."

Gabe clenched his jaw even tighter. "And yet, you left me anyway. You threw away everything we had."

Kayla huffed. She'd thought they'd made progress this morning, but maybe she was wrong. "I left you, but not the way you thought. The last few months we were together, your attitude changed. We were still moving forward with the engagement, but you became cocky. Arrogant. You were planning a life for us, but there was no room for me to tell you what I wanted. Maybe I didn't want to work for your dad. Maybe I didn't want to move into the guesthouse in back of their house until we had enough money to buy a place of our own."

She paused and inhaled. "Even with that being said, when I came back to Bella Cove, I had every intention of returning to you — but as I've told you, I didn't realize how screwed up my family was. I also had no idea you were also going through your personal hell. Had I known, I would have handled things differently. But I had no way of knowing I was abandoning you because you never told me."

Gabe's jaw was still clenched. "What would you have done differently?"

"I don't know," she whispered. "Maybe I would have spent the weeks with my family and the weekends with you. I honestly don't know, Gabe. But I would have done *something* differently."

They stared at each other for another moment. Then Gabe nodded and started to walk away.

"I'll be back with the ladder."

Kayla sat on the stepstool and placed her head in her hands. She wanted to cry. She even tried to force the tears to come, but her eyes remained dry. Maybe she was just tired, fed up, and angry.

Five o'clock came, and Gabe still hadn't shown with the ladder. She tried using the stepstool again, but it wasn't any use. She still couldn't hang the hearts. Sarah tried, too, when she got back but she struggled as well, and she was tall. Unfortunately, she hadn't brought back a firefighter. Although, Sarah talked Kayla's ear off about the firefighters she had met. She even had a date with one, but she reiterated that she had no intention of getting married or being in a long-term, committed relationship.

Kayla rolled her eyes at her sister. Love had a way of sneaking up on people. She didn't want to admit it had happened to her, but it was the truth. She still was in love with Gabe. Spending time with him this morning had confirmed her feelings. Too bad they had to get all serious when he caught her on the stepstool. At least she'd found the courage to communicate with him. Without communication — even communication that might hurt sometimes — they didn't stand a chance.

Gabe showed up at 5:10. Kayla was adding descriptions of new toys into the computer database, and Sarah was on the floor, rearranging the bottom shelf of family board games.

"Hey, Gabe," Sarah said. She stood, brushed off her jeans, and gave him a huge hug.

Kayla's heart tightened. Sarah hugged him naturally, and yet, Kayla couldn't imagine throwing her arms around him so casually like that, even though she had a strong urge to do so.

He hugged Sarah back with one hand while holding the ladder with the other. Kayla was grateful. No matter how upset he was with her, at least he was still kind to her family.

"You brought your ladder." Sarah clapped and jumped up and down.

Gabe smiled at her.

"Gabe to the rescue!" she yelled, punching her fist into the air.

"Thank you, Gabe." Kayla smiled warmly.

Gabe didn't say anything. He simply nodded. Still, she caught the look in his eyes. She'd do anything to be able to read his mind.

"Okay, I'm ready. Where are the hearts?"

Sarah ran to the register desk and grabbed the adhesive stickers and hearts.

"Do you know where to hang them?" she asked.

"I think I do."

Sarah told him anyway, pointing to each place while giving him her most flirtatious smile.

Gabe smiled back, that charming smile that Kayla always loved. Then he climbed the ladder and began hanging them, making the job look easy as could be.

"Hey, Gabe?" Sarah asked.

"Yeah," he said, his focus on placing the stickers in the exact spots Sarah had indicated.

"Did Kayla tell you the great news?"

Kayla looked up at Gabe. He had stopped hanging hearts and had turned to look down at Sarah.

"What's the great news?" he asked.

"We're going to split the storage room in half. One side will still be for storage, and the other side will be an area where we can hold classes. We were thinking of having Mommy and Me classes and maybe art classes for kids. And Kayla said I can run them."

"You wouldn't know my sister was twenty-seven," Kayla told Gabe.

"Hey! I'm young at heart," Sarah responded.

"And that's why I love you." Kayla couldn't help but tease.

"I think it's a great idea. And I know you'll make it a success." Gabe smiled at Sarah. "And I like your young-at-heart attitude. It's who you are, and that's why you're so adored."

"Thank you, Gabe," Sarah said sweetly, batting her eyelashes dramatically as she pretended to flirt.

Kayla thought of something. "Oh God, you're not going to raise the rent now, are you? Kidding. Okay, maybe I'm not."

Gabe's gaze tore through her, making Kayla feel as if they were the only two people in the world.

"No," he said looking directly at her. "But that's not the only power I hold over you."

Kayla swallowed hard. She wanted to tell him she agreed. He held her heart and her body. She clenched in her deepest places just from his tone alone. Was he referring to that, too? God, she missed having sex with this man.

Sarah cleared her throat. "Hello? Have you forgotten I'm here or do you guys need to get a room?"

"Sarah!" Kayla's cheeks heated. Actually, for a minute there, she *had* forgotten her sister was in the room.

"What?" Sarah asked. "I know you guys used to be together, and then all hell broke loose with our family, but the tension in the room seems to rise the minute you two are together. This is one of the reasons I have no interest in being in a relationship. You guys have a second chance of being together, and yet you can't get out of your own way."

Kayla had no idea what to say. She looked over at Gabe, who was pushing his hands through his hair.

"You're right, Sarah," he began. "But, please, don't let what happened between your sister and me screw up any chance you might have to form a great relationship. It wasn't just the situation with your family that had an impact on breaking us up. Apparently, I was also being hard-headed toward the end. I had a vision of what I wanted Kayla's and my life to look like, but I failed to consult my partner."

"Gabe," Kayla cut him off.

"Let me finish. But while the Conway family was going through hell when your nana passed, I was going through my own hell."

"What happened?" Sarah asked, leaning against the wall.

Gabe continued hanging the hearts as he spoke. "My parents were going through a divorce, and I felt abandoned all around. My parents were barely communicating with me, and my brother chose that moment to move with his new wife to Oregon. We spoke a bunch of times about it, but he didn't want to have to deal with it, so when his wife got a new job, he left."

"I'm sorry, Gabe," Kayla said quietly, meaning it with her whole heart.

"I'm sorry, too," Sarah said as she looked at both of them. "But Kayla's here for you now. And I don't believe in abandonment issues. I took a yoga class once where my teacher said the only people who are truly abandoned are babies who rely on eating through the help of their moms or someone to give them food. You had a shitty situation, and Kayla did, too. But you both survived. You didn't die from it."

"Sarah," Kayla said warningly, as she straightened the toy cars.

"No. If you both don't want to be together, that's fine by me. But please do something to relieve the tension I feel whenever you two are together. The way you guys look at each other makes me want to run home and touch myself."

"Thanks for the visual, sweetie," Kayla said.

Sarah blew her a kiss. "No problem, beautiful." Then she looked at Gabe. "And hurry up hanging up those hearts so I can drive you crazy and make more."

Gabe chuckled. "You Conway women are so demanding."

"That's right, we are. Conway women power." Sarah raised her fist in the air.

A few customers came in, so Kayla couldn't say anything else. What she wanted to tell Sarah was that she wasn't going to abandon Gabe ever again.

A few minutes later, Gabe finished hanging the hearts and left. He said goodbye to Sarah, but he barely glanced at Kayla.

It was turning out to be a week of discoveries. Today alone, she'd learned two very important things. One, she understood why he couldn't let go of what had happened between them, and two, she needed to make sure they spent more time alone together. As long as he wasn't dating anyone else, maybe they could get out of their own way, as Sarah put it, and have their second chance.

13

ONCE KAYLA CLOSED THE SHOP, Sarah ran to the gym as if she had no cares in the world. Kayla envied her sister's lighthearted attitude, especially since Kayla's own cares seemed to be growing. Once Sarah had said her piece to her and Gabe earlier and gotten it off her chest, she was happy as a clam.

By the time Kayla walked up the back porch to her house, she was wiped out. The sun hadn't set yet, so she sat on the rocking chair and rocked back and forth, drawing in deep breaths of the fresh air coming in off the bay. The smell of Bella Cove always soothed her. There was nothing in life more peaceful than this.

She glanced toward Gabe's property, which was a mistake. Why did she automatically always look there? He stood there as strong and determined as always, looking over the work the builders had done so far. Kayla couldn't believe the progress, but Gabe had hired them to work seven days a week.

Her dad walked onto the back porch and sat on the chair next to hers. He didn't say anything at first. He just leaned forward, resting his arms on his knees.

"Beautiful view," he said finally.

"I love it here," she said, continuing to rock back and forth.

Her father grew silent again, and then he took a deep breath.

"I wasn't talking about the bay. I was talking about the gentleman standing over there. Gabe Wademan."

Kayla's heart froze. "He's a nice-looking man." She didn't know what else to say. A part of her wanted to tell her dad everything and cry on his shoulder, but if her mom found out she had told her dad before sharing her secret with her, it would only ignite another battle between them. And that's the last thing she wanted to do.

"I thought the sparks between the two of you were going to light the barbecue on fire the other night at dinner. You wouldn't have needed me to cook."

Kayla bit her bottom lip to keep from laughing. Sarah had said something similar earlier. "He's my landlord and my new neighbor."

Her dad looked her straight in the eye, like he had when she was a little girl, and he was trying to get his point across.

"We don't choose who we're attracted to or who we love. Love doesn't make sense. Our minds give us reasons why we shouldn't love that person and tell us how wrong they are for us, but our hearts tell a different story. If everyone chose love by logic, the world would be one boring place." Her father stood. Instead of looking back at her, he made eye contact with Gabe and nodded at him.

Then he walked inside the house, leaving Kayla with her conflicting thoughts and heart.

She was tempted to tell her dad that she already made up her mind that she'd fight for Gabe. Her problem was figuring out how, since Gabe was so stubborn.

But her dad was also referring to her mom. If her dad allowed his head to rule over his heart, he never would have chosen or stayed with her mom. But in his heart, he loved her. He always had, and he always would. Kayla had known that deep down, but now he'd confirmed it for her. She'd have to tell Sarah what her dad said. Maybe Sarah wouldn't have such a warped view on love if she knew.

Kayla briefly closed her eyes. When she opened them, she chose to take her dad's advice.

Without thinking twice, Kayla stood and ran across the back porch, down the stairs, and across the grass to Gabe's property. He was still talking to the builder, but when he saw her running toward him, he said something briefly to the other man, who glanced at her and then walked away.

By the time she reached him, she was out of breath, huffing and puffing. She thought she was in good shape, but she had never run so fast in her entire life.

"Gabe," she said, trying to catch her breath. "I really am sorry." When she looked at him straight in the eye, she had forgotten the speech she had mentally prepared while she was running. Which was something like, *Can we stop talking and just have sex?*

Gabe stared back at her, not responding. Damnit, he was making her work for this.

"I didn't know I'd left you at the same time your parents were getting a divorce," she said, her tone strong.

Gabe chuckled and then looked up at the sky before turning his attention back to her.

"You told me that already. Why are you really here, Kayla?"

"Gabe, why can't we fight this out like normal people?" she asked, raising her voice.

He became really quiet. At the same time, a breeze blew, making her shiver. She crossed her arms over her chest, but she wasn't sure what felt colder, the wind touching her body or the look in Gabe's eyes.

"What kind of fight are you looking to have?" he asked, raising his eyebrow.

Kayla clenched her vagina. "Maybe the kind we used to have?" Her tone grew softer.

Gabe chuckled again, as he shook his head. "You mean when I ended up fucking you hard?"

She bit her bottom lip as she nodded.

"And what would you like the end result to be? After I fuck you. What are you looking for?"

Kayla threw up her hands. "I'd stop walking around horny whenever you're near." She paused and then said, "And maybe we could start fresh. Without the past hovering over us."

"Are you wet, Kayla?" he asked, smirking.

Her face heated up. "I am."

"You're beautiful. You can have any man you want. Go out and have sex. You can start fresh with any man."

Kayla's heart fell. "You really want me to date another man?" If he did, he truly wasn't interested. She'd die if she found out he was dating another woman.

It felt as if hours had passed before he responded.

He groaned. "No, I don't want you to be with another man. If I saw you out to dinner with a guy, I'd probably want to kill him."

Kayla busted up laughing.

"This isn't funny." His jaw clenched. "But I told you…baby steps. Fucking each other will momentarily feel good. But it won't solve our problems. It won't solve the fact I have no idea what you've been up to the last two years. And it won't help if you filled me in. I have to get to know the woman who left our life and created another one with her family. I need to find out if I can fall in love with that Kayla, like I did with the one I was hoping to spend my life with. And frankly, you need to do the same with me. I was naïve when it came to love when we were together. But after my parents' divorce, my views on love and life changed. You need to learn if that's the Gabe you want in your life, too."

Kayla looked at her sandals. He was right. She'd assumed sex would wash away all their problems, but she was wrong. "Okay, you're right. So what do we do from here?"

Gabe smiled. "Why don't I meet you by our rock tomorrow morning. Same time, same place?"

Kayla's heart flipped. He'd said *our* rock. "I'd like that."

He walked up to her and kissed her on the top of her head. "I have to go back to my grandfather's, but I'll see you tomorrow."

She smiled at him as he walked up the hill, got in his SUV, and drove away.

Kayla stood there and thought about everything he'd said. Unlike Gabe, *her* views on love and life hadn't changed. She was and always would be a hopeless romantic. After all, when they were together, she was the one who had been secretly planning their wedding. They hadn't set a date or booked a venue, but she had cut out pictures from magazines of the perfect wedding dress and the flowers she'd like on the tables. When Nana had called her home, Kayla had packed one suitcase with what she'd need most to survive. And one of the things she'd packed were those magazine pictures. On the airplane to Bella Cove, she had looked at those pictures as if they were her lifeline. And to some degree, they had been.

When she came home and everything went from bad to worse, she'd still looked at those pictures every night…until things became even worse. Then, finally, she'd put the pictures away. But the night before she signed Melody's contract to buy the store, she'd looked at them again. Deep down, she'd still hoped they could be together. Deep down, she still did.

So tomorrow morning, she'd meet him by the rock, and maybe that would be the beginning of their second chance.

As she walked back to her house, she could see her mom sitting on the back porch. Kayla sighed. She needed to be alone, not deal with her mother.

"Hi, Mom," she said in a quiet tone.

Her mom looked at her suspiciously. Kayla groaned inside.

"What were you and Gabe talking about?"

She hated lying to her mom, but if she told the truth right now, her mom would ask her so many questions she'd never be able to relax.

"Sarah had this great idea to turn part of the storage room of my shop into a room where we can hold classes. I was telling him all about it, hoping he wouldn't raise the rent." Kayla opened the back door, praying her mom wouldn't ask her more questions.

"It didn't look like that to me."

Kayla took a step inside and then paused. "What did it look like to you?"

"Like two lovers having a fight."

Kayla huffed. Of course that's what her mom thought. She had fights like that with her dad all the time. Kayla turned back toward her mom, gripping the doorknob.

"It was nothing like that. He was putting his two cents in with his own vision of my store, and I didn't like that. You know how I have to always feel in control, Mom." She could barely look her mother in the eyes.

Her mom sighed. "You wouldn't be having a love relationship behind your family's back, now, would you?"

"Why would you ask that?" Kayla was clenching the doorknob as if it was her lifeline.

Her mom cleared her throat. "Sit down, sweetheart. There's something I've got to say."

Kayla reluctantly let go of the doorknob and sat on the rocking chair next to her mother.

Her mom continued. "You know how sick Pop was toward the end?"

Kayla nodded.

"Well, he was sicker than you realized. But he always got better, until the end. He had a really bad leg and back. Some days, he couldn't get out of bed."

"I remember, Mom." Kayla had never seen such intensity on her mom's face. Whatever she was about to say was important enough for Kayla to stay and listen.

Her mom cleared her throat again. "One time, it lasted three months, and then he was fine for the next two weeks, and then in bed again for about another month. The business wasn't affected because your father pretty much ran the show by that time, but Nana was very affected. You were about twelve years old at the time. Nana was sick of watching him in bed. She loved him, and it was tearing her apart. She wanted to feel something other than despair. She wanted to escape and feel joy again, even for just a moment or a few hours."

"What are you telling me, Mom?" Kayla whispered.

"Nana cheated on Pop. Only once."

Kayla gasped.

Her mom continued. "She told Pop after she cheated. But she never told any of us; I found out on my own."

Kayla's heart was beating faster. She started rocking back and forth on the chair to calm down. Her mom might as well have poured a gallon of ice water on her head. Nana cheating on Pop was huge. Devastating. They were the only love relationship Kayla looked up to. The only relationship that made her believe in true love.

"How did you find out?" Kayla asked quietly, continuing to rock.

"I didn't know Nana had cheated on Pop. I never thought my mother would do that. She was always so perfect. I never knew her to make a wrong choice. She was the epitome of what the matriarch of the family should be. Then one day, Pop and I were home alone, and he was still in bed, unable to move. A strange man knocked on our front door. You know how it goes…if someone knocks on the front door, it means we don't know them well."

"I know," Kayla said.

"The man kept knocking. He was being persistent. I opened the door and asked if I could help him. He was a nice-looking man with salt-and-pepper hair and clear blue eyes. He handed me Nana's pearl bracelet. You know, the one she used to wear all the time?"

"I remember the bracelet and how one day she stopped wearing it. Pop had bought her a diamond tennis bracelet she wore all the time instead."

Her mom nodded. "He did, and I'm going to tell you the real reason why. I took the bracelet he handed me and asked how he got it. He said Nana had left it at his place. He said she never told him her address, but he remembered her saying she was from Bella Cove. He went into town and asked around, and they pointed him here."

"Oh, Mom!" Kayla's eyes widened. "Did everyone in the town find out and gossip?"

"They may have at first, but Nana went into town the next day and told everyone how he was a business associate of Pop's, and that they'd gone to his house one night, and she'd left the bracelet. Apparently, he lived in Montauk. Nana never would have slept with a man here in Bella Cove. Everyone in town seemed to believe her. Even if they suspected she was lying, no one would have dared to say anything. Nana held that much power."

Her mom paused and took a deep breath. "So, back to the man handing me the pearl bracelet. I was stunned, but I felt as if I had to invite him into the house. I was afraid the neighbors would wonder who he was. He didn't want to come inside. In fact, I remember him telling me how funny he felt about coming into Nana's house where she lived with her husband. I knew right then and there that Nana had been with him. Imagine that realization?

"Unfortunately, Pop picked that moment to get up out of bed. He said he'd heard the knocking. He'd grown concerned. It took a lot of effort for Pop to get out of bed, but he was worried. He looked at the man standing in his living room and at me holding Nana's bracelet, and he knew exactly who that man was. Then Pop introduced himself. He said he was Nana's husband and that she was the love of his life. He asked what his intentions were toward Nana. The man said Nana had made it very clear their affair was a one-night thing. Then he told Pop he was a lucky man, and Nana was beautiful. I'd never seen Pop turn so white before. I went up to him to help him, but he shook his head. Later, he told me he had pride, and even if the man had his wife for one night, Pop was determined to have her for the rest of his life.

"The man left, and I broke down and cried. I knew Pop wanted me to be strong, but the vision I had of my mom being the perfect woman had disappeared in that moment—not to mention the fact she had hurt Pop so deeply. As I led Pop back to bed, I told him how sorry I was. He told me not to be. Instead, he told me to feel sorry for Nana because she got dealt with a husband who for months on end couldn't move or be the husband she deserved. She had so many responsibilities on her shoulders. He said she needed to feel alive and free for one night. He wasn't happy the man had come to their house, but he was sure he wouldn't come again. And he didn't. Then Pop told me not to say anything to anyone. I agreed. I didn't want anyone else in the family to be disillusioned about Nana either. Pop took the pearl bracelet that I hadn't even realized I was still holding, and then I left him alone. But the moment I closed the door, I heard him sob. That was one of the worst sounds I've ever heard. Pop never cried."

Kayla was crying, too. "What happened when Nana came home?" she asked, sniffing back tears.

Her mom sighed. "I didn't tell her. I pretended nothing had changed. I promised Pop I wouldn't say anything, and I didn't want to disappoint him. He was disappointed anyway. It wasn't until a few days later that Nana pulled me aside and told me that Pop had told her what had happened. Then she said that sometimes even the matriarch needed a break from life. She told me that having the weight of every member of the family's problems on her head was sometimes too much, but she wouldn't trade it for anything in the world. She said the man in Montauk made her feel as if she didn't have that weight, and she'd needed it as much as her next breath. And that's all she said. She didn't give me any more excuses. All she said was she needed it. And who was I to judge?

"You were born to be the next matriarch, Kayla. I knew that since you were a little girl, and I hated it. When Nana was dying, I asked her if I could be the next matriarch. I begged her."

"Why?" Kayla asked softly. She'd never had any idea about any of this.

"Because I didn't want you to have the responsibility. I didn't know the toll it took on Nana until she cheated on Pop. I didn't want you to have that added weight. I wanted you to live your dreams. I wanted you to graduate with a degree in psychology. I wanted you to stay in Bella Cove if that's what you chose, or leave if that's what you wanted. You're the most intelligent one in the family. You have ambition, determination, and a strong sense of self. But Nana refused me. She said I was too obsessed with my own problems to solve everyone else's. And she was right, but I had to fight for you anyway. Then, when my mother died and everything was going so wrong with the family, I was devastated that you were forced to leave school and never return. That's not what I wanted for you. That's not what any mother would want for her daughter. But I was too weak to stop it then, and I'm too weak to stop it now."

"Mom, I'm *not* the family matriarch. I've told you. I love helping others, ever since I was born. That's what fulfills me. When Nana passed, the whole family was unhinged. Of course, I wanted to help all of you get back on your feet. I love my family, and if I want to help them, while keeping my word to Nana, there's nothing wrong with that. But I don't want to be branded as a matriarch, because I'm not. And one day, I plan on getting married and having my own family to worry about and take care of."

Her mom stood and looked at her straight in the eye. "You would have been married ages ago if it wasn't for helping us."

Kayla swallowed. "Maybe, but I won't settle just to get married. Nana never settled with Pop. She made a mistake by cheating on him, but she never settled. In that regard, I want to follow in her footsteps by being with the love of my life."

"I hope you find that, sweetheart. Don't let our family stop you from having a life."

"I have a life. Maybe I haven't accomplished all my goals, but I will," Kayla said. "But Mom, do you miss having a matriarch in the family, like Nana?"

Her mom took a deep breath. "I miss my mother every damn day." She walked back into the house without saying another word.

Kayla sat rocking on the chair long after her mom had gone. She couldn't stop thinking about why her grandmother had cheated. If she was alive today, Kayla would have a billion questions for her. She decided not to judge her, because knowing Nana the way she'd thought she did, she must have had a pretty good reason. And it wasn't her job to forgive her. It was Pop's. And he had forgiven her. The only thing that Kayla missed about Nana was how she loved unconditionally. No matter what problem Kayla went to her with, her grandmother helped her figure out a solution. Even on her deathbed, she encouraged Kayla to return to Gabe when the family was healthy again.

Maybe it was a good thing Nana had never seen how fucked up they all were when she died. Or maybe she'd been watching in heaven, hoping Kayla would leave the family in their screwed-up state and return to Gabe. Kayla would never know the answer to that question, but when she went to heaven, hopefully a million years from now, she'd ask Nana. In the meantime, if her grandmother was watching over her, Kayla hoped she was proud that her granddaughter was fighting for Gabe now.

Kayla must have fallen asleep because the next thing she knew, someone was shaking her.

"Kayla, wake up!"

Kayla slowly opened her eyes. Lauren was standing beside Kayla's chair, looking frazzled and stressed out. It was dark outside, so she had no idea how long she had been asleep.

"What time is it?" she asked.

"Eleven o'clock," Lauren said.

Kayla had slept for two hours. "Is everything okay? You look a mess."

Lauren exhaled and then sat on the chair next to Kayla, where her mom had sat earlier.

"No, everything isn't okay."

Kayla was exhausted. All she wanted to do was go upstairs and crawl under the covers, but her sister needed her.

"What happened?" she asked.

"I went out with Jordan again. We were having the best time until he blurted out that although he loves Bella Cove, he isn't sure he could move here. His law firm won't let him work from home."

"Then what happened?" Kayla asked.

Lauren blew out air. "I flipped out. I told him we should break up. I have no intention of moving to Manhattan, and if he can't move here, I might as well break things off with him now before I become even more attached."

Kayla grabbed her sister's hand and squeezed it. "It seems you're pretty attached already."

"I am," Lauren admitted. "I realize I barely know him, but we've spoken on the phone every day for hours on end."

"Lauren, we've talked about this. The city isn't far away. We can visit you, and you can visit us."

"But I don't want to leave Bella Cove. I love it here."

"Your dream is to be married, and I think you have a real chance with Jordan." He was the first man her sister had liked in a long time. Kayla didn't want Lauren to lose what might be her one opportunity at true love.

Lauren slumped back in the chair. "No, my dream is to be married to a man and live in Bella Cove forever. I love both ideas equally. If I marry and leave Bella Cove, I'll only have half my dream. I'd be miserable."

"How did Jordan react?"

"He was devastated. He told me not to give up on us. That he'd figure out a way to make it work."

"And what did you say to that?" Kayla asked.

"I said that was fine, but between you and me, we're doomed."

Kayla pushed the hair out of Lauren's eyes. "I wouldn't give up hope if I were you."

"What do you mean?" she asked softly.

"I'd trust Jordan. If you're truly meant to be, then he'll do whatever it takes to be with you."

"He's not going to quit his job, Kayla. He's happy there," Lauren said.

Kayla shrugged. "Maybe not, but let's see what he *is* willing to do. I think he'll fight for you. I think he'll want to be with you no matter what."

Lauren sniffed back tears. "How do you know that? We've only just started dating."

Kayla stroked her sister's hair gently. "I have a feeling. That's all. Just don't give up on him. Let's see what he's made of. Do you trust him, Lauren?"

She nodded. "I do."

"Then trust he'll do whatever it takes to be with you."

Lauren sighed. "Thanks, sis. You always make me feel better." She gave Kayla a quick kiss on the cheek. "Are you coming in and going to sleep?"

Kayla sighed. "In a few minutes. I'd like to enjoy the peace and quiet out here for a bit more."

"Which you were doing, until I ruined it."

They both laughed, and then Lauren went inside and up the stairs to her bedroom. Hearing about Jordan kept Kayla outside thinking. If he was willing to do everything and anything to keep Lauren, why hadn't Gabe? True, she was the one who had left him, but he knew where she lived. Why hadn't he fought for her? Love was a two-way street, after all.

Kayla rocked back and forth, pondering that idea for a few more minutes before she thought she'd fall asleep again. So she stood, took one more glance at the breathtaking bay with the moon reflecting off the water, and then walked inside and upstairs to her room, closing the door behind her.

When Kayla opened her walk-in closet, she paused. She had a small dresser on the back wall. The second drawer held the pictures of different wedding ideas she'd had when Gabe was saving up for a ring. She opened the drawer, took them out, and held them close to her heart. After Gabe and she stopped speaking, she viewed these pictures as her lost dream. But maybe her dream wasn't lost after all.

KAYLA ARRIVED AT THE ROCK exactly the same time as yesterday, but Gabe beat her to it.

"I thought you'd get lost," she said, extending one of two iced coffees she'd brought with her to Gabe.

"No, smartass." He took the cup out of her hand. "Thanks for this." He took off the straw wrapper and took a sip. "It will go with what I brought."

Kayla hadn't paid attention to the rock. She'd only noticed the gorgeous man in jeans and a black polo shirt standing next to it. When she looked down, she saw he'd laid out a blue blanket. On top of the blanket was a picnic basket.

She couldn't help but smile. "Are we having a morning picnic?"

"Come see for yourself." He held out his hand to help her sit.

She took it only so she could hold his hand. The physical contact alone, even as innocent as it was, caused goosebumps to erupt on her skin.

He raised his eyebrow as she got comfortable on the blanket, making sure to push down her white skirt.

"Cold?" he asked.

Kayla chuckled. "No." She hadn't let go of his hand yet. "I like the feel of your hand."

Gabe smiled in that charming way she loved. He squeezed her hand before releasing it.

So much for that, Kayla thought.

"So…what did you bring?" she asked.

She watched Gabe open the picnic basket.

"I'll open it, but you can't make fun of me."

Kayla smiled softly. "I'd never do that."

"Oh, yes, you would." He took out a paper plate and put two square pieces of crumb cake on it. "I made these myself. When I was at your house a few weeks back, your mom made a crumb cake. Do you remember?"

"I remember." She remembered every detail of their time together since he'd shown up in her life again.

"Well, your mom said crumb cake was your favorite."

Kayla licked her lips. "It is. I love crumb cake."

Gabe chuckled. "So…my mom also loves it. In fact, when I was growing up, she made it her mission to bake every crumb cake recipe in the entire world until she found the one she liked best."

Kayla put her hands on her hips. "Gabe Wademan, are you trying to tell me my mom's recipe wasn't the best?"

Gabe chuckled again. Kayla adored the sound.

"That's exactly what I'm trying to say. And you'll agree once you've tried *my* mom's. She's made this recipe so many times, I know how to make it by heart. Are you tempted?" He broke off a piece of the cake and held it right under her nose.

Kayla inhaled the delicious smell. "Yes, I'm tempted." Although what she really wanted to taste was his finger that was so close to her mouth. All she had to do was stick out her tongue. But she resisted. He'd said baby steps, after all.

Gabe moved the piece even closer. Kayla opened her mouth and ate the piece out of his hand. Her tongue "accidentally" touched the side of his finger.

The second the cake was in her mouth, she moaned. The crumbs melted on her tongue. She loved her mom's, but his version had even more brown sugar and butter added to it.

When she swallowed, she looked into his twinkling eyes. "This is the best damn cake I've ever tasted."

He grabbed the back of her neck and pecked her hard on the lips. Then he licked her bottom lip before pulling away.

"I had to get some sugar off your lips."

Kayla smiled. "Uh-huh."

He handed her another piece, and she took it.

"Mmmmm, I'm impressed with your baking skills," she said once her mouth wasn't full.

He sipped the iced coffee and took a bite of cake, too. "So do you think it's better than your mom's?"

She took another piece of the cake. "It is, but if you tell her, I'll deny it."

Gabe laughed. "I promise, I won't tell her. But I have to admit, your mom makes incredible brownies."

"She really does." Thinking about her mom made her think of what she had said about Nana last night. Part of Kayla wished she could be in denial about it. But another part felt as if she was in mourning over her grandparents' love for each other.

"Hey, Kayla," he said. "Where'd you go?"

Kayla blinked. "Sorry." She sighed. "My mom told me some seriously disturbing news last night."

Gabe sat up a little straighter. "Is everything okay?"

She took a sip of the iced coffee. "Yes and no," she began. "Can I tell you a secret? And you won't tell anyone?"

He grinned. "Well, I already promised I wouldn't tell your mom that my mom's crumb cake is better, so what's one more secret?"

She smiled softly. "Mom told me last night that my nana cheated on my grandfather. It was only one time. But I don't know what to do with the information."

He grabbed Kayla's hand and moved his thumb along her palm. "What do you want to do?"

"I mean, I don't know where to place it. All I know is that I feel such a loss. Almost as if Nana cheated on me."

Gabe nodded while continuing to move his thumb in slow circles. "That makes sense. You looked up to their love for each other. You always said they were your example of true love. Once you even said you aspired to have a love just like they had."

She glanced at his eyes, which were filled with warmth. "I did," she whispered. "I do."

"Cheating is a huge deal. But there had to be a pretty big reason for why she was intimate with another man."

"I know there was."

She looked down at her iced coffee until Gabe lifted her chin.

"And they stayed together afterward."

She nodded.

"Love can be messy, Kayla. Love can be ugly. But no matter what happened, they found a way to get through it. Their love overcame her being with another man." He paused and then said, "So let them still inspire you. Still use them as an example of what you want for yourself. And trust your nana cheated for an important reason."

Kayla put her iced coffee on the rock and then threw her arms around Gabe, holding him tight. Gabe moved his coffee out of the way and hugged her back. He maneuvered so her head rested against his chest. They both turned to look toward the bay, gazing out at all the boats in the water.

"Our love is messy," she whispered.

"It is." Gabe paused, then kissed her on top of her head. "Baby steps, Kayla. Baby steps."

Kayla briefly closed her eyes and inhaled his intoxicating scent. After a few minutes, Gabe rocked her back and forth, just like the boats. She'd never felt so safe and peaceful in her life. That feeling was what she remembered from their time together at school. Being in his strong arms always made her feel as if everything would be okay.

They must have stayed like that for minutes, hours, Kayla had no idea, until Gabe glanced at his watch.

"Our hour is up. Unfortunately, it's time to go to work." Gabe kissed her on the top of her head again before breaking their hug.

Kayla smiled wide. "Thank you for the crumb cake and for cheering me up."

"My pleasure. Would you like the remainder of your piece?"

She grabbed it off the plate. "How could I refuse?" She put tissue she'd found in her purse around the treat and placed it inside.

Gabe put his piece in the picnic basket and stood. Kayla followed and picked up the blanket they'd sat on and folded it.

"I'd forgotten how good you are at folding. You used to fold all of our laundry."

She handed him the blanket and then picked up their iced coffees. "I have to admit, I'm a bit of a perfectionist when it comes to folding."

Gabe chuckled as he put the blanket under his arm and grabbed his coffee out of her hand. "I remember that, too."

They walked in silence until they reached Main Street.

"I'm actually going up to my house to meet with a builder before I go to my office," he said.

"Oh, okay," she said, as she shifted on her feet. "Thanks for meeting me."

She turned to walk in the opposite direction, but Gabe grabbed her elbow and moved them behind one of the stores.

"But I'm not leaving until I do this." He dropped the blanket and the picnic basket, being careful not to drop his coffee, too, and pulled Kayla toward him.

When they kissed this time, it was no peck. His tongue slid inside her mouth, and she sucked on his tongue until her lips meshed with his. Sexual tension that had been out of control between them came to a head. Kayla kissed him with all the tension she felt inside, and he kissed her back the same way.

Out of the corner of her eye, she saw someone walking close enough that any second they would see them, and reluctantly, she stepped back. Gabe turned his head and saw the man passing.

He chuckled under his breath. "I should have kissed you by the rock, instead."

"Next time," she said, before biting her bottom lip.

He nodded. "Next time." Then he picked up his stuff and walked away.

Kayla closed her eyes and sighed. Her love was messy just like Nana and Pop's. With the feeling of Gabe's lips still on hers, Kayla thought maybe her and Gabe's love would survive...just like her grandparents' had. A girl could certainly wish.

When Kayla made it back to the store, she was ready to do something. So she walked into the storage room and looked around. Getting the room ready for their classes required a lot of work. She might as well start unpacking some of the newer toys that had recently come in. Maybe that would get her mind off Gabe's beautiful lips.

An hour later, Kayla was sweating and covered with dust when she heard someone come into the store. Her heart instantly beat faster, and a sudden burst of hope lit up inside her.

"Hello?"

Kayla sighed, her excitement deflating like a burst balloon. Not that she wasn't happy to see Melody. Kayla missed her friend terribly, but she had hoped to see Gabe. She had just seen him an hour ago and she already craved him. How pathetic was she?

"Hi, Melody," Kayla said, striding toward her friend, smiling with honest joy. "I'm sweaty and gross from working in the storage room, but can I give you a hug?"

"I wouldn't have it any other way." Melody laughed and gave Kayla a hug.

"I missed you," Kayla said, as she blinked back tears and wished she wasn't so damn emotional lately.

"Me, too, honey. Now, let me look at you." Melody stepped back and looked Kayla up and down. "You have a light about you that I've never seen before, but you also don't look happy. Are you miserable that I made you take over the store?"

"You didn't *make me* take over the store. I wanted to." Kayla smiled.

Melody rolled her eyes. "Whatever. But on a serious note, are you glad you took over this place?"

Kayla thought about that for a second. "I *am* glad. I was a little nervous at first that I wouldn't be able to fill your shoes, but so far, none of the customers or vendors seem to be complaining."

Melody placed her hands on her hips. "Oh, please, what's there to complain about? You pretty much ran the place when I was here anyway. They're used to you."

Kayla smiled again. "Thank you. So... what about you? Why aren't you traveling the world?"

"We were away for over a week and my homing device kicked in. I missed Bella Cove, so I told Harry we should stay home for a few days, do the laundry, clean the house, make sure you're doing okay, and then fly away again. He agreed."

"Thanks for making me part of your excuse to come home." Kayla laughed.

"It worked! Now, tell me why you have that look on your face. Have you been working too hard?"

Kayla walked to the register desk and started cleaning it. She grabbed the dust rag on the counter and began dusting everything and anything she could get her hands on. There was no way she'd tell her friend what was going on with her and Gabe, especially when she was trying to figure it out herself.

"No, not at all. I asked my sisters to come and work here with me." Kayla paused. She must look like a crazy lady, cleaning like mad. "Would you like to sit down? I can bring you a chair. I hope you don't mind me cleaning."

"No, I'm fine. Do whatever you need to do. So, you hired your sisters? How are you paying them? I know it's not my business anymore, but I'm concerned for you," Melody said.

Kayla grabbed one children's book at a time and dusted them. "I'm taking less of a salary."

Melody opened her mouth as if to argue.

"I know what you're going to say, but it has been great with them here. Sarah has never been able to hold down a job. She's always gotten too bored. But she loves it here. I knew she would, and she's been thinking of creative ways to enhance the store. And Lauren always walked around miserable because she wasn't married. On one of her first days here, she met a man."

"Really? Who?" Melody's eyes grew wide.

"His name is Jordan. He was on his way to the Hamptons, and he needed to buy a toy, so Google sent him here."

Melody clapped her hands. "I love it. I remember you telling me you hoped Lauren would meet someone. The fact it happened at Magical Toys brings tears to my eyes." Melody was always such a romantic. "But I still don't like that you had to take a pay cut in order to help your sisters. You're too nice, Kayla. One day, it's going to come back and bite you in the ass."

Kayla smiled. Melody always told it like it was. "I like making others happy."

Melody snorted. "I know you do, but for once, I'd like to see you make *yourself* happy."

"I am happy," Kayla said softly.

"You can fool your family, Kayla, but you can't fool me."

Unable to look at Melody, Kayla looked at the book she was dusting.

"I'm okay, Melody," she said.

"A second ago, you said you were happy; so, which one is it? Are you happy or just okay?"

Kayla sighed. "I'm happy."

Melody grabbed the book out of Kayla's hand and threw it onto the counter. "Really? Because you've got man troubles written all over your pretty face."

Kayla rolled her eyes. She and Melody had spent hours together at the store, just the two of them. Kayla had spent more time with her old boss than anyone else.

"Don't roll your eyes at me. I know man trouble when I see it. I may be older than you are, but I remember man-trouble days, and they weren't pleasant. And you look like a woman who has a man but feels conflicted. I don't have to be psychic to know that. But do you remember when I took that clairvoyant class? They tried to teach me tarot, but I kept forgetting what all the cards meant."

Kayla laughed. "I remember the class very well." She had to tell her at least something about Gabe, so she could change the topic.

"There's an ex from my past who is sort of back in my life, and the situation has kind of thrown me off. That's all. But I'll be fine."

"I knew it. I'm never wrong with these things. Do you still like him?"

Kayla sighed. She seemed to be doing a lot of that lately.

"I do, but it's complicated. But can we please keep this between us?"

Melody looked at Kayla with compassion. "I know how private you are. I promise not to tell anyone, including your family."

"Thank you," Kayla whispered.

"But are you sure he's not the one?" Melody asked.

Kayla smiled faintly. "I'm not sure about anything these days."

"Then let's not talk about him a minute longer. But in all the time you've worked for me, I've never heard you not sure about anything."

"I know, and I hate feeling so unsure about everything."

Melody smiled. "You'll figure it out."

Kayla gave her a hug. "Thank you."

Melody returned the embrace, and Kayla resumed dusting the books. Most likely, she'd told her friend more than she should have, but she couldn't take back what she'd said now.

"So, tell me, did you ever connect with Mr. Kleiner's grandson?"

Kayla dropped the book she was dusting. "Yes, I did. I contacted Alice the day after I signed the contract like I promised you I would." She coughed, pretending something was stuck in her throat, hiding her expression from Melody. Usually, Kayla was so good at disguising her emotions, but apparently, not today.

"Are you okay?" Melody slapped her back.

Tears appeared in Kayla's eyes, but that was from the fake coughing.

"Sorry. I swallowed the wrong way."

"I hate that. So? Tell me about his grandson. What's his name?"

Kayla cleared her throat.

"His name is Gabe Wademan, and he has been so nice to us. He hasn't raised the rent, so that's a good thing. He also has a ladder, so Sarah, in her own sweet way, asked him to paint the yellow border around the ceiling." She could have told Melody the truth, but she had to tell her parents first. And she wasn't quite ready to tell them yet.

Melody glanced up at the ceiling. "I hadn't even had a chance to take a look around the store. I was so happy to see you." She looked at the yellow border and the hearts and snowflakes they'd hung. "Very nice. I love the changes."

"Thank you. At first, I was upset Sarah had asked Mr. Wademan to paint for us, but like I said, he had a ladder, so I was grateful. The minute I have a chance, I'm going to buy one," Kayla said, keeping her tone light. "Did you know Mr. Wademan moved his office across the street?" Melody was friends with Alice. She'd find out sooner or later.

"No. Where?"

Melody turned, and Kayla pointed to his office.

"Oh, my goodness. I've missed a lot while being away—even in just a week! I called Alice earlier and left her a message to tell her I was in town, but I had no idea they'd moved across the street."

"And you're going to love this. You know the piece of land next to my family's house? Well, his grandfather owned it, so now he's building a house there, which he plans to move into." Kayla filled Melody in on all the gossip. If she didn't, Melody would wonder why Kayla hadn't said anything. And speaking of gossip… Kayla tried to think of an innocent way to ask Melody if Alice had a boyfriend. Kayla would love to know, but only if she could come up with a way to ask without drawing suspicion.

Gabe and Alice weren't dating, but Kayla wondered if Alice had a crush on him.

"He's your new landlord and your soon-to-be neighbor?" Melody gasped.

Kayla nodded. "I know. The only positive thing I could come up with is maybe he won't raise my rent at the end of the year." Kayla studied Melody's expression. So far, she didn't seem to suspect anything.

When Kayla heard her front door open, she turned to see who it was. Her heart stopped when, of all people, Gabe stepped inside. Melody looked at her and then at Gabe, and her mouth hung open. Kayla wasn't surprised. She'd left him just an hour ago and she felt the same way.

"And who, may I ask, is this?" she whispered in Kayla's ear.

"Mr. Gabe Wademan, himself," she whispered back.

"Did I just hear my name?" Gabe asked.

Kayla rolled her eyes. "Mr. Wademan, this is Melody Fischer. The woman who you thought owned my store. Melody, this is Gabe Wademan, my new landlord."

Kayla immediately saw the hurt in his eyes when she'd introduced him as her landlord. She wanted to explain to him that Melody was a huge gossip, and she couldn't tell Melody the truth about them until she told her parents.

Why was Gabe here anyway? He extended his hand to shake Melody's.

"Nice to meet you," he said.

"Likewise." Melody extended her hand to Gabe.

He took it, but kissed her on the cheek anyway.

"Ohhhhh." Melody laughed once Gabe released her hand. "He's a charmer." She paused. "I'm sorry about your grandfather. Mr. Kleiner was such a kind man."

Warmth filled his eyes, but a second later, it was gone.

"That's why I'm here," Gabe said.

"It is?" Kayla blurted out.

"Yes. Alice told me you called her, Melody, because you were in town. My grandfather had mentioned how wonderfully you always treated him. He told me he always enjoyed coming to Bella Cove to see you. Before he died, he asked me to come here and tell you thank you for always being warm and friendly with him. He considered you a friend."

"I always enjoyed talking with him, too, when I'd pay the rent. As a matter of fact, I used to talk to him and Alice for hours on the first of the month, and then I would meet Mr. Kleiner at the coffeeshop down the street. He told me once he loved their coffee, so I insisted on meeting him there once a month. He was such an interesting man. Thank you, Mr. Wademan, for telling me this." Tears formed in Melody's eyes.

Kayla had known they'd used to meet at the coffee shop, but she didn't realize it was such a big deal. Mr. Kleiner would also come into the store a whole bunch of times, asking Kayla odd questions, and then he'd leave. Kayla always answered him. He seemed harmless and nice. He was always warm with her, but they hadn't been as close as he and Melody had been.

"Please, call me Gabe. Everyone does but Kayla," he said. "He also insisted I give you this." Gabe handed Melody a large blue box, which she reluctantly took.

"What is it?" She looked at Kayla and then at Gabe.

Kayla shrugged.

"Open it," Gabe said.

From the look in his eyes, Kayla wasn't even sure if he knew what it was.

Melody slowly opened the box, careful not to drop it. The moment the lid came off, Melody gasped. Then she showed the contents to Kayla, as a tear slid down Melody's cheek.

"They're beautiful," Kayla said, as she found herself gazing at two exquisite pieces of jewelry. One piece was a gold necklace with a large diamond in the center. The other was a ring in platinum with the largest diamond Kayla had ever seen. It was definitely an engagement ring.

"Oh, wait, there's a note in the box." Melody handed the bottom of the jewelry box to Kayla and took out a note from the top. Then she read out loud.

"My Dear Melody,

"I'm sorry I couldn't tell you myself that I was dying. I hope you can forgive me. I'd also like to thank you for always

being kind to me. Both you and Magical Toys always had a special place in my heart.

"My loving grandson will be handing you a box of jewelry. There are two precious pieces in it that belonged to my beautiful late wife, who I will be seeing soon. The necklace is a gift for you. You're probably wondering why I'm giving you an engagement ring, too. The ring is not meant for you, but there will come a time in the near future when you will know who it belongs to.

"Congratulations on winning the lottery. I'm glad you'll be handing over the store to the beautiful blonde who works with you. She's a very special young lady. The store will flourish under her, and she will finally find peace. She's a rare gem. My only regret is not to have gotten to know her better.

"Take care, Melody. May you always be the happy, vibrant, and incredible woman that you are. Your husband is a very lucky man.

"Love,
"Mr. Kleiner

"P.S. Don't stress over not knowing who the ring belongs to. Trust me, you and only you will know."

Tears poured down Melody's face when she finished reading the letter. Gabe looked as white as a ghost, and Kayla felt shaken to her core. She had no idea how he knew all that about her. From the look on Gabe's face, they both knew who Mr. Kleiner thought the ring belonged to.

"Melody, did you tell Alice I was taking over your store? Because I thought Alice didn't know, and it was my job to break the news to Gabe." Kayla tucked her hair behind her ear.

Melody shook her head. "No, I swear. I left a message on Mr. Kleiner's phone about two weeks before he passed away, telling him we won the lottery. I never heard back from him. I never told him I was giving you the store. I was hoping to tell him in person, but that obviously didn't happen. I never told Alice anything."

Gabe chuckled, and both women turned toward him.

"You didn't know my grandfather like I did. If he knew you won the lottery, then he knew you'd eventually give up your store. And since you didn't need the money, he assumed you would have given it to Kayla."

"But he never even knew my name," Kayla said.

"He knew it," Gabe responded.

Kayla didn't say anything after that, but everything became clear. Gabe had spoken to his grandfather about her, and his grandfather believed they were meant to be married. He thought the store would bring them together, and Melody would know when to give her the ring. It all made perfect sense. His grandfather was partly right. This store had brought them together, but Gabe hadn't forgiven her. They may have made some progress, but she doubted Gabe was ready to completely forget what happened in the past.

Kayla also found it odd that she hadn't met Mr. Kleiner until a year after she started to work there. One random day, Melody had told her Mr. Kleiner specifically wanted to meet her. So at the beginning of the next month, he'd come into the store and had introduced himself. She had told him her name, but when he came in the month after that, he told her he had forgotten it, but Melody called her beautiful, so he would, too. From that day on, he'd only called her "beautiful." He hadn't forgotten her name, after all. He would also ask her odd questions. Once, he'd asked her why she wasn't dating. Another time he'd asked her to describe her dream house.

Another thing Kayla thought odd was something Lauren had recently told her. Her sister said she had run into one of the real estate agents from her old job. He said they heard a house was finally being built on the property next to their family's house. Then he said the lot had remained vacant for years until Mr. Kleiner had purchased it ten months ago. Right around the time he had asked her about her dream house…

Kayla glanced at Gabe, who still looked as white as a ghost.

Melody must have thought he seemed troubled, too.

"Are you okay, Gabe? The letter must have been hard for you to hear," Melody said.

Gabe shook his head. "It was surprising, that's all. My grandfather liked to surprise people. He was a generous man and always one step ahead of everyone else."

"What do you think he meant when he said I'd know who to give this ring to when the time was right?" Melody asked.

Kayla stared at Gabe, wanting to know that answer herself.

Gabe exhaled. "Hold onto it and see what happens. My grandfather was never wrong. Only time will tell, I guess."

"But what happens if he was wrong about this? Then what should Melody do?" Kayla asked. Since Gabe insisted his grandfather was never wrong, had he finally forgiven her?

Gabe looked at her strangely. She really wished she could read his mind. "Melody should keep it then," he answered.

"Oh, I won't be able to keep it," Melody said.

"You can and you will. My grandfather said when the time was right, you'd know. If he was wrong, then the ring will remain yours. And he specifically gave it to you, regardless. But knowing my grandfather like I do, I think he had a premonition about something. And as you know, he was a smart man."

Kayla swallowed. The way Gabe was talking, he thought they were meant to be together, but only because that's what his grandfather thought. Kayla wanted to so badly feel hopeful, but she was terrified of getting hurt again.

"You should keep the ring," Kayla said softly.

"Why don't you take it?" Melody held the ring out to Kayla.

She took a deep breath as her adrenaline rose. "No, thank you. If he had wanted me to have it, he would have given it to me. In the letter, he seemed pretty adamant about you having it."

Melody sighed. "Okay, fine. I'll keep it, but let's hope I'll know who it belongs to. I'm no good with puzzles. And with Harry and I traveling so much, unless it's a woman in France, it'll be hard for me to figure it out."

"I have faith in you," Gabe said, giving her that charming smile of his.

"All right, well, I have to get going. Harry wants to take me into the city tonight to see a Broadway show." She put the jewelry in her large beige purse and then turned to Gabe. "It was lovely meeting you. Your grandfather told me how handsome you are, and he was right. Let's hope he's right about the ring, too." She hugged Gabe and kissed him on the cheek. Then she turned toward Kayla and gave her a huge hug. "I may not see you again before I leave, but you never know."

Kayla hugged Melody back, eyes closed to prevent the tears from escaping. Kayla loved her friend. "I'm going to miss you again."

"You only miss me telling you all the gossip going on in Bella Cove."

"I do miss it, I have to admit." Kayla smiled.

Melody gave Kayla a quick kiss on the cheek. "The store looks fabulous, as I knew it would. Until next time, beautiful." She waved at Kayla and Gabe and then walked out of the store.

The moment the door shut, Kayla laid into Gabe.

"You do realize your grandfather was talking about us?"

Gabe nodded. "I do."

"What did you tell your grandfather about us?" she asked.

Gabe shrugged. "Not much. When I called him and told him about my parents divorcing, I told him how I was also hurting over a woman who lived in Bella Cove. That's when he told me how close he lived to here, and he visited at least once a month. He asked me your name, and I gave it to him, but then he didn't say anything else, so I figured he didn't know you."

"But he did," Kayla added.

"Yes. Then he asked me to tell him why I loved you and what I missed about you the most. So I did. I told him about your beautiful smile. I told him about how contagious your laugh was. I told him how you try to help everyone you meet. But I told him what I missed most of all was my best friend. I told him I could tell you anything, and you never judged."

Kayla sniffed back the tears. "Then what did he say?"

Gabe sighed. "He asked if I felt better, and I said I did. He said I should only think of the positive times in the relationship. And only of the goodness I saw in you. He explained the breakup was only one part of the relationship, not all of it. Holding on to the hurt and the pain wasn't honoring us and what we had."

"He wanted you to forgive me," Kayla whispered.

Gabe nodded. "Very much, but I couldn't. I just felt so betrayed. I'm trying to forgive you now, but all those bad feelings I felt when you left come back sometimes. Like now."

Kayla huffed. "I get those feelings, too. But I did tell you to wait for me. And even though dealing with my screwed-up family took me longer than I would have liked, I would have come back to you. Even after you gave me the ultimatum. At the same time, you never fought for us. If you really didn't want to lose me, you could have gotten on a plane and come here."

"You made it clear you didn't want me around your family then, especially since some of them didn't even know I existed."

Kayla's heart sank. "You're right, but if you showed up, I wouldn't have turned you away. You may have needed me when your parents were divorcing, but I may have needed you, too."

They were both silent.

"What are you thinking, Gabe?" Kayla asked softly.

He ran his hands through his hair. "I'm thinking I feel just as confused by my grandfather giving Melody the ring as you do."

Kayla looked at her hands; they still had some dust on them. "You told Melody that your grandfather was always right. Well, for the first time ever, I guess he was wrong."

Kayla tried to brush past him, eager to escape to her office, but Gabe grabbed her arm to stop her.

"Are you trying to tell me you think we should get engaged? You want us to skip the baby steps we're taking and just get married?" Gabe said the words as if he'd just voiced the most awful thought ever.

Kayla's heartbeat was pounding. "No, I'm not saying that," she said, even though marrying him was still her dream. "But I miss the Gabe from earlier by the rock. Because that Gabe didn't seem to be stuck in all the bad stuff that happened in the past. He was only remembering the good parts of us. Kind of like what your grandfather was trying to get you to see when you talked about me." She pushed Gabe gently so he would release his hold on her arm. Then she walked into her office, closed the door, and put her hands over her face.

"I'm sorry, Mr. Kleiner," she whispered. "I don't know how else to show your grandson that I still love him."

15

KAYLA STAYED IN HER OFFICE until she heard Gabe leave. He didn't go right away as she'd hoped he would, as if he were debating what to say. The sound of his heavy footsteps told her he'd hung out there for a while, pacing back and forth like crazy. Finally, he'd left, slamming the door behind him. Kayla was lucky it was still too early for customers to come in. But any second now, her sisters would arrive. She was surprised they hadn't gotten there yet. She wouldn't complain, though. It was nice to have a moment to herself.

Twenty minutes later, she was still in her office when Sarah opened the front door.

"Hello?" Sarah called out.

Kayla brushed away some tears, which seemed to have stuck to her face.

"Hold on. I'm in the office. I'll be right out," she yelled back. Quickly, she reapplied her makeup and smoothed down her yellow sundress. If it was up to her, she would have closed the store for the day and hid in her office. Unfortunately, that wasn't an option with her sisters working here.

"Hi, Sarah," she said when she stepped out of her office.

Sarah was putting her purse away in one of the register-desk drawers.

"You look terrible," she said as she locked the drawer.

Kayla rolled her eyes. "Thanks."

"Are you going to tell me why you were crying or are you going to hide your feelings like Nana always did?"

Kayla was surprised Sarah said that. She was right, though. Nana never shared her feelings when it came to her own life.

"I'm okay. It's just that Melody came here earlier, and then Gabe stopped in and gave her some jewelry Mr. Kleiner wanted her to have. Then when Melody left, Gabe was an asshole toward me. One moment he's so warm, and the next, he becomes a dick."

"Awe, sweetie." Sarah ran over and gave Kayla a huge hug. "I've been meaning to ask you about him, especially since I told you guys that the tension in the room was so intense when you were together that I needed to go home to touch myself, but I'm a little self-absorbed, so…you know."

That made Kayla laugh. "I know," she said, hugging her back. "I'm sorry. I'm okay." She stepped out of the hug. "Men can be so infuriating sometimes."

Sarah rolled her eyes. "Tell me about it. Here." Sarah unlocked the drawer and handed Kayla some tissues from her purse. "I know exactly what you need to cheer you up."

"What?"

"An iced coffee from down the street. And then when I return, we're going to dive into cleaning the storage room. I want to start classes in a few weeks."

Despite having had an iced coffee earlier with Gabe, Kayla agreed; today was definitely a two-iced-coffees kind of day. "I worked on the storage room a little this morning, but that's a great idea. Let me give you some money."

She turned to grab her purse, but Sarah stopped her.

"Are you kidding? You pay me really well. Don't think I don't know that you took a pay cut so Lauren and I can both work here." Sarah grabbed her purse and started walking toward the front door.

"Sarah?"

Sarah turned.

"Thank you for being there for me," Kayla said, smiling warmly.

Sarah sighed. "I want to be there for you, like you're there for us. At least, to some degree. I'm way more selfish, you know."

Sarah paused, and Kayla noticed tears in her sister's eyes.

"Sometimes, I would have liked to have helped Nana, too. She wouldn't let us. I know she had issues, too, like the rest of us." Sarah turned and walked out the door.

Sarah hadn't waited for a response, but she was right. Kayla would have liked to have been there for Nana, too. Maybe if she had leaned on her family, she wouldn't have felt the need to cheat on Pop. Or maybe she still would have cheated, but the family would have realized that sometimes her grandmother needed help, too.

From the minute Sarah left to get coffee, Kayla continued cleaning out the storage room. Doing something productive made her feel better. In fact, she felt better all around. Sarah being there for moral support really meant something. Even though she didn't know the full truth, it was nice she cared.

Kayla went to retrieve a bigger trash can from under the register desk when she saw Jordan, Lauren's new love interest, standing in the middle of the store.

"Hi, Jordan. You scared me. Is everything okay?" Kayla thought Jordan looked as if he hadn't shaved in a few days.

"I'm sorry, Kayla. I hope you don't mind that I stopped in. Lauren always says you're the voice of reason in the family, and I'm a mess right now."

Kayla sighed. "Wait for me in my office."

She pointed Jordan toward her office, then walked to the front door to change the open sign to closed. Sarah had the key. She would let herself in like she always did. This morning was obviously meant for drama and not for making money.

When she walked into her office, she saw Jordan had already taken a seat. She sat in the chair across from him.

"So tell me, Jordan, what's going on?" She clasped her hands on the desk and waited for him to speak.

"Lauren almost broke up with me. I thought she was giving us a real chance, but this morning at six o'clock, my boss called and told me I had to get to the office. A transaction was going sour, and I had to save it. But I was already in my car on my way here to see Lauren. I had to make sure she was okay and that she was still going to give us a chance. I told my boss I was on my way to Bella Cove, and I was planning on working from here, and he threw a fit. He said I'm needed in the New York office, and if I wanted to be in Bella Cove, I should find a job there. I told him I was almost here, so he said I had to be back by noon. I was on my way back to the city, but I felt like I should stop and talk to you." Jordan's eyes were bright red. He was leaving something out.

"Did you see Lauren?" she asked.

He nodded. "I did. I stopped at your house. Your mom is very nice, by the way. She made me take some brownies for the ride home."

Kayla smiled. "Go on."

"Your mom led me up to Lauren's room. She had just finished getting dressed and she was doing her makeup. At first, she was surprised to see me, but I told her I wanted to make sure we were okay. And she said she trusted me to make the right decision. Well, that threw me off because of my boss's threats. And I'm on the fast track to becoming a partner. So I told her I had to stay in New York, but I made enough money at the firm to buy a house here. We could come here every weekend if she'd like. She said she didn't want that. It's all or nothing. Then I said I would commute by train or car every day. But the thing is, I have to be at work most mornings by seven. The morning traffic would be over two hours, and the train ride is just as long because out here, you have to transfer trains. I'd be willing to do it, though, for Lauren. But she said she couldn't ask me to do that because eventually I'd resent her." Jordan ran his hands over his face. "What should I do, Kayla?"

Kayla sighed. "You don't need my advice."

"I do."

Kayla shook her head. "I already know what you're going to do."

"You do?"

Kayla smiled. "Yes, you're going to do whatever is necessary to be with Lauren. She already made it clear she won't leave Bella Cove. That's a deal-breaker for her. But the good news is, that's her only deal-breaker. Besides the normal things like no cheating. And even though you two haven't dated for long, she really cares about you."

"And I care about her," he added.

"I know. So my question is, what's your heart telling you? What can you do to make your relationship with Lauren work, and at the same time be true to yourself? My only advice is to listen to your heart. Your mind may be fighting against you, but eventually, the heart leads the way. Listen to your heart, and stop creating obstacles to be with Lauren."

Jordan stared at her. Kayla could tell he was thinking.

"I know what I have to do," he said. "You're right." He stood, leaned over the desk, grabbed her face, and kissed her on the cheek. "I'm sorry, but I've got to go."

Jordan ran out of the store without looking back. When he opened the front door, he almost ran into Sarah, who had her hands filled with iced coffees.

"Whoa," Sarah said.

"Hey, Sarah, I'm Jordan. You look exactly like the picture Lauren showed me. I'm her boyfriend. I'd like to talk, but I have to go." He kissed her on the head and then ran out the door.

Sarah looked at Kayla, and they both laughed.

"That was Lauren's new man?"

Kayla grabbed her iced coffee out of Sarah's hand. "Yes, it is. I've decided to close the store for the day. You and I have a date in the storage room. Do me a favor and call Lauren. Tell her to take the day off. She won't be in the right frame of mind anyway."

Sarah smiled. "Okay!"

Kayla was about to enter the storage room, but she remembered something.

"Oh, and one more thing. Please tell Mom to make extra brownies for us tonight. I think we'll definitely need them."

Sarah laughed and immediately dialed home.

16

THE NEXT MORNING, Kayla went to the rock just in case Gabe was there. They didn't have a standing rock appointment, but she'd hoped he'd be there anyway.

When she didn't see him, she stormed to his office and knocked on the door.

Gabe answered the door, looking frazzled. His thick hair was in disarray, and he had dark rings around his eyes.

"Are you coming to the rock?" she asked before he could even say hello.

Gabe chuckled. "Do you want me to come to the rock?"

She put her hands on her hips. "I wouldn't be standing here if I didn't. Unless you're still holding a grudge."

He ran his hands through his messy hair. He must have done a lot of that this morning.

"You confuse me, woman."

"Well, get unconfused."

She turned and starting walking, not even waiting for him. If he wanted to come, he'd follow. As she reached the trees, she sensed Gabe behind her.

"You didn't give me a chance to lock my door," he said, catching his breath.

"I've given you enough chances. Now, it's up to you." She'd made up her mind she was still going to fight for him, but he had to meet her halfway. Him deciding to join her this morning was a sign that maybe he would.

They were silent until they reached the rock.

"I didn't bring a blanket."

"That's okay," she said as she sat down. "But I brought us a snack." She opened her purse and took out two large brownies.

Gabe took a brownie out of her hand and joined her on the rock. "Crumb cake yesterday and today brownies. Maybe we should run around the rock instead of sitting on it."

She laughed. "I wouldn't mind if you got fat."

He raised an eyebrow as she took a bite of her brownie. "You want me to get fat?"

She laughed again. Gabe always made her laugh. "I'd like that. That way, you wouldn't be so damn attractive, and every woman in Bella Cove wouldn't be checking you out."

He smirked. "You're jealous of the women here who check me out?"

She sighed. "I've only seen the women we pass when we walk here, but, yes, I'm jealous."

Gabe looked at her, but suddenly, his eyes turned serious. "I hate watching men checking you out, too. While I was catching up to you just now, I saw at least four guys checking out your sexy butt."

She busted up laughing. "You did not."

He nodded. "I wouldn't lie about something like that. I was picturing myself hitting all of those guys over the head with my grandfather's signed Mets baseball bat."

She smiled wide. "The cops would arrest you, but don't worry; I'd bail you out of jail."

He looked out into the bay, taking another bite of the brownie. "You wouldn't abandon me?"

She looked at the bay, too. "I'd never abandon you again."

They were both silent after that as they sat looking at the water and the boats and munching on brownies. After a while, she couldn't take the silence.

"Are we going to talk about the ring?" she asked.

He didn't even glance at her when he answered. "Do you want to talk about the ring?"

She sighed. "No."

He chuckled. "I don't either."

Kayla scooted closer to him. He put his arm around her and she leaned against his chest. She didn't want to talk about the ring, so she was glad he didn't either. Sitting here like this was exactly what she wanted to do. This was one of the first times they were on the same page since he'd showed up at the store.

They remained silent for a long time until Gabe put his nose in her hair and inhaled. "Lavender. You always used lavender shampoo and lavender oil on your skin."

Kayla smelled him, too, but she didn't make it as obvious as he did. She missed his woodsy smell so much that about a year ago, she'd gone into a candle shop in town, smelled each one, and then tried to explain to them what he smelled like. It hadn't worked; nothing they sold came close.

"You used to love the smell of lavender. Do you still like it?" she asked.

He groaned. "You have no idea." Gabe inhaled her hair again. "I can't do this anymore."

"Do what?" It didn't take long for her to find out.

Gabe grabbed the back of her head and gave her the kiss of the century. His lips pressed into hers as if he was starved. She opened her mouth, welcoming the feel of his tongue, and he did not disappoint. He moved his tongue around hers, as if she was his favorite flavor of ice cream.

Kayla wrapped her arms around him as he guided her back against the rock.

"I should have brought the damn blanket," he whispered against her lips.

"It's okay. I'm fine."

He leaned his forehead against hers before slipping his hand underneath her tank top.

"I know it was my idea to take things slowly, but every time I see you, I can't get enough of you. And when I'm not with you, you consume my thoughts. Fuck, I'm struggling here."

"I'm struggling, too."

He kept his forehead against hers as his hand touched her bare stomach.

"Your skin was always so smooth." He moved his hand in circles until he reached her bra; in one swift motion, he unhooked it.

When his fingers grazed her nipple, she moaned, dying for him to remove her shirt. But he didn't. His thumb circled her nipple, but other than that, he didn't move. With his head resting against hers, neither could she.

Gabe pinched her nipple, exactly how she liked it. He remembered.

"Your nipples are so hard for me."

She wanted to tell him how wet she was, too, but she refrained, afraid he'd stop touching her.

When he touched her other nipple, she about lost it. She lifted her pelvis slightly in the air.

"Easy, baby," he said. "If you think I'm going to fuck you against the rock, I'm not. I only want to touch you. I miss how you feel so much. You're my drug."

"A good drug? Or a harmful drug?"

He chuckled. "Sometimes good and sometimes harmful."

"I don't want to be a harmful drug, Gabe," she whispered.

He continued pulling her nipple. If he didn't stop this torture, she was definitely going to come, even without her clit being stimulated. And she didn't want to come this way, as much as she loved what he was doing.

But before she could tell him to, he stopped touching her, clasped her bra, and pulled her shirt down. His forehead stayed against hers, so she reached up and quickly kissed him on the lips.

"I could have touched you all day, but I think we're being watched," he groaned.

"What? Where?" She turned her head and saw a boat not that far away.

Gabe sat up and ran his hands through his hair. Kayla followed.

"You run your hands through your hair when you're frustrated," she said.

He smiled. "True. You frustrate the hell out of me."

She stood and wiped sand off her clothing. "Me? Why?" She batted her lashes at him.

"Don't look all innocent," he said and then became serious. "When we stopped talking, I was done with you. But now, since you're back in my life, I can't stop thinking about you and your sexy body. You're dangerous."

She tilted her head and looked at him. "I don't think anyone's called me dangerous before."

"That's good to know. But only because they haven't touched or tasted you the way I have. You were supposed to be out of my system two years ago, and clearly, you're not. You confuse the hell out of me, woman."

Kayla smiled softly and repeated her wish from earlier, more gently this time. "I hope you become unconfused soon." She grabbed the remains of her brownie, wrapped it up, and threw it into her purse. Then she grabbed Gabe's and handed it to him, touching his fingers as she did. "And by the way, Mr. Wademan, you're my drug, too."

They walked back to Main Street in silence. The entire time, Kayla felt the imprint of his fingers on her nipples. She had never felt so horny in her entire life. At the same time, she was through asking him to meet her at the rock. Nope. The ball was officially in his court.

Two weeks later, she still hadn't heard from him. Obviously, she wasn't that strong of a drug because he was able to resist her. And she couldn't figure out why. He seemed into her at the rock. Yet, everything else was pretty much the same…everything except for Kayla's fragile heart. She went to the rock every morning to see if he was there, but he wasn't. His car was always in front of his office. She could have knocked on his door, as she had that other morning, but she wanted to see if Gabe would start to pursue her. He hadn't…not even a little bit.

That didn't stop her from missing him. In fact, she missed him more and more each day. With the pain came the realization she was more in love with him than ever. It didn't help that he had touched her intimately.

So she threw herself into cleaning the storage room with Sarah. Together, they made the room look great. Kayla even succumbed to buying a ladder so she could paint the room. Sarah thought Gabe should do it, but Kayla said there was no way they could ask him for another favor. Besides, they wanted to paint flowers on the wall, and Gabe wouldn't be able to do that. Once they bought the ladder, Sarah even painted a superhero figure. She printed out a picture of one on the internet and then traced it onto the wall. Kayla was super impressed with her sister's artistic skills. She had never seen Sarah so determined before.

Their first class was scheduled in three weeks—a Mommy and Me yoga class. Sarah would be in charge, but a yoga instructor in Bella Cove had agreed to teach it at no cost. She thought it would be a great way for her to generate some business for her yoga studio. She also agreed to supply the yoga mats. Sarah was also planning a Mommy and Me art class. An art teacher from town had agreed to teach the class. The fact Sarah had orchestrated this all on her own thrilled Kayla.

Jordan continued pursuing Lauren, but he had pulled back a lot. He still called but now only once a day. Lauren walked around looking miserable again, but Kayla told her not to give up hope; she believed Jordan was up to something. He didn't want to lose Lauren.

Her mom still yelled at her dad. Unfortunately, nothing had changed there. Kayla hoped her dad wouldn't leave her mom. No matter how many times Kayla told her mother to cool it, the stubborn woman just wouldn't listen.

Josh still walked around acting as if Kayla was doing a terrible thing by not giving him some of Nana's money to buy a car and not paying him for his work at the family's furniture business. Eventually, she'd have to give him a little money, just to make sure he didn't do anything dumb. She had to sit down with her dad and talk about it. Josh would drink with or without her giving him money. At the same time, he needed to grow up and act like a man—no matter how he felt. With him having to ask for every little thing, he couldn't be feeling like much of a man, regardless of how he'd harmed the family.

Matt and Jessica seemed okay. Jessica had called Kayla a few days before and told her she was continuing with the acupuncture and taking the supplements Erica had given her. She was also sleeping with the rattle underneath her pillow every night. Every time it moved, it would wake Matt, but it was good preparation for when the baby woke during the night. They would make wonderful parents. Kayla hoped Jessica would get pregnant soon.

Jessica asked when she could come to a family dinner, so Kayla had planned one for tonight. Her mom was more than happy to cook.

Even with the dinner planned, Kayla had stayed at the toy store late, needing to finish some accounting. The rent was due next week, and she'd have to see Gabe.

Kayla wished her grandmother was alive. She could sure use some advice. When she told Nana about Gabe, Nana had said not to worry. "True love always wins," she'd said. Kayla wondered if Nana had been thinking about her and Pop when she'd given Kayla that particular piece of advice.

By the time Kayla arrived home for dinner, the tension in her house was so palpable, she already felt suffocated. When she walked into the kitchen, her mom was screaming at Josh to put on a nicer t-shirt. Kayla looked at Lauren to see what the problem was. Lauren mouthed back that their dad was running late. Kayla rolled her eyes. She needed a calm family dinner, not a chaotic one.

"Hi, Mom. Do you need help carrying things outside?" During the summer months, they always ate on the back porch.

Her mom was stirring the pasta pot. "There you are. Between you and your father, we'll be eating dinner for breakfast."

Kayla grabbed the salad bowl. "Hush, Mom. I'm sure Dad will be home soon."

"He won't. He's been staying late for the last three nights. He says he has some large pieces of furniture due, but I think he's having an affair."

"Mom! He's not having an affair." Kayla almost dropped the salad all over the floor. Luckily, she had good reflexes.

She opened the back door and placed the bowl on the table. At the same time, Matt and Jessica were walking up the back-porch stairs.

"Hey, sis, we were just grabbing something from the car."

Matt kissed Kayla on top of her head, and Kayla gave Jessica a hug.

"That's okay. I just got here, and Mom is already on a tirade. Dad's running late."

"I know. We have a bedroom set due in a few days. Dad's been working like crazy on the bed. I told him I'd help him, but he wanted me to start on another order, which is due shortly after this one. Business has been crazy. In a good way, but crazy all the same."

Kayla sighed. "Please do me a favor and tell Mom that."

"All right." Matt walked into the kitchen.

"How are you doing?" Kayla asked Jessica.

Jessica smiled. "I'm good. I absolutely love Erica."

"I'm so glad." Kayla inhaled. "We better see if we can help Mom before she completely loses it."

Jessica laughed, but Kayla didn't. She hoped she had it in her tonight to be there for her family. Right now, she didn't think she did.

As they were about to enter the kitchen, Matt came out with a huge bowl of spaghetti. Her mom followed with meatballs.

"Kayla, grab plates and bowls. Jessica, sit down and relax."

"But I'm family, too," Jessica said in the strongest tone Kayla had ever heard from her.

"Yes, you are," Kayla responded. "Help me grab everything."

Jessica followed Kayla into the kitchen, where they grabbed plates, bowls, and silverware.

"Hey, Kayla, do you approve of this shirt?" Josh asked, running down the stairs.

"I didn't even see the shirt you originally had on. Mom made the comment. Not me."

"But you'd probably agree," Josh said in a tone Kayla did not appreciate.

"Josh, let's try to get through this meal in a civil manner. Please?"

Josh gave her a dirty look and stormed out the back door. Kayla rolled her eyes and shook her head at Jessica, who smiled warmly at her.

Jessica and Kayla joined everyone else outside. Her mom grabbed the plates out of her hand.

"It took you long enough," her mom said.

"Mom's in rare form tonight," Sarah said sarcastically, as she chewed on a carrot stick.

Kayla turned toward Sarah to respond when she felt her hairs stand on end. Her heartbeat thudded wildly.

"Is everything okay? You look pale all of a sudden," Sarah said.

Kayla swallowed hard. "Yes, I'm just worried about Mom's attitude ruining this dinner." But she was far from okay. Somehow, she knew if she turned around, she wouldn't be able to take the sight in front of her.

"You can't control everything, Kayla."

Sarah was right, but not for the reasons she thought. Without any other option, Kayla turned toward the table. Her breath caught in her throat. Standing on his property, surveying his house, was Gabe. Aside from the mornings, she'd been outside every night for the last two weeks, hoping to catch a glimpse of him. She was starting to feel like a stalker. Figured—of all nights, he had to be around tonight. Was she still his drug or had he spent the last two weeks detoxing from her? She was dying to know, but, of course, she couldn't ask him that. At least, not now.

The builder had been making progress, and Gabe must be glad about that. But ever since she realized Gabe's grandfather had bought the property for the two of them, she'd never looked at the land in the same way.

"Oh, there's Gabe," her mom chimed in. "Should we ask him to join us?"

"He seems busy," Kayla said quickly.

"He had a very nice time last time he came for dinner," her mom said, clearly not letting it go.

"I was hoping for a night with family only, Mom. Jessica and I have some news," Matt interjected.

Kayla looked at the two of them. She suspected what the news was and briefly closed her eyes. She needed this news, and by helping them, she was a part of it.

Still, Matt had said he had hoped it was a night for family only. Gabe was supposed to be a part of their family. She needed to tell her parents and brothers about him soon.

Kayla's father finally arrived and walked up the back stairs slowly. He looked exhausted. With the business being busier than ever, he was working too hard. Kayla needed to talk to him about that.

"You look exhausted, Paul," her mom said in a sharp tone.

"Mom, don't start. Let's make this a peaceful meal," Kayla said sternly.

"That's easy for you to say. Your husband hasn't cheated on you."

Kayla's eyes grew wide. "Enough, Mom."

Luckily, no one else heard. They were all grabbing plates and filling them with food. On instinct, Kayla looked at Gabe. He always made her feel calm, which was one of the reasons she had fallen in love with him.

Her family all sat around the table. Kayla stood and made the toast like she always did since Nana had passed.

"To the Conway family. May we always stay happy and healthy."

"And rich," Josh yelled.

Kayla ignored him. Then, as everyone clicked their glasses, she turned toward Matt.

"Matt, is this a good time to tell the family what you'd like to say?"

"Yeah, it's the perfect time." Matt stood and nodded at Jessica.

She blushed and shook her head. Kayla watched them silently communicate. She had done that with Gabe countless times. And as a silent communicator herself, she knew what Matt was saying. He wanted Jessica to stand with him, but she felt too shy, and she opted to remain seated. Kayla wondered what it would have been like for Gabe and her to tell her family news like this.

"Jessica and I have been struggling with fertility since we've been married. I'm sorry we didn't tell anyone. We needed to work through this on our own, except Kayla found out recently. And because she's brilliant, she recommended an acupuncturist. The woman Kayla introduced us to is still in school, working toward her certification, but her grandmother had taught her the tricks of the trade. And let me tell you, the lady was incredible." Matt looked down at Jessica with tears in his eyes.

She was beaming up at him.

Kayla was relieved when Jessica stood and joined him.

"We're pregnant!" Jessica yelled at the top of her lungs.

Kayla's mom let out a happy scream and then kissed Matt and Jessica. Kayla ran up to them, unable to stop the tears flowing down her face, and hugged Jessica. While they waited for their turn to hug them both, Sarah and Lauren clapped and screamed. Her father, bless his soul, wiped tears out of the corner of his eye while slapping Matt on the back. Even Josh smiled.

"Congratulations, guys," he said.

Kayla glanced at Gabe, who was staring back at her. Even from this far away, she could feel his eyes penetrating her soul. She had such a strong urge to run up to him, throw herself into his arms, and tell him the good news. Then she'd ask him why he was avoiding her. But she couldn't.

"Now let's eat!" her mom yelled.

Reluctantly, Kayla turned back toward the table and began eating with the rest of her family. But not a moment went by when she didn't feel Gabe. God, she missed him.

"It's nice to know true love exists," her mom blurted out. "I also have news I'd like to share with the family."

Her mom cleared her throat as Kayla's heart clenched. She had to stop her mother from speaking. But she couldn't think of the right words to make her stop.

"Your father is cheating on me. He's having an affair."

"Mom!" Kayla said sternly. "He is not."

"Dad, are you cheating on Mom?" Sarah stood and pushed her plate of pasta away, causing it to spill all over the table. "Just because Nana got away with it doesn't mean you can."

Kayla gasped and stood, too. "Sarah!"

"That's right, Sarah. My mother cheated on Pop with a man from Montauk. The man came to this house and gave me Nana's pearl bracelet to give back to her. Pop came into the living room to see who was at the door. When he saw the bracelet, he knew who he was. So Pop forbade her to wear the pearl bracelet anymore. That's when he bought her the diamond tennis bracelet, which she never took off until the day she died."

"Was that the pearl bracelet I tried to sell?" Josh asked.

"Yes," Kayla said. "Among other pieces of her jewelry."

"How did you know Nana had cheated?" Kayla asked Sarah.

Sarah shrugged. "On my tenth birthday, Nana and Pop gave me the gold chain I wear with my initial in diamonds on it. I loved it so much, I wanted to tell Nana and Pop thank you. So I went to their room, and I was about to knock on their door when I heard Pop yelling at her. I'd never heard him raise his voice before, to anyone."

"I have, and trust me, it's not pretty," her mom said.

"It was terrible. I stood there shaking, and I didn't know what to do. I was afraid to knock on their door, but I was also curious. So I listened in, but it wasn't my fault. Pop was super loud. Anyone could have heard them. Nana said she didn't regret cheating at all as it had saved their marriage and saved her life. I was so surprised she had cheated. I ran to my room. Luckily, they didn't hear me. No one ever knew until now. I decided to keep it a secret. And I didn't know you and Mom knew, too."

"Oh, I knew," her mom said. "And I just recently told Kayla."

The family grew silent after that as everyone processed the fact their beloved Nana had cheated on Pop. But Kayla learned two powerful things from Sarah that she didn't know when her mom had told her. Nana had said by cheating on Pop it had saved her life. And Gabe had saved Kayla's life. Before she went to graduate school, she lived for pleasing her family. She was always the good girl in the family, constantly helping others. Meeting Gabe had saved her from herself. Gabe's love had saved her even more.

The second thing she learned was that Sarah had been carrying the knowledge of Nana cheating for a long time. Kayla would bet the reason her sister had no interest in marriage was because Sarah felt disillusioned about love. Their grandparents had always acted as if they were in love, and they were. But they weren't perfect. They were both human. But Sarah couldn't figure that out on her own. Somehow, Kayla had to help her believe in love again.

"And all of you think *I'm* messed up." Josh threw his pasta plate across the table, joining in the mess Sarah had made. He stood, forcing his chair back, which fell onto the floor with a loud thud. Then he stormed inside the house, slamming the door behind him.

"I'm sorry, Jessica and Matt," Kayla said softly.

"No, this is what family is about. I haven't been present in your family the way I should have been. I thought you were all perfect, unlike my family. It's important to be here in the good times and the bad," Jessica said.

Kayla smiled warmly. "Discovering Nana cheated has had a huge impact on all of us."

"I'm so shocked I can barely speak," Lauren added.

"Lynne, I didn't know about this. If I knew you were carrying this on your shoulders, I would have taken it from you," Kayla's dad said. "I swear on the family, who I love more than anything in my life, I didn't cheat on you. I never have, and I never will." Her dad looked at all the siblings. "Nana let us down. If I had known, I would have taken charge more. I allowed Nana to run the show. I allowed her to run my wife's life. I watched it happen over and over."

Her dad paused and cleared his throat then turned toward her mom. "I love you, Lynne. I love you so much. You can be annoying when you yell at me, I can't deny that, but you're the love of my life. I've been working late on that big furniture deal, but I've also been secretly making you a new wooden bed. Remember the one you always wanted? Well, I've been working on it from scratch. To surprise you for our wedding anniversary next month. I know I don't tell you I love you like I should, so I wanted to show you instead."

Tears poured down Kayla's face and those of both her sisters. Even Jessica was crying, although that was easy for a pregnant woman. Kayla's mom wasn't crying, though. She looked serious and deep in thought.

"No, Paul, you're wrong. There was nothing you could have done to release my mother's hold on me. It was who she was, and I allowed her to take my power. I'm bored without her though. I feel an emptiness. During the day, I'm so lonely. And I know you have to work. I think I knew deep down you weren't cheating. What my mother did to my father scared me. And I was blaming myself. I was so lonely I took it out on you. I'd yell and criticize you whenever I had the chance. I was wrong."

Her mom threw her arms around Dad and kissed him. "Thank you for making me the bed, baby. Thank you for being my husband and sticking by me. I love you, too. Marrying you was the best choice I ever made. And I made it on my own, without my mother's approval."

Her dad chuckled. "Did she approve of me?"

"She did because you allowed her to continue running the show."

Kayla looked over at Gabe's property, hoping he'd still be there. She yearned for him, especially now. But she didn't see him. When she turned back toward her family, her dad was staring right at her. He gently released his wife's hug but continued to stare at Kayla.

"Lynne, there's one thing I regret more than anything. I regret the responsibility Nana put on Kayla's shoulder, especially before she had a life of her own."

"But she was the only one who could handle it," her mom said.

"No, we need to stop relying on Kayla the second something goes wrong with one of us."

Then he addressed Kayla directly, and she got a sick feeling inside.

"Kayla, Nana never should have made you leave school. It was wrong."

"Dad, she was dying," Kayla cut him off.

"Please hear me out. You could have come home to say your goodbyes to her. I get that. But then you should have finished school. Your dream was to become a psychologist, not own a toy store. Not that there's anything wrong with that, and you've been doing a phenomenal job, which doesn't surprise me. Whatever you touch becomes a success. And the fact you included your sisters was selfless, as usual. But you staying here cost you a lot. And I've been doing some research, so I have an idea of what the cost was."

"Dad!" Kayla said sternly.

"When there's a new man hanging around my three beautiful daughters who will be our neighbor soon, I want to know exactly who he is, so I hired someone to do a little investigating. He gave me the gist, but I told him not to give me the details. Because you're the one who should tell me that story, not a stranger I hired."

"What's going on, Kayla?" Matt asked.

One tear ran down Kayla's face. Quickly, she wiped it away. Lauren handed her a tissue and rubbed her back. She was grateful. This was her family. And it was time they knew the truth. She took a deep breath and looked around at her family as she spoke.

"Gabe Wademan isn't only my new landlord or our new neighbor. Gabe was the love of my life."

Her family members gasped, and Sarah squeezed Kayla's hand under the table.

"Gabe *is* the love of her life," Sarah corrected.

"Go on, Kayla. You need to get this off your chest," her dad said.

Kayla inhaled. "I met him at graduate school on my first day. It was love at first sight. I wanted to tell you and Mom I'd met the most wonderful man." Kayla looked over at her mom. "But I was scared, Mom, that if I told you, Nana would find out. And you and Nana would freak out because he lived in California. And for the first time in my life, I didn't want to second-guess my decision to be with Gabe out of fear of what the family would say."

"I understand, honey," her mom said.

"Anyway, we started dating. As you all know, I stayed at school over the summer between my first and second year to take classes. We rented an apartment together. We loved each other so much." Kayla had to get everything out, once and for all. So she told them everything, from the moment they met, to that fateful call when she made her choice. "When I finally told him I could return, he told me I was too late."

Kayla looked at her mom, who was fully sobbing.

"We were all so messed up when Nana died. You were the only one who was strong. So you helped us. But you lost the love of your life because of us. And I understand why you never told your father and me, because I did the same thing." Her mom turned toward her dad. "I never told you this, Paul, but when you and I started dating, I didn't tell my mother. I was afraid she would judge you so much that I would end things with you because she didn't approve of you. So I'd tell her I was at Leslie's house."

"Your best friend?" her dad asked.

"Yes, but then once you and I got serious, I told my mother, and she told me she'd adore whoever I chose. And when she met you, she did."

"Thank God, or none of us would never have been born," Matt chimed in.

Kayla smiled. "I told Lauren and Sarah, who were super supportive. And I ended up telling Nana when she was dying. She told me to be there for the family when she dies and to always manage her money. And then she made me promise to return to Gabe. Because that's where my heart lay. But I was too late, I guess."

"Do you still love him?" Lauren asked softly.

Kayla sighed. "I love him so much."

"Then why aren't you two back together?" Matt asked. "And by the way, sis, thanks for telling Sarah and Lauren about Gabe but not telling me."

Kayla rolled her eyes. "I love you, Matt, but you've always been a little bit too protective over who I've dated. Remember threatening my high school boyfriend with his life before we went on a movie date?"

"You did not," Jessica said, hitting him on the arm.

Matt smiled. "I love my sister, and I don't trust men. Because I know how we can be when we like a woman. But back to the important subject. Why aren't you two back together? He's here in Bella Cove. That makes no sense."

"Because he still hasn't fully forgiven me. I thought we'd made progress, but lately, I'm not so sure. He felt alone and abandoned by me. I've tried to fix that, but I guess I can't."

"Would you marry him if he forgave you?" Jessica asked.

Kayla looked at her hands, unable to face her family. "Yes, I would marry him. I've always loved him, and I always will. But I'd also be here for all of you guys when you needed me."

"Kayla, we're always going to come to you with our problems. We always have and we always will. Even if we don't, you figure them out, and help us fix them. I'd like to help you now." Sarah looked at everyone in the family. "Nana felt the need to cheat because she needed a break. I heard her tell Pop. I don't want that to happen to Kayla. I think we all need to join together and help Kayla out. It's time."

Kayla started crying again. She couldn't help it. She heard a noise at the door and turned. Josh was standing by the back door.

"Did you hear what Kayla told us, Josh?" Matt asked.

"I did." He stepped outside. "I heard the whole thing. I caused your unhappiness, Kayla. This is all my fault." Josh ran down the steps.

"Josh," Kayla yelled, hoping he'd return so they could talk it out.

"Let him go. He needs to think about this. He had his part to play. We all did," her dad said. "Kayla, you've done a brilliant job helping us when we were falling apart, but we're not falling apart anymore. Sarah is right. We need to make fix this."

Sarah bounced in her seat. "Please let us help you."

"I appreciate that, but I don't think there's anything you can do."

"We haven't applied the Conway magic yet," Lauren chimed in.

"Whatever that is," Matt said, smiling.

"We haven't united as a family until tonight. I think we could do anything together," Lauren continued.

"I agree," her father added.

Kayla briefly closed her eyes, absorbing what they were all saying. "I'm sorry I lied all those years ago. And I'm sorry I've continued to lie. Nana would never have done that. I feel as if I've failed her."

"Nana cheated on Pop and thought she was keeping it from us. So. Not. Healthy." Sarah smiled at her.

"I love you, but don't keep a secret from me again," Matt joked.

Everyone joined in, telling her how loved she was.

"Thank you. But please, don't waste your time on Gabe. Nana said true love always wins. So if we're truly meant to be, it'll happen."

"Okay," Sarah said, looking around the table and winking at everyone.

Kayla had a feeling they would try to bring her and Gabe back together. And maybe it wasn't such a bad idea. She'd tried on her own, but maybe the Conway magic would work better. Nana had told her to always believe in miracles. And if Jessica could become pregnant, who knew what other miracle was in store for the Conway family?

17

KAYLA, SARAH, AND LAUREN were working on finishing the storage room. After about three hours of work, they were exhausted. During the entire time, no one mentioned Nana cheating or even Gabe. It almost felt as if the dinner three nights ago hadn't happened. No one in the family had spoken a word about it. Kayla wasn't sure if that was healthy. She was debating bringing up the subject when Sarah plopped down on the floor.

"I don't know about anyone else, but I need a break. I can't move." Sarah groaned.

Lauren threw down the dust rag. "I feel the same way," she said as she joined Sarah on the floor.

Kayla sighed. "Okay, let's take a break." Not that she had a say in the matter. She sat next to them and looked at her two sisters. "So, are we going to talk about me still being in love with Gabe and wanting to marry him? Or are we going to continue to ignore it?"

"We sort of already knew," Sarah blurted out.

"Yeah, we suspected it," Lauren agreed.

Kayla laughed. "What do you mean?"

"It was kind of obvious. I caught you blushing a million times when you'd look at Gabe," Sarah said, taking her shoes off and lying flat on the floor.

"Yeah, you do blush when he's around." Lauren followed Sarah and took off her shoes, too.

"I'm so embarrassed." Kayla blushed and laughed again.

"Don't be. It was nice to see you into something other than solving our family's problems," Sarah said.

Kayla looked at her sandals before pulling them off. "Can I change the subject for a second and talk about Nana?"

Her sisters didn't say anything, but they both looked serious.

"Even though she cheated, she loved Pop very much. Sometimes in life, you do things because you've reached your limit, and you need a break. I'm not making excuses for Nana, but I think that's how she felt."

Sarah broke in. "It was the wrong thing to do, but I have a great idea. Why don't I buy all of us iced coffees, so we'll have more energy to finally finish this room?"

Sarah looked at Lauren as she spoke, which seemed odd. They obviously wanted to change the subject. *Fine*, Kayla thought, but she'd have to bring it up again at another time. Too many unresolved issues because of what Nana did.

"I think that's a great idea. I'll buy the next time," said Lauren.

"And I'll buy the time after that," Kayla added.

"I can't hold all three, and this morning, they ran out of cup holders. Do you want to come, Lauren?"

"Absolutely," Lauren said.

One minute later, they had both left the room. When Kayla heard the front door close, she exhaled and remained on the floor, deep in thought. Her sisters wouldn't understand what their grandmother had gone through because they'd never been in her position, but to a certain degree, Kayla had. What scared her the most was the way they perceived Nana. And she wasn't here to defend herself. Kayla thought it was wrong for Nana to have cheated on Pop, too, but she understood.

Ten minutes later, the front door opened, and she still hadn't moved from her spot on the floor. Her sisters had returned rather quickly. Usually, the lines in the coffee shop this time of day were super long. But it wasn't her sisters. It was Gabe with his ladder.

"Resting on the job?" Gabe asked.

Kayla quickly stood. "What are you doing here?"

"That isn't a nice way to greet me."

Kayla sighed. "I'm sorry. You caught me off guard, that's all."

Gabe crinkled his forehead. "Really? Your sisters said you needed some work done in here."

A second later, she heard her sisters run into the store, laughing. They were clearly up to something. When they reached the storage room, Sarah ran in and placed two iced coffees on the floor. And Lauren pushed Gabe further into the room. Obviously, he hadn't been expecting the push, and he almost fell over his own feet.

"Whoa," he said.

"Sorry," Lauren said—which from the way she was laughing, was a total lie.

Sarah placed her hands on her hips. "You've both been misbehaving, and it's time you had a talk."

"We have talked," Kayla insisted.

"Well, you've been saying all the wrong things." Sarah nodded at Lauren.

Then the two of them walked out of the room, closed the door behind them, and locked it. Kayla sighed. She never should have given Sarah the key.

Looking up at Gabe, Kayla realized he seemed as surprised as she was.

"Sorry. I didn't know they were going to do that," she said.

"I figured as much."

Kayla sat back on the floor. She had a feeling they were going to be in here for a long time. She should have known her sisters were up to something. Earlier, Sarah had insisted she leave her purse in her office. She told Kayla she was worried paint would get on it. That, too, was a lie. Her keys were in there.

Kayla exhaled. "I told my parents and brothers about you at our family dinner last night. My sisters and the rest of them are plotting to get us back together."

"I had a feeling." Gabe ran his hands through his hair.

They were silent for a few minutes.

"You might as well have a seat. I think we're going to be in here for a long time," Kayla told him.

He sighed dramatically. "I should have known. They both were wearing huge grins and giggling when they said you needed my help. And you'd only ask for my help if you desperately needed it, and even then, you probably wouldn't."

"I finally bought my own ladder. See?" She pointed to the ladder in the corner.

Gabe nodded. "So why did you tell them?"

She was waiting for his questions.

"My dad suspected there was something going on between us. He wasn't sure what, so he hired a private investigator to find out for sure."

"He did *what*?" Gabe raised his voice.

"Don't be mad. You were new in town, and all of a sudden, you were my new landlord and my new neighbor, and being friendly with my sisters…and me. My dad has always been protective over his family. The investigator told him some things, but Dad said he wanted to hear the details from me. So I told them pretty much everything. It was hard. They didn't judge me, though." Kayla paused and took a deep breath. "It felt good to clear the air."

"I guess it's better late than never, but you should have told them years ago."

"I know, and I'm sorry. I can't apologize any more to you than I have already. And I don't want to fight anymore. I'm tired." Kayla rubbed her temples. "So why have you been avoiding me? I haven't seen you in more than two weeks. I thought we would have hung out by the rock again — unless you've been detoxing from your drug of choice." She smiled wide.

Gabe sighed and succumbed to joining her on the floor. Then he did something she didn't expect.

"Scoot forward," he said, as he leaned against the wall and moved Kayla slightly forward, so her back was facing him. Then he slowly started rubbing her shoulders. "You're right. I tried to detox from you, but it hasn't worked. I failed. And I don't want to fight either."

Kayla inhaled with relief and closed her eyes as he continued to massage her shoulders. It felt so good, she never wanted him to stop. "Thank you," she said.

They were both silent as Gabe moved to her neck and then her back. She heard him laugh softly.

"This room reminds me of when we painted our apartment," he said.

Kayla swallowed. "I remember. Do you like it?"

"I do." He paused and moved to her lower back.

Kayla couldn't help but moan, and she clenched her vagina muscles. Massages always turned her on. Had she ever told Gabe that?

He continued talking. "I remember you saying we should paint flowers and hearts on the walls. And a puppy. You had a thing for little dogs."

"I still do," Kayla said.

They both laughed.

"You wanted to paint everything you and I loved on the walls. You wanted hearts, because you loved me. You wanted flowers, because you loved planting flowers. You wanted baseballs, because you knew how much I loved baseball. You wanted books, because they represented the way we met at school. You wanted to paint chocolate bars, because I loved chocolate."

Kayla swallowed hard. "You remember everything I said." His warm breath brushed against her ear, causing her to shiver.

"I do," he said as he kissed her neck once, twice, then a third time. He remembered that was her most sensitive spot, too.

Kayla leaned into him as he continued massaging her shoulders and every few seconds placing another kiss on her neck.

"I'm tired," she whispered and then moaned.

If he continued to massage her like this, she would probably come on the spot, even without any other stimulation.

They were silent again.

"So what else happened at dinner? I heard all of you congratulating Jessica and Matt."

She kept her eyes closed as she responded. "She's pregnant. I'm really happy for them. They were having trouble with fertility, and I found an acupuncturist to help them." Kayla smiled to herself. Jessica's pregnancy was the light in her life right now.

"Please congratulate them for me," Gabe said.

"I will, and thank you." Kayla sighed, feeling more relaxed and content than ever. She also had the strongest urge to make love to him. So she placed her hand on his thigh, not too high but high enough he'd get the hint. The sexual tension between them had to end. He'd already touched her breasts. She'd love for him to touch her everywhere else. And with her sisters locking them in here, they might as well take advantage of the situation. "So should we take a nap or something?"

Gabe was silent for a minute. She hoped he understood that "something" meant sex. He was a smart man. She was sure he'd get her meaning. She almost regretted asking him, since she'd sort of implied it a few weeks ago, but that was before they almost had sex on the rock. If it wasn't for that damn boat, they probably would have.

"It's been over two years since I've been inside you," Gabe responded.

"When you touch me, you drive me crazy. Please, don't leave me horny like you did a few weeks ago," Kayla blurted, as she leaned her head back against his shoulder.

Gabe didn't respond because his cellphone rang. He took it out of his pocket and immediately stood, causing Kayla to catch herself before she fell onto her back.

"Hello, Alice?"

Kayla's entire body was pulsing as she tried to regain her composure. All she wanted to do was touch herself and make herself come. But when she watched Gabe stare off into the distance as he listened to what Alice was saying, she realized he was still torn when it came to her, and that killed her sexual feelings.

"Yes. Tell him I'll be right there. And Alice, do you have the key to the storage room at Magical Toys? Great. Would you mind coming across the street with it? Kayla and I are locked in here. It's a long story. Thanks." Gabe hung up and looked at Kayla. "Problem solved."

Kayla took a deep breath, not realizing there had been a problem. "How come you didn't call Alice right away?"

Gabe grabbed his ladder. He seemed to be contemplating his answer. "Because I liked being alone with you and I missed our time on the rock."

Kayla opened her mouth to respond, but she heard her sisters groaning when Alice walked in. She also wanted to ask Gabe if Alice had a crush on him. A second later, Alice opened the door to the storage room. Kayla's heart sank. She had liked being alone with him, too. Right before he walked out, she grabbed his arm.

"I liked it, too, as well as our time on the rock," she whispered. "Very much."

He nodded and then walked away with Alice, talking to her about something Kayla couldn't hear. But she could see well enough, and judging by his body language, he didn't seem to be attracted to his assistant. But not knowing the woman well enough,

Kayla couldn't be sure about Alice. She knew it didn't make sense, being so jealous, but when it came to Gabe, she was. Before Kayla walked out of the room, she saw the iced coffees still sitting on the floor. She picked them up. She had forgotten all about them.

"Gabe?" she yelled, running out of the store.

Luckily, he was right outside.

"Here you go," she said.

He looked as if he thought she'd say something else. She didn't know what he wanted her to say; if she did, she would have said it. She'd practically asked him to have sex with her. Wasn't that enough?

Gabe took the iced coffee but barely looked her in the eye. Were they back to that again? Kayla thanked Alice for rescuing them, and then she walked inside the store, closed the door, leaned against it, and exhaled.

"Why did you do that?" She looked at her sisters.

Both women were dead silent for a moment.

"We wanted to help. Did it work?" Lauren finally asked, clearly hopeful.

Kayla sighed and briefly closed her eyes. "No, I told you; Gabe's a stubborn man when he wants to be."

"Then we'll keep on pushing," Sarah said.

"You'll do no such thing," Kayla reprimanded, as her mind flashed back to all the mixed signals Gabe had given her in the storage room. One minute, he'd been massaging her and taking them for a trip down memory lane, and the next, he was telling Alice to come unlock the door to the room.

"I don't understand. It's not like you committed murder or anything," Lauren blurted out.

"I did," Kayla said. "I murdered his heart."

"Aw..." Sarah ran up and gave Kayla a huge hug around her waist. "You didn't murder it. You damaged it, that's all."

"And damaged hearts heal," Lauren added.

Kayla smiled. "Thank you both for helping and for trying to make me feel better, but I think the damage I caused is too deep to heal."

Lauren joined them and threw her arms around both of them. Kayla hugged them back tightly. She had no idea what the future held for her and Gabe, but she and her sisters were closer than ever.

18

TWO NIGHTS LATER, Kayla came home to another family dinner. This one had been her idea, too. She thought it would be nice to invite Erica and little Ben to their home to thank Erica for helping Jessica become pregnant.

Kayla was helping her mom put the salad together when Jessica came into the kitchen.

"Hi," she said.

"You get out of the kitchen and relax. Stay off your feet as much as possible," her mom said.

Jessica was newly pregnant. When Matt and she shared the good news, they were aware of the possibility of a miscarriage before the end of their first trimester, but they'd both wanted the family to know early on.

"Can I talk to Kayla for a minute?" Jessica asked Kayla's mom.

"Sure." Kayla washed her hands and then moved into the living room with Jessica. "What's up?" she asked.

"I know it's super early, and I know I could still lose the baby, but my mother is already planning my shower. Before she goes any further, I told her I wanted both of my families to be involved. Is that okay with you?"

Kayla threw her arms around her sister-in-law. "Yes! Absolutely. I'd love to help, and you know Sarah and Lauren will be elated. Do you want to have it here?"

Jessica smiled. "That's exactly what I was thinking. This house is so pretty, and with the view it'd be the perfect place for my shower. I know it'll be in the winter months, but you can still see the beautiful view from inside."

"Perfect. If you wouldn't mind, I'd love to talk with your mom and tell her all this. You shouldn't have to worry about the shower. Your only job is to take good care of yourself. And you're not going to lose the baby. Trust your body to take it from here."

"I know, and thank you."

Jessica was beaming, and Kayla couldn't resist giving her another hug.

"I need help in here," her mom yelled.

Jessica and Kayla laughed.

"And I don't mean Jessica," Mom added.

"I'll wait outside for Erica and Ben."

Jessica walked outside, and Kayla grabbed plates and silverware and joined her. She hoped this dinner wouldn't be as intense as the last family gathering. She had already confessed about Gabe. What else could go wrong?

Kayla opened the back door and saw her dad and Gabe talking. Her heart fell. She hadn't invited him. In fact, when she and her mom had planned the meal, they'd said there needed to be enough food for ten people. Gabe made eleven.

She put down the plates and silverware, took one look at her dad and Gabe laughing together, and stormed back inside the house.

"Mom, what's Gabe doing here?" Kayla asked.

Her mom was placing chicken and shrimp on a large plate and not looking Kayla in the eye.

"Your father and I thought it'd be nice if we invited him. He was a huge part of your life, and we want to get to know him better."

Kayla sighed and rolled her eyes. "That's not the complete truth, Mom. You and Dad are trying to get us back together, like Sarah and Lauren are. I appreciate the trouble you're all going through, but it won't work. Trust me. He refuses to forgive me." She wanted to add that he'd been avoiding her, too, but she chose not to say anything. Then again, if he was avoiding her, why was he here?

Her mom stopped what she was doing, grabbed Kayla's face, and kissed her on the cheek. "He'll forgive you, sweetheart. *Trust me.*"

"He won't, Mom. Please don't push this," Kayla said.

Brushing away a strand of hair covering Kayla's eye, her mom said, "You've been there for the family more than you should have. We're all giving back to you now. Your problem is, you've always given, but you've never received. It's time to be open to receiving."

Kayla nodded slightly. It was no use. Her family would do what they were going to do. She didn't think any of them would change Gabe's mind, but if they all felt good helping her, she wouldn't stop them nor could she.

"Okay, Mom," she said.

"Excellent, now take out this plate of chicken."

Kayla took one more deep breath before she walked back outside, chicken in hand.

"Chicken parmigiana. One of my mother's many specialties." As she placed the plate on the table, Kayla looked at Gabe. Why had he agreed to come here for another dinner? Hadn't the first time been enough?

"Hi, Gabe," she said, as she raised her eyebrow.

He looked back at her with a twinkle in his eye. Looking more relaxed than she had seen him in ages, Gabe leaned back in his chair and took a sip of beer. Kayla wanted to pour the beer over his head for showing up without warning her first.

"Hi, Ben," Jessica said from the other end of the table.

Kayla blinked to break the hypnotic spell Gabe seemed to always cast on her and turned to Ben and Erica, who were walking up the back stairs.

Kayla ran to Ben and gave him a huge hug, then tickled him until he laughed. She loved the sound of children laughing.

"Why don't you go inside and ask Mrs. Conway if she'd like some help," Erica said to her son.

He ran inside without a second glance.

Kayla laughed and threw her arms around Erica. "Thank you so much for helping us."

"Oh, please, it's the least I could have done. You've done so much for Ben and me. I'm relieved it worked so fast, but Jessica was incredibly open to whatever I told her."

Kayla smiled. "Being open seems to be an important lesson for our family."

Jessica pulled Erica away from Kayla and gave the woman a hug. Kayla watched them with a smile as she felt eyes boring into her back. She knew who those eyes belonged to. They were very familiar to her. Slowly, she turned and caught his gaze, which held an intensity she hadn't seen since the first time he came to her store. What the hell was he thinking? He'd practically rejected her the other day in her storage room. Had he changed his mind?

Kayla's dad nudged him to show him something on his phone. Gabe reluctantly moved his eyes from her.

Kayla's mom came out, holding the shrimp parmigiana plate in one hand and Ben in the other. Sarah and Lauren were behind them, laughing. It was nice to see Lauren smiling. Maybe something good had happened with Jordan and her.

"Hey, Lauren, would you like to come back inside with me? I brought home a ball for Ben. I have to find where I placed it."

"Sure," Lauren said as she gave Kayla a big smile.

Yeah…something definitely must be going on.

"So, tell me why you look so happy," Kayla said.

Lauren grabbed Kayla's arm.

"You," Lauren said, laughing.

"Me? Why?"

Lauren sighed. "You're not with the love of your life, and yet you seem happy…even if you're struggling inside. It made me think. Since working at the store, I've been really happy. And then it occurred to me: I'm happy with or without a man. That's because of your influence. You were forced to give up the love of your life and yet you still smile and laugh."

"I wasn't forced, Lauren. It was my choice," Kayla emphasized. "But I'm so proud of your epiphany."

Lauren giggled. "Yeah, it's pretty huge."

"Do you still want Jordan, though?"

Lauren sighed. "Yes, I do. I'm crazy about him, but he'll have to think of a way to move to Bella Cove. I'd feel empty leaving here, even if I am in love."

Kayla had been willing to move to California permanently when school finished and she and Gabe became engaged. She questioned her choice, though, and since she had been back in Bella Cove, she wasn't so sure she could leave again. It was a beautiful place to live, a great place to raise children, and her family was here.

"I understand," Kayla said. "Let's find Ben's ball and eat. I'm starved."

By the time Kayla had joined the others with Lauren, she had made the decision to follow her sister's lead and be happy — with or without Gabe's forgiveness. She loved him, but life was too short to be miserable.

"Look what we brought you from Magical Toys," she said.

Ben ran over to her, grabbed the ball out of her hand, and started bouncing it.

"Thank you," he said, grinning from ear to ear.

"You're welcome, sweetie." She winked at Ben. Then she raised her glass of water. "Okay, time for a toast. Thank you, Erica, for helping Jessica and Matt's dream come true. We all feel grateful and blessed that you and Ben are in our lives."

"To Ben and Erica," Matt yelled.

Everyone clicked their glasses. When Kayla clicked glasses with Gabe, he raised his eyebrow at her, like she had earlier. She wasn't sure why.

"Thank you for always welcoming Ben and me into your lovely home. Bella Cove is a special place to live because of folks like you," said Erica.

Kayla's dad stood and raised his glass. He never made a toast. She needed to sit for this one.

"Thank you, Erica. You've made this entire family happy." He looked at Erica and then turned toward Gabe.

Kayla's heart sank. *Oh, no…*

"I'd also like to make a toast to Gabe, as well as extend an apology. Kayla had told us the two of you were about to get engaged, which meant you were going to be part of our family. It was our fault that didn't happen."

"Dad," Kayla said, her tone louder than normal.

"Let me finish, beautiful. Your mom and I have been talking, and we came to the conclusion we wronged the two of you. We knew you were in school, enjoying yourself, and you were about to complete your grad degree. But when Nana died, we were one messed-up family. Kayla helped us get back on track, but we should have insisted she return to school, instead."

"Dad, please, we went over this the other night. Let's drop it and eat," Kayla insisted.

"Everyone dive in," Sarah said enthusiastically.

Kayla looked over and smiled, grateful Sarah had Kayla's back.

When she looked at Gabe, he had an odd look in his eyes. Maybe if he didn't look so damn hot in his green polo shirt, which was the exact same color as his eyes, she'd be able to figure him out better. Or maybe he was sitting there thinking of a way he could sell his property next door and move far away from her beautiful but wacky family.

Kayla's mom began serving everyone. Her dad reluctantly sat back down and grabbed some shrimp off the plate, but he looked serious. Maybe Kayla shouldn't have cut him off, but it was all too much. She didn't want to ruin this family dinner, especially since it wasn't about her. It was about Erica and Ben, who were eating and laughing with Jessica and Matt.

Sarah told everyone about the Mommy and Me classes coming up. Enthusiastically, she explained in detail how the room looked. Gabe chimed in a bunch of times and joked about what they'd painted on the walls. His mood was lighter, which seemed to take some tension off of her dad.

Everyone continued to joke around. Every so often, Kayla glanced at Gabe, and he'd immediately glance back at her. Her mom went into the kitchen and brought out a large sheet cake, which read, *Thank you, Erica and Ben.* And right under that, it read, *Welcome to the family, Gabe.*

Kayla cringed. She looked at Gabe and mouthed, *sorry.* He smiled back at her. At least he didn't appear to be mad.

"Thank you again, Erica and Ben. And please, Kayla, let me finish what your father started to say," her mom said in a stern tone.

Kayla looked at Gabe to make sure it was okay, and he nodded. It was up to her, then, to stop her mom, but she didn't have the heart. Maybe, in some way, this would help Gabe heal.

"Okay, Mom," Kayla said reluctantly.

"Your father and I want to officially welcome Gabe into the family. We're well aware the two of you aren't together at this time. But two years ago, you loved each other and we want to honor that."

Kayla's dad stood and placed his arm around his wife. "We like you, Gabe, and we wish you were a member of our family. But regardless of what happens between you and my daughter, this will be your home. Thank you for wanting to marry my daughter and spend the rest of your life with her. She's a rare gem, and if she chose you, then you must be mighty special."

Kayla's face heated up. She was debating sliding under the table when Gabe stood and raised his glass. Kayla briefly closed her eyes. Earlier today, she had actually been looking forward to a peaceful family dinner.

And then he spoke. "I'd also like to thank the both of you for welcoming me into your family. In school, Kayla always spoke so highly of all of you. She was right. It feels strange to sit amongst you all when I was almost a real family member, but I'll take anything I can get. We may not be real family, but we'll be real neighbors. That's for life, unless you move. Because I sure won't be moving. Once my house is finished, I'd like to invite all of you over for dinner."

"We'd love that, but only if you let me do the cooking in your new kitchen," her mom said.

"That's a deal," Gabe said, then took a sip of beer. "But on a serious note, I had a part in Kayla's and my breakup as well. She wouldn't come back to California on my timeline, and I sort of threw a temper tantrum because I was going through a hard time, too. But Kayla and I are learning how to be friends again. And I will always care deeply about your daughter."

Kayla's heart fell. She loved him and Gabe only cared about her. She always hated when men said they "cared." What did that even mean? At the same time, her parents seemed to be happy with what he said. He always knew the right thing to say, whereas she always had trouble communicating. And he wasn't planning on moving. So she was stuck with him. Maybe not as her husband or lover but as her neighbor, at least. Her friendly neighbor, who'd be coming over to her house for dinner and whose new home they would be visiting, where they'd share meals now and then, too. But would that be enough?

Kayla was obsessing over the situation until the back door slammed shut. She quickly turned and saw it was Josh.

"Gabe, the reason my sister didn't marry you was because of me. I messed up Kayla's life. It's my fault. She loves you, and I ruined everything." Josh ran down the stairs and left before anyone could respond, a repeat of the previous dinner. Just great.

"That's not true, Gabe," Kayla said. There was no way she'd let Josh take the blame.

"It sort of is," Sarah said. "Gabe, are you still a psychologist?"

"I have a bunch of patients I still Skype with from California. I told them all last week they'd have to find a psychologist in California. To be able to practice in New York State, I'd have to take more classes and tests, and I don't want to do that. My dad is a psychologist. I went into the profession because of him, but when they divorced, I did enough analyzing to last a lifetime. I like handling my grandfather's properties. Plus, I know I've made my grandfather proud."

Kayla loved hearing him talk, but she wished she could run after Josh.

"The reason I'm asking is because I want to know what you'd tell Josh if you could. What advice would you give him?" Sarah asked.

Everyone at the table waited for Gabe to answer, except for Ben, who was asleep on his mom's lap.

"Erica, you don't have to stay for this," Kayla said.

"I want to. I want to be there for your family like you've been there for mine."

"You have been," Jessica said, reaching to squeeze Erica's hand.

"I want to help more, please. It helps me get my mind off Ben's father. That's what you all do for me."

"And we'll continue." Kayla smiled at her.

"So tell us, Gabe, what would you say to Josh?" Matt asked.

Gabe inhaled. "I'd do whatever Kayla suggests. She was the top psychology student in our program. We had a class together where each of us acted as the psychologist. Each class member would mention a problem they were having, and in less than two minutes, the student acting as the psychologist had to think of a way to help solve their problem. Kayla did the best job, hands down. In fact, after that class, all the students continued to go to her for advice."

"She has had a lot of experience dealing with all of us. We've been a handful," her dad said.

Kayla's face got hot again, so she looked at the plate of food she'd barely touched. Gabe always had a way of making her feel better…like now. He knew how to build her up when she needed it and how to keep her there. She was sure he'd have some brilliant advice regarding how to deal with Josh, but by saying what he'd said, he was respecting her.

"Thank you, Gabe," she said softly.

Gabe winked at her.

"Kayla's been giving us advice since she was a little girl," her mom said.

"She's saved all of us," Sarah added.

"I haven't. I may give advice, but you're all in charge of your own lives."

"Was it always your dream to be a psychologist?" Sarah asked, turning toward Kayla. "I don't remember you talking about wanting to be a psychologist as a kid."

She took a deep breath. "I love helping others. It makes me feel good."

"And you're the best at it. That's why I'd listen to Kayla." Gabe smiled.

The warmth in his expression made Kayla's body pulse. He was acting like her best friend again. It made her want to run up to him and throw her arms around him.

Gabe changed the subject and asked about the family's furniture business. Matt and her dad spoke about some of the pieces they had made over the years. And her dad described the bed he'd been making for Kayla's mom. Gabe asked a ton of questions. Jessica told him about the furniture Matt had made for their house and Erica described the piece of furniture Matt was making for her as a way of showing his thanks for all of her help.

No one brought up Josh's name again. Lauren and Sarah talked about Bella Cove in the winter and how beautiful it looked in the snow. Her parents gave Gabe the history of Bella Cove, and Kayla sat there in awe. If someone would have told her two years ago that Gabe would be having dinner with her family, laughing and talking and looking relaxed and happy, she would have said it would never happen. Throughout parts of the evening, she closed her eyes and then reopened them to make sure she wasn't dreaming. It felt as if she was. And in those moments, she pictured Gabe forgiving her and telling her he loved her. That he always had and always would. But deep down, she knew that was an illusion. After all, he had said they were lifelong neighbors. And being a lifelong neighbor wasn't the same as having a lifelong husband.

19

KAYLA AWOKE THE NEXT MORNING to the sound of pebbles hitting her window. She opened her eyes a little wider and glanced at the clock on her bedside table. 6:10. Who would be throwing pebbles at her window this early? Who would be throwing pebbles at her window at all? Her first thought was Josh. Maybe he'd broken his sobriety last night and had lost his key in a bar. But then she shook her head. Josh knew where they hid the spare key.

She got out of bed to see who it was. As she walked toward her window, she thought about throwing on her bathrobe but was too lazy to go find it. Her green silk nightgown hung low in the front. She'd always had a thing for sexy lingerie, and the nightgown only reached mid-thigh, but that didn't matter; it wasn't as if they could see her from all the way down there.

When she reached her window, she opened her shade and looked down. Gabe was standing there, his arm back as if he were ready to throw another pebble. She opened the window and leaned out.

"Hi, Gabe, is everything okay?"

His hair was a mess, probably from running his hands through it a million times.

"I need your help. Sorry about the pebbles. I tried calling and texting you, but you didn't respond."

"I was asleep. Do you need me to come down?"

He nodded. "Yes. Something isn't right with my house. I need your opinion."

Kayla bit her bottom lip. Gabe was staring at her cleavage, she had no lip gloss on, and she probably looked a mess.

"All right, give me five minutes and I'll meet you over there."

Gabe nodded again and headed toward his house. She didn't understand why he would want her opinion, but she assumed it was important. She ran into the bathroom to brush her teeth, comb her hair, and apply light-pink lip gloss. She didn't have time to get put together; this would have to do. She ran into her closet and slipped on her favorite jeans and her large yellow sweatshirt with a hood that had *Bella Cove* written on it in big white letters. Then she put on her white sneakers. She didn't look her best, but it was early.

When she got to his house, she found him pacing back and forth; she'd never seen him look so stressed.

"What's going on?"

He turned her way and made a grunting noise. "Thank goodness you're here. I woke up at four in the morning because I felt like something wasn't right with how they laid out the house. The size of some of the rooms seemed off." Gabe grabbed her hand and walked her closer to the frame of his house. "This room here looks small, but it's supposed to be my office. It's too small for my office. And then here," he said, as he pulled her further into the house. "Be careful where you step. This room was supposed to be a small sunroom where people can sit and look out onto the bay. Remember when we talked about this room? We knew our house would have a view, even if we weren't sure where it would be built. This room looks way too big to be the small sunroom we had in mind. What do you think?"

Kayla looked around at the outer wooden frame of his house. At first, when he'd grabbed her hand, she hadn't been able to focus on anything but the feel of his hand in hers, but now she couldn't take her eyes away from the house. This wasn't any old house. This was the exact same house they'd dreamed of together. Walking through the house was way more difficult than seeing the plans his architect had drawn up. When they had envisioned this over two years ago, Gabe had started describing his dream house, and Kayla had suggested changes she thought should be made. Originally, Gabe never wanted a sunroom, and he had wanted his office to be upstairs.

Thinking about their time together brought tears to her eyes, but she blinked them away before he saw. He was waiting for her to say something, but she felt too humbled to speak.

"Kayla?" Gabe asked, running his hands through his hair for probably the millionth and one time.

"You're right. The sunroom should be smaller, and I remember wanting the room to have a cathedral ceiling." Kayla cleared her throat.

"Oh, yeah, I totally forgot about the cathedral ceiling. I'll have to tell the builder."

"And your office is in the wrong place altogether. It should be here." Kayla walked around to the other side of the house, careful not to trip over any of the pieces of scattered wood, and stepping over the framing that would hold up the floor joists. "And is this your kitchen?" She had trouble saying *your* when she meant *our*.

"Yes. Is there something wrong with that, too?"

"It's supposed to be a long rectangle. Right now, it looks like a square."

Gabe groaned. "You're right. Would you mind going over each room in the house and making sure they're exactly how we planned them to be?"

Kayla swallowed hard. Last night, when she couldn't sleep, she had pictured herself living here with Gabe. "Sure," she answered.

For the next hour or so, Kayla went over the entire house, with Gabe listening intently. He even typed in notes on his phone. Some of the questions he asked were hard for her. He wanted details on how she would decorate the place. Finally, she sat down in the dirt, and Gabe followed.

"Why would you put a yellow couch in the sunroom? And do they even *make* yellow couches?"

Kayla laughed. "I don't know, but that's what I'd want. A yellow couch with floral throw pillows would look lovely, especially if you're sitting there watching the sunrise."

"And how many times have you watched the sunrise?"

"I watch the sunrise a lot from my bedroom."

"While you're in bed, but I don't think you'd go downstairs to the sunroom and watch it."

"I would," Kayla insisted.

Gabe chuckled. "I remember you being too lazy to even go to the library and study, which was across the street from our apartment. I can't imagine you going downstairs to watch the sunrise that early in the morning."

If you came with me, I would, Kayla thought. "Would you like to make a bet?"

Gabe chuckled again. "Okay, what would you like to bet?"

Kayla thought about it. She really wanted to bet him a dinner date, but she was afraid to break the newfound easiness between them, so instead, she said, "I'll bet you an iced coffee." She smiled.

Gabe shook his head. "No, I bet you a meal at Bella Edge."

Kayla swallowed hard. Bella Edge was the nicest restaurant in Bella Cove. It overlooked the bay, and was very romantic. "Okay, deal," she replied. "But you do know I'll have to spend the night for us to find out." Her heart thudded.

Gabe nodded. "I know."

Her heart filled with hope, and he still hadn't released her hand. Unfortunately, her cellphone rang at that moment. Kayla reluctantly took it out of her pocket. She couldn't imagine who would be calling at eight in the morning.

When she looked down at the phone, she didn't recognize the number.

"Sorry," she said softly to Gabe before she answered. "Hello?"

"Is this Kayla Conway?"

"Yes." Her heart beat wildly. She didn't have a good feeling. She looked up at Gabe, nervous butterflies in her stomach.

"This is Bill Emerson down at Bella Hideaway. Your brother Joshua Conway has been here for over ten hours. He has a glass of scotch in front of him, but he hasn't touched it. He's just been staring at it and talking to himself. He keeps mentioning your name. Finally, he gave me your phone number. I thought I should call you. We took the glass away at one when we closed. He kept sitting there, so we didn't have the heart to kick him out. I was here all night, anyway, cleaning up the place. We reopened the bar a few minutes ago, and he asked for a scotch again. I thought I'd let you know."

Kayla sighed. "I'm sorry for the trouble he's given you, sir. I'll be there shortly to get him. Please don't tell him I'm coming; I'm afraid he'll run," she said. "And thank you for calling me."

She hung up but kept staring at her phone. She wasn't sure if she could face Gabe.

"I'm sorry. I have to go," she whispered.

She stood, and Gabe did, too.

"What's wrong?" He grabbed Kayla's arm. "You can tell me, Kayla. Please let me in."

The intensity in his eyes shook her. Even though they weren't back together, she had a chance to make a different choice than she had two years ago.

"Josh has been at Bella Hideaway for the last ten hours. It's a bar located on Raven Avenue, a few blocks from Main Street." Kayla blew out a breath. "He must have gone there after dinner last night. I should have followed him and talked to him."

Gabe was still holding her arm. Then he pulled her into his chest and held her tightly.

"It's not your fault. Not everything your family does is your fault."

Kayla hugged Gabe back. It felt good to be in his strong arms. He hugged her as if he loved her. But as much as she loved the way his arms felt around her, she couldn't keep standing there.

"I have to go get him," she said softly.

"I'm coming with you," Gabe said, releasing her.

She shook her head. "You don't have to."

"I do. I wasn't there for you two years ago. You went through everything with your family alone. I won't let that happen again."

"But I chose to go through it alone."

"You did, but as I said, I won't let that happen again. I should have come here to see what was going on with you, and I didn't. I didn't fight for us the way I should have," Gabe confessed.

"It wasn't all your fault. It was mine, too. I should have communicated better."

Gabe ran his hands through Kayla's hair and kept his hands there. "We can't go back, Kayla. But today, you let me in, and I know how huge that is for you. So today, I'm going to be there for you. Now, let's go."

Gabe grabbed her hand, and together they hurried to his car.

A few minutes later, they arrived at Bella Hideaway. Kayla stepped out of his black Range Rover. Gabe climbed out and came around to her side of the car. He grabbed her arms before she went in.

"Are you okay? You were too quiet in the car."

"I'm okay because you're here."

Gabe kissed her on the top of her head. "Are you ready?"

Kayla nodded. Gabe grabbed her hand and only let her go when he opened the door of the bar for her. Once inside, Kayla stopped and pointed to Josh. He was sitting by himself at the bar, staring at his glass of scotch, exactly as the man on the phone had said. Kayla swallowed hard as she walked toward him. She needed this to be the last time she caught him with alcohol.

"Hi, Josh," she said, coming to a stop directly behind him.

Josh jumped and knocked the glass of scotch over. It flew off the other side of the bar and hit the floor, shattering.

"Kayla, look what you did," Josh yelled.

"I see what I did. I did you a favor," she said calmly, even though it wasn't her fault the glass of scotch had fallen and broken.

Josh fully turned toward her, and he glanced over her shoulder toward Gabe.

"What's he doing here?" her brother asked.

"I wanted him to come with me. I needed him."

Josh looked at Gabe. "You know I'm the reason you two aren't together. I'm the cause of her leaving you."

"Josh…"

"Let him speak," Gabe said into her ear.

Kayla sighed. "Okay," she whispered.

Gabe's gaze turned a darker shade of green.

"Please, continue, Josh." Kayla turned to Josh and sat on the barstool next to his.

Gabe moved to her and placed his hand on her shoulder. Kayla wasn't sure what Josh would say, but it didn't matter. If it helped him to get everything off his chest, she'd be grateful. And if Gabe heard everything she hadn't been able to tell him in the last two years, she'd be okay with that, too. It was time to come clean.

Josh looked back and forth between them.

"You were saying Kayla breaking up with me was all your fault," Gabe said, encouraging him.

"You say it like you don't believe me, but it's true. I'm the one who ruined both of your lives," Josh said.

"Why do you think that is?" Gabe asked.

Kayla almost smiled. He may have decided not to be a psychologist anymore, but he was good at it.

"When Nana died, the entire family went crazy, and I took advantage. I was sick and tired of Bella Cove and the family. I grew up with Nana telling me what to do constantly. I couldn't breathe. You have no idea what it feels like to have to listen to everything the matriarch says or you get into trouble. Then Nana put Kayla in charge of her money and asked her to keep the family together. But I didn't care about the family staying together. I wanted out. I wanted my own life. I was nineteen years old. With Nana dead, I could finally do what I wanted to do. So the first thing I did was drop out of college. I wanted to drink every minute of every day simply because I could. It was my life. If I chose to drink, it was my business. But I needed money. Badly. I had this vision of going to Florida on my own and buying a house.

"So, I stole Nana's jewelry. I was also working part-time for the family's furniture business, and I wanted no part in that. About a month after Nana died, I hid her jewelry. My plan was to sell all of it. I went to my dad's biggest competitor and told them about the new furniture line he was putting out in a few months.

"Then I told them about my mother. The moment Nana died, my mom screamed and cried for hours and didn't get out of bed. I told them my dad would close the store because he couldn't handle my mom. And I told them to spread the word. I was so angry, and I wanted to ruin the family name. Customers began asking my dad about Mom's health, and my dad fell into a depression. Kayla made him go to the doctor to get antidepressants."

Josh kept rambling on until, finally, Gabe cut him off.

"Did all of this happen at the same time?" Gabe asked.

Kayla remained quiet. All their family secrets were being revealed, and she couldn't stop it from happening. Nor did she even want to.

"Yes, I had to act fast. Between Nana's jewelry and the money I got from telling our competitors about the furniture line coming out, I'd be rich beyond my wildest dreams. At the same time, I was ruining the family name. And my family was in bad shape. Mom was hysterical all day and refused to leave her bed. She was borderline suicidal. Dad was depressed. Matt was exhausted from having to do most of the work at the furniture factory, and he ended up in the hospital with pneumonia. And Sarah and Lauren moved out of the house to stay with friends because they couldn't stand hearing Mom scream anymore."

"And what was Kayla doing this entire time?" Gabe asked, clenching his jaw.

Josh looked at Kayla, and she nodded for him to go on.

"Kayla was doing what Kayla always did. Picking up the pieces of our lives while she lost hers. First, she—"

Kayla cut him off. "Please, Josh, let me tell it."

"Okay," he said.

Gabe pulled over a barstool and placed it in between them. Kayla couldn't look him in the eye, but she grabbed his hand. At least they were pretty much alone. The bartender—probably the same man who had called her—kept looking at them from the other end of the bar, but he gave them space. He hadn't even bothered to clean up Josh's mess. She was grateful. Kayla inhaled before she began.

"My mom's screaming and crying was so bad, I didn't know what to do. You've heard her acting hysterical when we spoke. Anyway, I was debating checking her into the hospital out of fear that she would kill herself, when I had an idea. If Mom held one of Nana's pieces of jewelry, she'd feel close to her, and maybe she'd calm down a little. One morning, I went to look for my grandmother's jewelry. I wanted to bring Mom her diamond wedding band, which she'd never taken off. I went to where Nana had told me she'd hidden her jewelry, but everything was gone. I panicked. And then I remembered seeing Josh sneak into her room one day. When I had asked him why—"

"I said I missed Nana, and I wanted to sit on her bed and have a little cry," Josh added.

Kayla nodded. "I wasn't suspicious then. My main concern was my mom screaming, but when I looked for her jewelry and found it missing, I had a feeling, so I went into Josh's room and searched. I remembered when we were kids, he told me he hid everything from Nana under his mattress. So I lifted up his mattress and found all the missing jewelry right there."

"What did you do then?" Gabe asked, taking a deep breath.

She sighed. "Look, I've told you a lot of this when we spoke, but I left out Josh's role."

"And Josh's role played a huge part in what happened with your family after your grandmother passed. I'm starting to get it, Kayla, so, please, continue."

She nodded. "So I sat on his bed, trying to figure out what Nana would have done. As I sat there, I heard my mom's continued screams. My dad was in a full-blown depression by then. He was beside himself, and he couldn't even sleep in their bedroom. So I had to trade rooms with him for a while. Luckily, he agreed to take antidepressants. I practically begged my dad to take them because without my dad and Matt working, the business wouldn't survive.

"So as I sat there, I looked up to Heaven and asked Nana if someone up there was pulling a trick on me. Then I looked out the window, and I saw a bird flapping its wings really fast. I felt like it was my grandmother, watching over me. You see, she loved birds, and when I was younger, she and I would sit on the back porch for hours and watch them.

"A second later, it hit me. There was no way the customers would know about my mom unless a family member had told them.

"So I sat there and considered confronting Josh, but Nana had taught me to always look at the bigger picture. I also thought I could call Matt and my dad and tell them about my suspicions. But calling them at this point didn't feel right. Instead, I called one of my old high school friends, who was one of the customers who'd asked about my mom but didn't buy anything. She was really nice and said she didn't buy from my dad because she found a similar coffee table elsewhere, but the bottom opened up and became a file cabinet. I froze when she described it to me. Then I asked if she had seen any other pieces of furniture lately. And she described my family's new furniture line, which was supposed to come out in a month or two.

"Suddenly, everything made sense. Josh wanted money to get out of Bella Cove. Enough money so he could take off for a few years and live a fancy lifestyle. Between stealing Nana's jewelry and selling our secrets to competitors, he'd have it made. Ruining the family name in the process was his revenge for Nana not leaving him any money, even though she didn't leave money for *any* of us. Not directly, anyway."

Gabe let go of her hand and, instead, caressed her back in slow circles.

"When I got home from the factory that night, I walked into the living room where my dad, Sarah, Lauren, Kayla, and my mom were all sitting. My mom wasn't screaming, and I assumed my sisters had come home to visit." Josh looked at Kayla, as if seeking her permission to continue the story.

Kayla nodded. She felt too drained to continue.

"Kayla had called an emergency family meeting. Everyone was there but Matt, since he was still in the hospital. But Kayla had him on speakerphone. From the disapproving glares of the family, I knew this meeting was because of me. And it must have been bad enough for my mom to stop screaming. Kayla told me to sit down. The first thing she did was take out Nana's jewelry and show me. Then she told the family how she discovered I had taken it. After that, Kayla told them about me selling secrets to competitors and spreading the word about Mom."

"I'll tell the rest," she said. "Once I had finished talking, I told my sisters it wasn't necessary to stay at their friends' again, because Mom had stopped screaming. I wanted to move back into my room, so I suggested my dad sleep in his own room. I told him to continue taking his antidepressants. I told my mom she was allowed to grieve, but she wasn't allowed to scream like that ever again. Nana's passing affected her, but it had affected everyone in the family, and right then, the family's problems were bigger than her. If she wanted the family business to remain profitable, she needed to go to the factory and start showing her face. And then I told Josh he had to work for free because his salary was going back into the business until the business recouped the money he'd made them lose. Then I divided up Nana's jewelry according to who she wanted each piece to go to. I was going to get around to it sooner or later, but I had my hands full up until that point."

"How did the family react?" Gabe asked, his tone soft, soothing.

Kayla couldn't speak again, so Josh chimed in.

"They all listened to her, like they would have if she was Nana," Josh said. "That night, my sisters unpacked. My dad slept in my mom's room. Kayla moved back into her room, and my mom stopped crying. The very next day, she visited the factory to show everyone she was fine. And I've been working off what the family lost every day, and I still am now. Without any money, it was hard buying alcohol, but I found ways. It took me another six months until I was forced to get sober. I'm not proud of those six months. I threw temper tantrums like crazy. Finally, Kayla put me on a strict schedule, and she said if I didn't follow it, she would tell the cops. I knew she wasn't bluffing. We agreed I'd go to five AA meetings a week for at least one year. It wasn't until a few months ago that she gave me spending money. And that's when I broke my sobriety. It was only one night, but I was a mess."

Josh briefly closed his eyes. "So you see, Gabe? Kayla put the family back together. Every one of us needed someone to step in and save them. Kayla did that for all of us."

Gabe didn't say anything for a moment. Then he nodded. "I have two questions, which I think are important."

"What are they? I'll answer anything," said Josh.

But Gabe wasn't looking at Josh. He was facing Kayla.

"In the last two years, have you had a chance to mourn your grandmother?" Gabe looked intently into Kayla's eyes.

She thought about his question. There were moments when she'd try to force herself to cry over her death. Kayla had read somewhere it was unhealthy not to cry over someone close who had died. But at the same time, her guilt over not returning to Gabe overshadowed Nana's passing. Kayla remembered constantly feeling torn.

She shook her head. "No."

"Question two. Who picked up the pieces of your life when the most influential family member in your life—someone you loved and respected—died?"

Kayla looked at her hands sitting in her lap. "I had the toy store to escape to, and Melody, who made me laugh. I had my sisters. And once Josh got sober, the family wasn't all that high maintenance anymore. They were all pretty much back on their feet."

"She had no one," Josh said.

"That's not true," Kayla retorted. "I wasn't mourning over Nana properly, because I was mourning over you, Gabe, and that made me feel like a terrible person. Nana died—a woman I loved deeply—but because of her death, I'd lost the love of my life." She put her hands over her eyes as she felt the tears threaten to come.

Gabe pulled her close and put his arms around her while she sniffled back tears. She put her arms around him, too, and snuggled closer. But she couldn't seem to get as close as she'd liked.

"I *wanted* to mourn over Nana. I miss her, Gabe. Every day of my life. I loved her so much."

Gabe tightened his arms around her and caressed her hair. She hadn't realized how badly she needed to feel this.

He continued caressing her hair as he spoke to Josh. "So here's how this is going to go down. From what I hear, you don't get to the furniture factory until one o'clock every day. I want you at my office from nine until noon, Monday through Friday."

"But I don't like getting out of bed until noon," Josh complained.

"Well, since I'm going to be paying you and giving you a chance to get out of Bella Cove sooner, you'll learn. From now on, you're not going to bother Kayla with your complaints. From now on, you'll be working for me in the mornings, like a man, and then going to the factory in the afternoons and working off what you owe the family for acting like a boy."

Kayla looked at him. "You don't have to offer him a job. I can talk to my dad. Maybe we can start paying him a little. I've been thinking we should lately."

"I think it's better if he got a job outside of the family business. He feels trapped in Bella Cove. Let him fly, Kayla. Your grandmother loved the birds because she craved freedom. She wasn't flying."

"Okay," she said.

"I'll be there every day at nine," Josh said.

"Good. You may not like the work I'll give you. I'm going to make you file and sweep and clean the bathroom. But I guarantee you a paycheck. It'll be up to you whether you spend it on alcohol and waste your life away or save it so you can see where your destiny lies."

Josh nodded. "Understood."

Gabe continued to caress Kayla's hair, although she didn't know if he was even aware he was doing it.

"Thank you, Gabe," she said, lifting her head.

Gabe's eyes glazed over. "For what? I should have done this two years ago. I should have known if you left me and kept telling me you couldn't come back and asking me to wait for you, something was very wrong. I should have come here and acted like your equal partner instead of wallowing in my own pain. I was an asshole for given you an ultimatum."

"You can't think that way. I never told you the full extent of what was going on here."

"But you told me enough. And I heard your mom screaming and crying in the background when we spoke. I should have fought for you. I should have fought for us," he said, his voice low.

Kayla moved her hands to both of his cheeks and held them there. "I loved you, Gabe. I loved you so much. The last time I called you and told you I was ready to come back, you texted me and said no thank you and to take care. I was sad, but I was also relieved. At that point, I didn't want to leave my family again. You made it very clear when we were planning our lives that you had to live in Los Angeles, and I didn't communicate properly that I wasn't sure if I wanted that, too. I made a commitment to you, even though my heart was split in two. When my grandmother died, I felt as if the universe solved that problem for me. I couldn't leave my family on your timeframe. So even though I was still in love with you, I was also relieved to be back here for good."

Gabe's eyes became more intense than she'd ever seen them. "Did you realize that when you left me the message, saying you were ready to come back?"

She let go of his face and shook her head. "No, I knew I felt relieved, but I didn't put the pieces together until a few months later. I didn't fight for us either, Gabe."

Gabe groaned. "I would have moved here. I'd have done anything to be with you and spend the rest of my life with you."

Kayla turned toward Josh. She hated him listening in on their conversation.

"I'm sorry, Josh. I didn't mean for you to hear any of this."

Josh frowned. "You loved Gabe, and yet, you felt relieved when Gabe told you not to come back to California? You fight for everyone in the family and you didn't fight for him?"

Kayla nodded.

"I'll answer that," Gabe said. "I was the unknown. And Bella Cove and the Conway family were her constant. Most folks choose constant over the unknown. But the unknown is more exciting and adventurous. At the same time, the unknown is a risk, and I was the biggest risk Kayla would have had to make in her life. Kayla was flying at school, but she always assumed she'd land. If she'd stayed with me, she would have continued to fly. There would be no landing. I was an asshole toward the end. I was planning our life the way *I* wanted it. In California, working for my father. I was mapping out our lives without asking her how she truly felt about it. I like to be in control and take charge. And by your grandmother asking Kayla to come home, it gave her an out."

"I can't deal with this," Josh said as he pushed his stool away, causing it to skid across the floor. He turned and left the bar.

Kayla looked at Gabe's intense eyes. "I'm sorry, Gabe. I didn't want there to be any more secrets between us."

"I had my part, Kayla. I didn't fight for us. At the same time, from what I've learned just now, I wouldn't have even known what the fight was about. I'm sorry I was an asshole the last few months we were together. And I'm sorry I didn't come with you or fly to Bella Cove to help you with your family. But had you communicated your feelings at any given point, we never would have broken up. I wouldn't have felt abandoned by the woman I planned to spend the rest of my life with, and we would be building that house next to your family's together, as husband and wife." Gabe stood. "I'm leaving. I drove you here, so if you're ready I'll drive you home."

Kayla nodded and followed Gabe out the door. She wished she'd brought her own car. The ride back to her house would be the most uncomfortable ride of her life.

THEY RODE BACK TO KAYLA'S HOUSE in silence. When she got home, Kayla called Sarah and told her to take over the store for the day. She needed to do something, but it took her a few hours to find the courage to actually do it. Instead of hiding in her room, she drove to Southampton, pulled over at the side of the road, and sat in her car, looking out over the Atlantic Ocean to give her plan some thought. She could have gone to the rock instead, but that didn't feel right now. She used to think that was *her* rock, but Gabe had claimed the rock as his, too.

By the time she'd made it home, it was after five. Her plan was to park her car in the driveway and then walk over to Gabe's to see if he was there. She hated the way they'd left things. But her plan changed when she saw her dad sitting alone on the porch. He was never home this early unless there was a big family dinner, and as far as Kayla knew, they had nothing planned.

"Hey, Dad, what are you doing home so early?" she asked, climbing the back stairs.

He was sitting on the rocking chair, drinking a beer. "You'd never guess what happened. Josh came to the factory and said he'd finish up the coffee table I was working on so I could go home and relax. At first, I didn't believe him, but then he got right to work, so I left. Your mom is so happy; she's in the kitchen cooking up dinner."

Kayla sighed. Maybe some good came out of her and Gabe showing up at the bar after all. Maybe Josh had decided to grow up. But something didn't feel right.

"Did Josh say anything else?"

Her dad took a sip of beer. "He told me some of the stuff you and Gabe talked about."

Kayla's heartbeat quickened. "And?"

He kept his eyes on the bay when he spoke. "And I think Gabe was right. You know how to take care of the family. You've been doing it since you learned to talk. But falling in love is scary. I know because I fell hard for your mom and nothing's been the same since."

"I planned on going back to him for the first few months, but then I got used to Bella Cove again. I had a new coffee shop to go to, and a new place to do yoga, and my old bed to sleep in. The idea of graduating and moving to Los Angeles and working for his dad became a distant dream."

"Did you fall out of love with him?" her dad asked, finally glancing at her.

She didn't even need a second to think of her answer. "No — if anything, I loved him even more. I craved him like there was no tomorrow, but my fear won."

Her dad grabbed her hand. "Fear isn't your biggest problem, Kayla. Your biggest problem is not communicating your needs. You were always like that, even as a little girl. You always solved everyone else's problems, yet when it came to what you wanted, you never said anything. Your mom and I would have to figure it out on our own."

Kayla laughed. "You guys did a great job. I loved my childhood."

Her dad didn't respond. He just kept looking at her intently.

"But you're right. If I had told Gabe I wanted to move here after graduation, we could have talked about it. At the same time, Dad, he was acting arrogant when he planned our future. He told me where I'd work, where we'd live, and even what restaurant we'd celebrate in when we each graduated. Gabe had a part in our breakup, too."

He chuckled. "Sweetheart, it takes two to break up. But you're not in charge of how Gabe acts or any choice he makes — or even how he responds when you communicate your needs. You're only responsible for speaking your truth and cleaning up your side of the street."

She smiled wide. "Dad, when did you get so wise?"

He sighed dramatically. "I've been doing a lot of thinking lately, especially when my wife accused me of cheating, and after learning that Nana actually *did* cheat. If I spoke my truth when I married your mom and told her I wanted to build my own house where we'd live and raise all of you, and told her we could make our own choices as husband and wife without asking Nana's opinion all the time, your mother and I wouldn't have had all the problems we've had in our marriage."

"You wanted your own house?"

He chuckled again. "Do you think a newly married man in his early twenties would *want* to live with his in-laws?"

Kayla burst out laughing. "I never thought of that, but you're right."

He winked. "Before your mother comes out with dinner, was there someplace you needed to be?"

Her dad was so smart. Kayla looked over at Gabe's property and found him pacing in front of it.

"Did you know he was there the entire time?"

He nodded. "I did. I'm surprised at how long it took you to notice."

She smiled softly. "I loved talking to you, Dad. We never get a chance to just talk. The two of us."

"Well, let's change that, then."

She kissed him on the cheek and released his hand. "I love you."

He smiled. "I love you, too. Now go get your man."

Kayla didn't need any more convincing. Everything her dad had said was right. She ran down the back porch steps right as she heard her mom's high heels tap-tapping in the direction of the back door.

When she got closer to Gabe's property, she saw him talking to a builder. She wasn't sure what to say, but her dad's words of wisdom reverberated in the back of her mind.

Kayla watched Gabe talk while he moved pieces of plywood out of a blue pickup truck. He looked sexy, especially the way his jeans kept falling slightly whenever he lifted his arms. The rust-red polo shirt fit him to perfection. He was one beautiful man.

Kayla waited until the builder was out of sight, then sighed loudly, which got Gabe's attention.

"Do you and Alice have a crush on each other?"

Gabe stopped what he was doing and stared at her. "What are you talking about? She's old enough to be my mother."

"Some men like that, and she's attractive enough."

"To other women, Kayla. She has a girlfriend in East Hampton. What's the real reason you're here?" he asked, continuing to take the plywood out of the truck.

"I came here because I'd like us to live in Bella Cove. I don't want to stay in California and work for your dad. I'd miss my family too much. And I think raising kids in Bella Cove would be perfect." She closed her eyes briefly, but the sound of Gabe dropping wood on the ground was so loud, she snapped them back open.

"Is that what you wanted to say to me two years ago?" He wiped sweat off his forehead.

Kayla had never seen anything sexier. "It is," she answered.

He chuckled as he shook his head. "When you and I pictured our dream house, it could have been anywhere. I thought we'd stay in California because you seemed happy there. I had no idea you'd rather be here. If I'd known, I'd have moved mountains to find a house for us near your family, but you never gave me the chance. You never gave *us* that chance. I admit I was cocky when I talked about our future because I was so proud that you would be my wife. I was so proud that I wanted to give you a perfect life. The idea of losing you scared the crap out of me. I think I knew deep down that our relationship was too good to be true." Gabe was now practically throwing the wood.

"Gabe, stop. You'll hurt yourself," she pleaded.

He stopped and stood still, breathing hard.

"What do you want from me, Kayla?" he asked.

"I want a second chance," she said instantly.

Kayla felt a raindrop hit her head. When she looked up, a dark cloud had rolled in—any second, they would be drenched. She usually loved summer storms, but why did the weather have to turn now? "I'm sorry, Gabe. I should have told you everything then." The rain began to fall harder.

"Why do you want me back? Why?" He threw his hands up in the air as rain poured down on him. But Gabe wasn't moving, so neither would she. "I should have come here and fought for us, and I didn't. You went through hell with your family, and I was so selfish and obsessed with my grief that I didn't come here and help you with yours. You told me about your mom and about your dad being depressed, so I knew some of what Josh told me, but you never said a word about Josh."

"Josh was hard to talk about. I could barely admit it to myself. Speaking it out loud made the situation more of a reality. And I hated what he was doing to our family."

"But I should have known, because I should have been right next to you when you found your grandmother's jewelry. Hearing all those things from Josh today made me feel like shit." Gabe ran his hands through his sopping-wet hair. "I was too fucked up to set aside my own issues and help you. And I *knew* you were going through hell. I heard it on the phone. You communicated a lot, just not about Josh. So, why do you want to get back together with me?"

The rain fell harder, and thunder sounded every few seconds, followed by flashes of lightning in the distance. They couldn't stay out there much longer.

"Why, Kayla?" Gabe asked her again.

"Because I still love you," she yelled over the rain.

"What?" Gabe asked.

"Because I love you."

They were both soaked. Her jeans and sweatshirt were drenched and sticking to her body. She was getting cold.

"What? I can't hear you," Gabe yelled even louder.

He had heard, but Kayla would say it again a thousand times if her declaration would change anything.

"I love you," she yelled louder. "I love you. *I love you!*" Tears sprang to her eyes, and she didn't fight them. Yet she couldn't tell the difference between the wetness from her tears or the rain.

The workers around them were getting into their cars and leaving. Probably the smart decision. Even the builder hopped into his blue truck with the wood and left, wood still in the back. Gabe turned his head and watched the lightning creeping up on them. He grabbed her hand and ran with her to his SUV. Once they were both inside, he slammed the door, shutting out the storm.

"What am I supposed to do with you?"

She briefly closed her eyes and rested her head against the headrest. "Love me back," she said over the rain pounding on the car, as she began to shiver.

"You're shaking," he said. He grabbed a blanket from his back seat and wrapped it around her, making sure to tuck her in.

He didn't pull away like Kayla thought he would. Instead, his eyes darkened, and his breathing quickened. "Is this the second chance you want?"

He clenched his jaw before grabbing the back of Kayla's head and doing the one thing Kayla had craved since the moment he went with her to find Josh. He kissed her. Hard. He'd kissed her a few times since coming back into her life, but he hadn't kissed her quite like this before, as if he was claiming her for his own.

His tongue brushed against her bottom lip. Kayla opened her mouth, inviting his tongue inside. And the moment she felt his tongue against hers, her passion broke loose.

Kayla grabbed his face with both hands and intensified the kiss, not caring that the blanket had fallen. Then she kissed his nose, his cheeks, his ear…but that wasn't enough. She needed to feel him skin to skin.

There was another loud boom of thunder. She stopped kissing him, pulled her drenched sweatshirt over her head, and threw it onto the floorboard. In one swift motion, she rid herself of her bra and tossed that aside, too.

Gabe's eyes grew huge as he inhaled. "I haven't seen those beautiful things in a while."

She grabbed her breasts. "Well, you *have* touched them. My only hope is that you don't leave me as horny as you did last time." Her nipples hardened under his penetrating stare.

He chuckled as he reached out to her, enveloping her in a huge hug and kissing her lips. Kayla wanted to get even closer, so she climbed over the divider and straddled his lap.

"Damn," Gabe whispered into her mouth.

Kayla pushed her pelvis against him, needing more. She moaned as her pubic bone touched his hard cock under his jeans.

"Gabe," she practically shouted, rocking her pelvis into him again and again.

"Shh, is this what you want? You want me to fuck you in my car?" he asked, pinching her nipples and massaging her tits just the way she liked.

Kayla looked him straight in the eye. With the rain still pouring on the roof, no one was going to bother them.

"Yes," she answered. "I want you any way I can get you, Mr. Gabe Wademan."

He didn't seem to need any more encouragement than that. He sucked her nipple into his mouth, causing her to moan again, while he pulled and twisted her other nipple with his fingers. Pain and then pleasure shot through her body. They never had boring, normal sex. It had always been raw and intense. He made her feel alive, free, and wild. At this moment, she had no idea how she'd given that up.

He released her oversensitive nipple, which had gone from pink to red, and with one hand behind her to keep the steering wheel from digging into her back, he reached with the other to unzip her jeans. Kayla lifted slightly, making it easier for Gabe to pull down her pants—not too far, but far enough to give him access to her most intimate part. The part that craved his attention badly.

He placed his hand over her panties on her crotch and groaned. "Woman, you're soaked."

Kayla laughed. "And so is my hair, my neck, my jeans."

Gabe laughed with her. "My hair, my jeans."

He pushed aside her panties and she instantly stopped laughing. His finger brushed her clitoris over and over and she moaned loudly, not caring how much noise she was making. The rain was still louder, continuing to pound on the roof. He pulled at her clit in the same way he had her nipple. Pulling, twisting, circling, all the ways that always drove her crazy. He remembered. He remembered exactly how she liked it.

"More," she demanded as she grabbed his face and kissed him as if they hadn't just kissed.

"More?" he breathed into her mouth, and then he gave her more.

He plucked her clitoris as if it was a violin string. Plucked and then stroked, plucked and then stroked. Then he stopped as Kayla stopped kissing him.

"Just as beautiful as ever—swollen, wet, and ready for my cock."

Kayla had never been so turned on in her life, watching him as his finger delved into her pussy. He dipped his head and sucked her nipple again, while thrusting one finger inside her, then two, and then three. Kayla was moving her pelvis, wanting his fingers to go even deeper. When he turned his hand and touched that sensitive spot, she almost came, but Gabe stopped cold.

"Tsk, tsk, tsk, not until I'm inside you. Is that what you want, Kayla? You want my cock in you, deeper and harder than my fingers?" Gabe asked, his voice soft, seductive.

"Yes," Kayla practically screamed.

Gabe smiled, unzipping his jeans. He took out his glorious cock. A little bit of precum glistened on the head. It had been over two long years since she'd laid eyes on his penis, and she craved it with every fiber of her being. How many nights had she stayed awake, touching herself while picturing his cock in her mind? So many, she couldn't even count.

"Lift for one quick second," Gabe said.

Kayla was straddling him in an awkward position. She lifted slightly off his lap and pulled her pants down further. Gabe bent over, opened his glove compartment, and grabbed a condom.

"Gabe, I haven't been with anyone since you." She had come clean with her thoughts; she might as well come clean with what her body had been up to.

Gabe stopped just as he was about to tear open the condom package. "I like that you haven't. I like that a lot. Too much," he said.

Kayla's heart sank, waiting for him to confess all the millions of lovers he'd had.

"I've been with a few women, Kayla. To get over you."

"I shouldn't have said anything. You don't have to, either." She'd never been so jealous before, especially over women she'd never met, but she hated every single one of them.

Gabe grabbed her face. "Kayla, please, look at me."

Kayla hadn't even realized she was looking at the pounding rain. "Okay."

"Those women didn't mean anything. They weren't you. There were days I was so lonely, I tried to find another you. But I couldn't. And I haven't been with anyone since I came to Bella Cove."

"Then why do you have condoms in your car?"

Gabe laughed. "I've been fantasizing over a million ways to sneak into your room and fuck you. My fantasies were so real, I knew any day I'd act on them. In preparation, I bought some condoms and stuck them in here." He grabbed her face and gave her a kiss, slipping his tongue inside.

He released her long enough to slide on the condom, then he lifted her slightly, pulled her panties aside, and jammed his cock so deep inside her, she screamed.

Lightning struck at just that moment, lighting up Gabe's intense eyes as he furiously thrust inside her, hitting her in that spot that ignited every one of her nerves.

She moaned, clawing at his hair, his ears, under his shirt, anywhere and everywhere she could reach. She missed this feeling so much, like they were wild animals mating, as if they couldn't get enough of each other.

Kayla kissed his lips, his hair, his cheek, trying to tell him without words how she felt.

Gabe groaned as he rubbed her clit in circles and continued thrusting into her deeper, driving her closer to the edge.

"Gabe," she said. "I'm close. Please be close, too." She wanted to come with him, but with the way he was touching her clit, she knew it wouldn't be long before she had the orgasm of her life. She pulled his hair as she fought a wave that was approaching.

"Don't hold back, baby. I'll be right there with you."

Gabe thrust faster, pressing into her most sensitive spot over and over, and an orgasmic wave consumed her. He continued thrusting in that torturous way that made the wave even stronger.

Gabe groaned as Kayla's muscles clenched around him, and he came hard inside her.

Thunder boomed as they were both coming down from their orgasms.

"Thank you," she whispered, touching her forehead against his.

Lightning lit up the car again, but she didn't care.

Gabe was quiet. Too quiet… making her feel all after-sex weird. So she did the only thing she could do with the storm raging above them. She grabbed her sweatshirt and put it on, careful not to touch him. She didn't even bother with her bra. Then, as gracefully as she could, she climbed off him, not daring to look him in the eye.

As she was climbing back over onto her side of the truck, thunder roared right above them, scaring her half to death and causing her to teeter a little. She grabbed onto the seat to keep from landing too hard, and her hand fell on something between the seat and the center divider.

"I think I almost sat on something." She pulled out a large bubble mailer envelope, which had a sticker on it with the words *fragile, insured,* and *international* stamped all over it. The package had been sent from France. From what she could tell, there was some sort of a box inside.

"Sorry," she whispered again, wondering what the envelope contained, even though it wasn't any of her business.

And that's when she saw Gabe looking at her strangely, as he tucked his dick back inside his jeans and zipped them up. His expression made her feel as if she'd stolen candy from a store and had gotten busted. Whatever was in the envelope, he definitely didn't want her to see it.

As she started to put the envelope back where she'd found it, a piece of paper slipped out. She knew the handwriting very well. What was Melody doing sending him mail? And then it hit her.

"Is this what I think it is?" she asked Gabe as she tucked the note back inside the envelope.

He nodded. "It is." He exhaled.

She wanted to read the note. Badly. So, keeping in mind all the lessons she'd learned the past few weeks, she came out and asked. "Can I read it?"

Gabe groaned. "Fine."

Her heart started to thud. With shaking hands, she took out the note and started reading.

Dearest Gabe,

> *I'm in Paris with Harry, and suddenly, everything hit me. About a year ago, when your grandfather and I were on one of our monthly coffee dates, he told me he had saved his wife's engagement ring. The ring meant the world to him, and one day, he said he would give it to his grandson. Of course, I didn't know at the time, but that grandson was you, Gabe. I asked him why he didn't give it to you then, instead of waiting, and he told me you weren't ready to propose yet. And when you were ready, he would make sure you had the ring.*

> *I asked him if you had a bride in mind. And he said yes — she's a beautiful blonde who has the weight of her family on her shoulders. Then he said she wasn't ready, either. And*

he said you would give her the world, but the only world she'd ever known was her family's, except for a brief moment in time. He said you and this woman loved each other deeply. Unfortunately, neither of you was ready to fight for your love, and you weren't aware of how rare and fragile true love is. And apparently, this woman had decided a life with you could never be more than a dream.

Once I figured out he was talking about Kayla, I asked my husband Harry if I should send the ring to her. He said the ring was intended to go to you. Then the next problem was when I should send it. I had no idea if you'd be ready to propose or not. So I asked your grandfather for a sign from heaven, which may sound strange to you, but I really believe in signs. My mother comes to me in my dreams all the time, and my father leaves dimes on the ground for me to find.

So anyway, I was looking for signs. I even told Harry to look for them. Two days later, our television in our hotel room went on and then off again, three times. At first, I freaked out, but then it hit me that it was your grandfather. I remembered him telling me that when he died, at the first of every month, he'd send me a sign to remind me to pay my rent. We joked about what the sign would be. He said he read somewhere that spirits can turn televisions on and off, so he told me he'd mess with my television. It wasn't the first of the month, but I just knew it was him. Isn't that hysterical? I believe this meant I was to send you the ring now, so here it is.

Please take care of Kayla. I love her like a daughter. Be patient with her. She's been through a lot with her family. She knows how to give, but she has trouble receiving. I wish I could have called you instead of sending you this in the mail, but Harry said if I called, you might tell me not to send it.

Good luck with Kayla. I think the two of you make a beautiful couple.

Love,
Melody

P.S. Don't forget to send me a wedding invitation, and tell Kayla I'm mad at her for not telling me the man she was talking about when I saw her was you.

Kayla folded the note back up and placed it inside the envelope.

"When did you get this?" she asked. Thunder boomed again, causing Kayla to feel even edgier.

"I got it yesterday. When I got home to my grandfather's house, after the meal with your family." Gabe turned and looked Kayla directly in the eye. "What did you think of it?"

Kayla exhaled. "I think it's interesting that Melody figured it out."

"Is that all you got out of that?" Gabe asked, his tone short.

The rain was still pounding hard on the car. When lightning struck, she got another good look at Gabe's expression. He looked as if he was ready to jump out of his skin. She knew the feeling… They'd just had sex for the first time in years. It would be nice if they were cuddling or something…anything but this.

"Your grandfather wants us to be married and live happily ever after. He believed in all that."

"Do you?" Gabe asked in a softer tone.

Kayla took a deep breath. "I do, but do you think you're ready to forgive the past and get married?" Impulsively, she took the box out of the envelope and opened it. The diamond shimmered. It was beautiful.

Gabe groaned. "I don't know."

The thunder and lightning were getting farther apart. Soon, the storm would be over, and she'd have to leave his car. "Well, it seems as if you have some soul-searching to do." She gathered her purse and bra to leave, but she still held the rock in her hand. She couldn't seem to let it go.

"You want to put the ring on? You want to wear it?" Gabe asked.

She took a deep breath. "I would," she said honestly.

"That would make us engaged."

"It would," she said again. "We could live in your house, which is our dream house. It's right next door to my family's house. It'd be perfect."

Gabe chuckled. "It'd be perfect until your mom knocked on the door crying. Your sisters will want man advice, so they'll call you at all hours of the night and expect you to run over to the house. Your dad will threaten to leave your mom because she's misbehaving, and who knows what Josh will be up to. Matt will be okay, though. He's happily waiting for his child to arrive. But who knows what will happen once the baby comes."

Kayla looked him directly in the eye. "Now who's allowing my family to get in the way of us being together?"

The thunder and lightning stopped altogether, though it was still raining.

Gabe chuckled as he ran his hands through his damp hair. "Do you still want children?" he asked.

Kayla closed her eyes briefly. "Every time I sell a doll to a little girl, my heart breaks a bit. We spoke so much about having kids. My heart aches because we never got that chance. I still want children with you, Gabe."

"So you're ready to get married now?"

She nodded. "I am. I love you, Gabe. And I know I'll never love another man in the same way I love you. Sure, I'll date and meet someone, but my heart will always belong to you." Without thinking, Kayla placed the ring halfway on her finger.

Gabe grabbed it out of her hand.

"Don't put the ring on your finger yet." He held the ring and her hand tight in his grip.

"You're not asking me to marry you?" she asked, her heart thudding like crazy.

He shook his head. "Not yet." He put the ring back into the envelope and threw it on the back seat.

Kayla's heart fell. "You want me to start dating other men?"

He clenched his jaw. "I'm not saying that, either. But like you said, I have some soul-searching to do."

Not even a second later, she heard her mom calling her name. Kayla was about to leave anyway. She opened his car door, not saying anything else. Before she shut the door, she smiled softly. He smiled back, but it didn't reach his eyes.

The ball was once again in his court, but she'd meant what she said. If he decided he didn't want to marry her, she was ready to date again. It was time she made a life of her own. She'd bared her heart and soul to him, told him she loved him, but he never said it back.

Maybe their problem wasn't that he couldn't forgive her. Maybe he'd fallen out of love with her.

The walk back to her house wasn't easy. Her lips were still tingling from his kiss, and she was already feeling slightly sore from sex since it had been so long.

Her mother stood on the back porch waving at her. Kayla waved back, letting her know she had survived the storm. Her mom nodded and went back inside the house.

When Kayla opened the back door, no one was waiting for her in the living room. She sighed with relief as she climbed upstairs. She closed the door to her room, threw her clothes off, put on her favorite camisole with matching silk shorts, and got into bed. Only then did she allow herself to finally process the most bizarre and most wonderful day of her life. Thinking that it might have been a dream, she touched herself. Nope, not a dream. Gabe had definitely been inside her. But the fact she'd told him she was ready to marry him and he clearly wasn't put a damper on the intimacy they'd shared.

Hours later, or maybe minutes, Kayla opened her eyes. Once again, she heard pebbles against her window. This time, she knew exactly who it was, but why was he here? Had he finished soul-searching already?

She threw off the blanket, ran to the window, and quietly opened it so as not to wake her family.

"What's wrong?"

Although it was pitch-black outside, he stood beneath one of their back spotlights, so she got a good look at his frustrated expression.

"I want to come up," he said, talking a little too loudly.

"Shh, you'll wake up my family," she said in a loud whisper. "Hold on."

Kayla shut the window and opened her bedroom door, making sure no one was around. The hallway seemed quiet, and no noise came from any of the other bedrooms. She tiptoed downstairs and down the hallway and through the kitchen until she reached the back door. Through the glass, she could see Gabe standing there with his arms crossed.

As she opened the door, a breeze from the water came in, causing her to shiver. She was only wearing the camisole and shorts she'd put on earlier.

"Why'd you come down like that? You'll catch a summer cold," Gabe scolded.

Kayla rolled her eyes. "Why are you here?"

He ran his hands through his disheveled hair. She could tell he was shivering, too. "I want you again, Kayla. I can't stop thinking about you. I can't stop picturing you naked. I'm a starved man, and you gave me just a tiny taste. Now, I can't get enough."

"You had a taste of me on the rock, too. Why was this different?"

"Because you said you'd marry me."

"And are you done with your soul-searching?"

He shook his head. "No."

She put her hands on her hips. "Then maybe you should come back when you know what you want."

Gabe huffed. "Oh, I know what I want."

Kayla tightened her jaw. "Gabe Wademan, I'm not talking about my body." She clenched her vagina anyway.

"I'm not just talking about your body. I also want your heart." He paused. "Because you own mine. You always have, and you always will."

"You *have* my heart. I told you that," she whispered.

He nodded. "I know. And you have mine. I didn't tell you in the car, so I'm telling you now."

He didn't say he loved her, but this was close enough. Kayla grabbed his arm and pulled him inside. Within seconds, Gabe was passionately kissing her. With all her might, she pushed away to close the door.

"Follow me," she said as she started walking toward the steps.

"No way." Gabe caught up to her and picked her up. "I lead, you tell me where."

Kayla sighed as she motioned toward the stairs. As Gabe was climbing them, she thought of what he'd just said. *I lead, you tell me where.* She wished she could have a relationship with him exactly like that.

When they reached the top of the stairs, she pointed toward the door on the left, then put a finger over his mouth to make sure he didn't ruin everything by talking. Her family were pretty light sleepers. The last thing she wanted was for them to catch her in Gabe's arms.

Gabe continued holding her, but he was still able to carefully push the door open. Once inside, he still didn't put her down. But he quietly closed her door and locked it.

Smart man, thought Kayla.

He walked over to her bed and dropped her right into the center.

"I want to fuck you, I want to touch you, I want to devour you," Gabe whispered as he started to remove his shirt. "What I *don't* want is for us to talk. About anything. Especially about what we spoke about in the car, unless it's how good we feel in each other's arms."

She figured as much, so she didn't argue. How could she? She wanted the same things. It would be nice to not have to talk about their issues for once.

Tentatively, she reached up to unbutton his jeans, and he let her. Screwing him in the car was one thing—impulsive, exciting because of the storm, and the sexual tension had been so strong since he showed up in town that their encounter had been long overdue. But tonight…this felt different.

Kayla wanted him so badly, her hands trembled. Once the button was undone and the zipper unzipped, she pushed down his jeans and his boxers at the same time. Gabe quickly stepped out of them.

She didn't have time to look at his glorious cock because he was already climbing onto the bed, grabbing her camisole and pushing it over her head. Before he could take off her shorts, she sat up, grabbed the back of his legs, and put his entire cock in her mouth. If he refused to stand still long enough for her to get an eyeful, she'd have to take matters into her own hands. Putting his cock inside her mouth was taking matters into her own hands.

Gabe groaned as she moved her mouth up and down, using his thighs for support. She licked the head and then slid all the way down. She continued doing that, even as her clitoris pulsed. She'd been dying to do this since the moment she saw him standing in her store. He tasted just as she remembered—raw wood and all man.

She grabbed onto one leg tighter, and with her other hand she massaged his balls. She remembered how this always drove him crazy.

"Baby, if you continue doing that, I'm going to come. And I only want to come inside your pussy," he said as he ran his hands through her hair.

She stopped sucking him because she wanted that, too.

Gracefully, or maybe not so gracefully, Gabe pushed her back onto the bed. The soft pillows met her fall. In one hell of a swift motion, he removed her shorts, leaving her naked and horny.

He told her he didn't want to talk, but there was one thing she had to say.

"I want all of you, Gabe. I want you raw, hard, and bare."

All he said was, "I'm clean."

"Me, too," she responded. "And I'm still on the pill."

Gabe kissed her mouth, then her neck, stomach, belly button, and finally, where she wanted him to kiss her and where he hadn't been able to kiss her in the car. Her clitoris swelled as he sucked it. Every nerve ending she had down there was at alert. Kayla lifted her pelvis as she grabbed his head, keeping him exactly where she wanted him. His tongue felt like heaven. He focused on the center of her clit and that was more than fine with her.

The moment she was about to come, Gabe pulled away, chuckling. Swiftly, he stuck his tongue deep inside her, exactly where she craved his cock. With his finger, he pressed on her clit. Between his tongue doing all sorts of naughty things and his finger on her most sensitive spot, Kayla came, and came hard. The power of her orgasm forced her back to lift into the air. Mid-orgasm, he moved his finger in circles, causing her to moan his name. In the middle of calling his name, she remembered her family sleeping. If one of them woke up and heard, she'd truly die of embarrassment.

"No one heard you, baby. You were quiet enough," Gabe said, reading her mind.

He crept up her body and moved his cock along her vagina a few times. She thought she'd die from that alone. With the extra lubrication, he thrust inside easily.

"You look so fucking beautiful with my cock deep inside you," he said as he went deeper and deeper. "I pictured this a million times in the last two years, but the vision in my mind couldn't compare to the real thing."

Aside from his words, at one point, she could have sworn he touched her heart.

Kayla was craving touching his chest, but he still had his shirt on. "Take it off," she whispered.

Gabe chuckled as he threw off his shirt. It landed somewhere on her floor. Not once did he break their rhythm.

"Much better," she said as she touched his chest all over, pinching his nipples and scratching him.

Gabe grabbed the cheeks of her ass, raising them slightly so he could hit all the right places.

Kayla wrapped her legs around him, making it easier for him to thrust and maneuver his cock to hit that one spot that drove her to another realm. And once she was there, all thoughts about what their future would look like were gone. All she could focus on was the man who was inside her and how much she loved him.

She grabbed him around the neck, wanting to be closer, but it still didn't feel close enough. So she rested her head against his neck, inhaling his scent, as he continued fucking her like he couldn't get enough.

With him hitting that one spot, it didn't take long for her to come again. She grabbed onto him harder as a wave hit her, and as she rode that wave, she held onto him for dear life.

A second later, he groaned. When she felt his sperm flood her womb, she wanted to burst into tears. It felt so good. So right. But she didn't want her tears to ruin this perfect moment. And perfect it was.

"Are we allowed to talk now?" she asked. "I mean, about real things?"

Gabe slowly pulled out of her, grabbed her around the waist, and pressed her back against his chest. She couldn't believe they were spooning, just as they used to do back in school.

"This *was* real." He kissed her on the back of her head. "Everything else will fall into place as it's meant to. Now, no more talking. Goodnight, Kayla." Gabe put his leg over hers.

When he was being all sweet like this, how could she argue? So she did what he told her. She closed her eyes, allowed sleep to consume her, and dreamed of the man who owned her heart but who still hadn't told her he loved her back.

21

NORMALLY, Kayla enjoyed watching the sunrise, but not this morning. Last night, she had slept two hours, at most, even while Gabe was holding her. She had made him leave at four o'clock. Not that she wanted him to, but her mom got up at around five.

But he'd refused to leave before they had sex again. Because they didn't have too much time, he had fucked her hard and quick. It was hot, nonetheless. He'd taken her from behind while touching her clit in the way that made her want to beg him to never stop. She came fast, and so did he. Having sex while lying on her stomach had always been her favorite position. Gabe remembered. He seemed to remember everything about her.

After he left, Kayla tried to go back to sleep, but she couldn't. She didn't like not having Gabe's arms around her. Finally, at six o'clock, she gave up and focused on what was happening between them.

By a quarter after six, she gave up thinking and got dressed. Before she left her room, she had a sudden urge to grab the pictures she had cut out—the ones that depicted her ideal wedding—and shoved them into her purse. Her mom and dad were already downstairs. As she walked down the stairs, they were laughing.

"Hey, Mom? Dad?" she asked as she grabbed a banana from the fruit bowl.

"Yes, beautiful," her mom said.

Dad looked up from his newspaper.

"I did it. I told Gabe I'd marry him and that I love him."

"Oh, honey, I'm so glad. What did he say?" her mom asked.

Kayla shrugged. "He said he had to do some soul-searching. He's not ready, I guess."

Her mom put her hands on her hips. "I don't like that. Any man should jump at the chance to marry my daughter."

Her dad put down the paper. "Men don't think that way, Lynne. Kayla and Gabe have both been through a lot. He probably wants to spend time with her without the drama of an engagement."

"Getting engaged is a beautiful time," her mom insisted.

Her dad smiled, shook his head, and went back to the newspaper. "Until the family gets involved. Gabe's a smart man," he said, chuckling. "If I was a gambler, Kayla, I'd make a bet that he'll ask you soon."

Kayla ran up to her dad and kissed his cheek, then did the same to her mom. "Thank you both. I'll see you later."

"Have a good day, and don't worry about Gabe," her mom said.

Kayla was already out on the porch, the door closing behind her, before she had a chance to respond. The truth was, she loved Gabe more than life itself. But since she'd decided to come clean and had spoken her truth, she felt a million times better.

If he didn't want to marry her, she'd be devastated, but she'd also start dating. She hadn't lied when she'd told him that. She was ready to live and have fun again. Nana's death had taken a toll on her in many different ways. But Kayla was alive. And life was for the living.

Before she opened her store, she grabbed an iced coffee. She was juggling her keys, her coffee, and opening the door to her shop when Sarah opened the door from the other side, almost causing Kayla to fall.

"Oh, shit, let me help you." Sarah grabbed the iced coffee out of her hand while Lauren held the door open.

"Hi," Kayla said. "What are you two doing here before eight in the morning?"

"We're preparing for the class that's coming up," Lauren said.

"And we wanted to ask you something," Sarah added, handing her back the coffee. Whatever she was about to say, she seemed nervous.

Kayla dropped her bag onto the floor. "Do we need to sit in a circle on the floor for this?" she asked.

Sarah laughed. "Yeah, I think we do."

The three of them sat on the floor by the register desk.

"What's going on?" Kayla asked. "Please don't tell me you're both thinking of quitting on me." She had gotten used to them working at the store.

"Quite the opposite," Sarah said as she looked down at her hands.

"We've come up with a different plan for the store." Lauren smiled.

They were *definitely* up to something.

"Out with it," Kayla said sternly.

Sarah sighed. "I want you to teach me the accounting side of the store and everything you can about how to run it, so you can take the rest of the online classes you need to finish your degree. You've always wanted to be a psychologist…that's where your heart lies, not in owning a toy store. But *I* love it. It's perfect for me. You can still own it. I'll only run it."

"And I'll continue to work here, as usual," Lauren chimed in. "Jordan is trying to start his own law firm here in Bella Cove, but he told me it'll take some time. I don't know what will happen between the two of us, but for now, I plan on working here. But instead of only listening to what you want me to do, I'll listen to Sarah, too."

Kayla swallowed tears. "Wow, I didn't expect any of this." Hope was bubbling up inside of her. "You're both willing to do this?"

"Yes, it's your dream to be a psychologist. We want to help you accomplish your dream, like you've helped us in every area of our lives," Sarah said, giving Kayla the biggest smile she'd ever seen.

"We want you to be happy," added Lauren.

"I told Gabe yesterday I'd marry him," Kayla blurted out.

Sarah sat up straighter. "Get. Out! And it's taken you all this time to tell us. What happened?"

Kayla held up her hand. "Do you see a ring on my finger?"

Lauren put her hands over her mouth and gasped. "Oh, my God, I'm so sorry."

Kayla smiled softly. "He hasn't rejected me yet. He said he needs to think about it, but we've also had sex. Three times."

Her sisters screamed.

"Was it good? I bet Gabe is a really good lover. I can tell," Sarah said, grinning.

"I'm not telling you that." Kayla's face heated up.

"It was good," Sarah said knowingly.

Both her sisters burst out laughing.

"So, what do you think is going to happen?" Lauren asked, her tone serious.

Kayla thought about that for a second. "I honestly don't know, but I love getting to know him again. There are moments when it feels like no time has passed. I'm so in love with him."

"I know what's going to happen," Sarah said, batting her eyelashes. "You're going to live happily ever after."

Lauren giggled.

"Wow." Kayla smiled wide. "That's huge coming from a woman who doesn't believe in marriage or happily ever after."

Sarah smiled back. "But you do, so that's what I want for you."

"I love Gabe," Lauren chimed in. "Since he offered Josh that job, our darling brother has been behaving like he used to. Did you know Josh left the house before we did this morning?"

"That's funny. I heard all of you leave the house, but I thought everyone was off to the gym or grabbing breakfast or something," Kayla replied.

"No, Josh told us how excited he was to start his morning job at Gabe's." Sarah slid over to Kayla and put an arm around her.

Kayla put her arms around Sarah, too. "Thanks for offering to run the store while I finish school. I love the idea."

"You do?" Sarah clapped her hands.

"I do, but I'll still be here. I like working with both of you. I have fun. But I'll need a few hours every day to finish my online classes. Then I'll have to find a supervisor to watch me give others therapy. That will take a few hours, too." Kayla paused. "Do you think Melody will be mad if I'm not working here every day?"

"Melody didn't work here every single day. She was always running off with Harry. And that was before he won the lottery. You used to complain about it all the time at dinner," Lauren said.

"That's true. And I'm not abandoning the store. I'm following my dream, that's all."

"So...it's settled?" Sarah jumped up.

Kayla laughed. "Yes, it's settled. And I guess I have to give you both a pay raise."

Lauren jumped up and clapped her hands with Sarah. Kayla stood and hugged them both.

"I love you guys so much," she said as a tear slid down her face.

"We love you, too," they said in unison.

Kayla wiped the tears with the back of her hands.

"Sarah?" Kayla asked.

"Yes?" Sarah responded.

"Eventually, we'll have to talk about what you went through when you heard Nana and Pop fighting about her cheating. You may not believe what I'm about to say, but I think it affected how you view love."

Sarah sighed. "Okay, okay…but not now. I want to create a career for myself before I worry about a man. But I *have* worked on flirting less."

Kayla nodded. Sarah wasn't ready to deal with it yet, but at least she had found some inner peace at Magical Toys. For now, Kayla couldn't ask for more.

That night, Kayla let Sarah close up the shop. She felt like walking while the sun was still up, and she wanted to talk to Gabe. She had been thinking about him all day, about their kisses, their intimacy, their everything. She didn't realize how much she'd missed the way he touched her, the way he grabbed her face and looked lovingly into her eyes. Without thinking, she walked past her house to go to his. If she married him and lived here, she'd walk past her house every day.

Gabe was sitting on the ground gazing out at the bay. She took a picture of him with her cellphone. He looked serene.

"Are you going to stand there taking pictures of me while I'm thinking of you or are you going to come and join me?" he asked, continuing to stare at the bay.

Kayla loved the fact he knew she was there even though he wasn't looking. She sat on the ground next to him and looked at the bay, too, rather than at him.

She opened her purse and took out the picture cuttings of her perfect wedding. She handed them to him.

"I'm ready to begin a life with you," she said, turning back toward the bay.

She heard him take a quick breath. "You do realize you'll have to make an effort to communicate your needs, and I will still be controlling at times and not realize it."

"I sure hope you're talking about our sex life," Kayla joked.

But he didn't laugh.

So in a more serious tone, she said, "I do."

Out of the corner of her eye, she saw him look through some of the pictures.

"And you're okay with that?" he asked.

"I am. I may struggle with it at times, but I'll work on it." Kayla fully turned to him. She couldn't help herself.

He turned his head toward her at the exact same moment. They were so close they could have kissed again, but she needed to tell him more.

"You're too important to me," she said. "I cut those pictures out during the last few months we were together at school. On my plane ride to Bella Cove, when I had to come home, I looked through them over and over again. I kept looking at them, even after Nana passed, until I finally forced myself to put them away. Even though I allowed my family's problems to consume me, I want you to know how serious I was about us — how serious I still am."

"I can see now that you had to take care of your family. I was never upset that you had to return here and hold down the fort until they got healthy again. I was upset that I had no idea how you still felt about us. A few months before you got on that plane to come here, you pulled away. It scared the hell out of me to think I was losing the love of my life, and I didn't know how to stop it." He paused. "But now I know."

Gabe reached into his pocket and took out the ring. Suddenly, the view from the bay slipped away. The only thing that mattered was Gabe and the ring his grandfather had given him.

"My grandfather was right. Getting back together was inevitable between the two of us. Neither one of us was ready to fight, but now we are. I wouldn't have accepted this ring a year ago, and he knew that, but now I'm desperate to put it on your finger. It's yours. It always has been and it always will be."

Tears of relief pricked her eyes. "Gabe Wademan, are you asking me to marry you?"

"Yes, I am."

"But I thought you had to do some soul-searching."

Gabe chuckled. "Nah, I only said that. I wanted to put the ring on your finger the second you admitted you loved me. But I wanted to ask you properly, not have you take the ring and just put it on. And I only thought to delay the engagement because once your family finds out we're getting married, there will be a huge amount of drama. I can see it now — your mom will want your wedding to be one place, and you'll want it to be somewhere else. Sarah and Lauren will be fighting over what dresses to buy."

Kayla laughed. "I could see those things happening, too. But I won't let them control my wedding. I want to get married in my parents' yard, overlooking the bay. My Pop built the house for Nana, and I think it will help me feel their energy more on our wedding day."

Gabe smiled. "You say you won't put up with any drama, but knowing your family, it will happen anyway."

She laughed again. "You're right, it will."

He grabbed her hand. "I wanted to spend some time with you as just us. Like we used to be. No pressure. No drama. Just us, enjoying each other. I love you, Kayla. I love you more than I've ever loved anyone."

A tear ran down her cheek. "So, do you want to put off our engagement?"

He shook his head. "No, I can't imagine allowing one more minute to pass before I put that ring on your finger."

"So put it on," she shouted.

Gabe put the clippings on the ground and got down in front of her on one knee. Kayla got the hint and stood.

"My beautiful Kayla, we've been through some intense ups and downs, but I love you more than anything. As much as I hated it, I think us separating for two years needed to happen to draw us closer together. I was a shell of myself during those years. Since you've been back in my life, I finally feel alive again. I want you to know I'll be here as your equal. If you want to move to Europe for a few years, I'll do it. I'll move or stay here. It doesn't matter so as long as I'm with you. You're the most caring, wonderful, generous, trustworthy, honorable, intelligent woman in the world. I want to spend the rest of my life with you. Kayla Conway, will you do me the honor of becoming my wife?"

Kayla knelt in front of Gabe. "Yes! I love you so much. And if you want to move to Europe for a few years or stay here, I will, because as long as I'm with you, I'm complete."

Gabe took her hand and placed the ring on her finger. He caressed her face and kissed her lips with passion, reverence, and a new promise of tomorrow. And then he abruptly ended the kiss. "Oh, wait, I forgot something."

He quickly stood. Kayla watched him run to his car and get something from the back seat. She couldn't imagine what it was. When she saw him run back, holding what looked like her favorite doll of all the ones she'd ever had on sale at her shop, she stood.

"This is for our son or daughter," Gabe said as he stood in front of her.

He handed her the rag doll with the long blonde hair and the piercing green eyes. Kayla took it and held it against her heart.

"It's from Magical Toys," she said.

Gabe nodded. "It is. I had Alice go get it a few days ago when you were at lunch. When I was painting your ceiling, a little girl came into your store and picked it up. You walked up to her and asked if she needed any help. She only wanted to hug the doll. But you looked at her and the doll with such yearning and sadness. It took everything inside me not to climb down my ladder and hold you, to tell you not to give up on our dream of having children together."

Kayla swallowed back tears of happiness. This beautiful man filled her heart with such love. "I loved this doll because she looked like a combination of us with her blonde hair and green eyes."

"I know," Gabe said.

Kayla smiled. "I can't wait to have your children, Gabe Wademan."

She threw her arms around him and held him as tight as she could, while also holding on to the doll. Gabe held her equally as tight.

"But I promise I'm on the pill. We're not pregnant yet."

Gabe chuckled. "So here's what I'm thinking. If you don't like the idea, just tell me. You may have a better one. I thought I'd move into your bedroom at your house until mine is finished. That way, I get to spend more time with you, and I'd like to sell my grandfather's house in East Hampton as soon as I can. Of course, I'll ask your parents first. Then, in about six months, our house will be complete. I'd like us to spend the first night there as husband and wife. What do you think?"

Kayla smiled wide and hugged him tightly. "I think that's perfect."

Gabe laughed. "Come on, let's go tell your family," he whispered in her ear and then kissed her on the forehead.

Before stepping out of his warm embrace, Kayla briefly closed her eyes. She hoped both Nana and Gabe's grandfather were looking down on them.

She grabbed Gabe's hand and started walking toward her house, but then she stopped. She wasn't ready to face them all yet. There was something she needed to do before that.

"Wait," she said. "We didn't seal your proposal with a kiss."

Gabe chuckled again. She'd never get tired of that sexy sound. "Yes, we did."

"You're right, but I want another one."

Gabe's eyes grew darker as he grabbed her and gave her his signature kiss, passion and love mixed together. Kayla pulled his hair and kissed him back the same way, but it wasn't enough.

"That was nice, Mr. Wademan, but I would have preferred if you'd kissed me behind that huge pile of wood over there." She nodded to the far end of his property, toward the area that was farthest from her house.

Gabe sighed dramatically, but his eyes held the most adorable twinkle. "I might as well start pleasing my wife-to-be now."

"That's right," she said as they started walking toward the woodpile. "It's good practice."

"Whatever you say, honey."

"I'll have none of that. My man can't lose his backbone."

When they were behind the pile of wood, their teasing stopped.

"I'll show you how strong my backbone is." Gabe's eyes turned intense as they darkened.

Kayla lay down on the dirt and spread her legs. "Show me."

Gabe swallowed and then lay on top of her. He kissed her gently, then slightly harder, then harder still until she opened her mouth, and his tongue slipped inside. Kayla threw her arms around him, while he continued making love to her tongue.

Reluctantly, he pulled back. "We officially sealed my proposal with a kiss…three times," he said. "Now I'm going to seal it with my cock."

Kayla moaned as he slipped his finger under her sundress and inside her panties. She was wet already. He turned her on so much.

"I'm so wet."

Gabe's breathing picked up. "My goal is to keep you wet forever."

That will be an easy goal to reach, she thought.

"You want me to be wet every minute of every day?" she teased between moans.

Gabe pulled down his shorts and took out his already hard cock. "Yes, because I'll be making love to you as much as possible," he said, before thrusting deep inside her.

Kayla couldn't say anything after that. Because he was kissing her like he couldn't get enough of her, and she was kissing him back in the same way.

She raised her legs slightly and wrapped them around his waist, so he could go even deeper. Gabe groaned. One thrust went so deep it felt as if he'd reached her heart, pushing away any sadness that lingered for living without him these last few years. He'd touched her soul as no man ever had. And every day, including today, she'd show him how much she loved him and make up for their lost time.

Gabe picked up the tempo. "Touch yourself for me, baby. I want to see you rubbing your clit."

Kayla had no problem doing that. Hell, she'd do anything for this man. She licked her finger, knowing she was driving him crazy. Then she put her finger on her clit and rubbed it in fast circles, making it swell even more.

"That's it, baby," he said, his tone filled with tenderness and lust at the same time.

Between his thrusts and her finger, she knew she was about to come, but she tried to hold herself back.

"I love you, Gabe Wademan," she shouted, right before an orgasmic wave hit her.

Gabe made a grunting noise. "I love you, Kayla Conway — soon-to-be Wademan."

He came then, too. Together, they rode the orgasmic wave, clinging to each other. Kayla thought it was a metaphor for their life. They'd already had ups and downs, and she expected to have many more, but as long as they clung together, they could get through anything, including telling her family.

She looked into Gabe's eyes and ran her hands one more time through his hair. "Thank you for sealing it with your cock," she said and smiled. "Now, let's rub off the dirt sticking to the back of my sundress so we can tell my family it's official; we're engaged."

She pecked him on the lips, as he slid out of her and then helped her to her feet.

Gabe helped her rub the dirt off her backside, which started to feel kinky, and they almost had sex again, so Kayla pushed his hands away and finished the job herself. But they were both laughing. Kayla hoped they'd always laugh like this. She'd make sure they did.

An hour later, the family was sitting in the living room at the house Pop had built for Nana — the perfect setting for Kayla and Gabe to tell her parents and siblings the news. Kayla had called an emergency family meeting. No one looked surprised. She had the ring on her finger, but she hid her hand in her pocket. Gabe stood next to her, taking his rightful place by her side.

She inhaled deeply. She stared at Matt, Jessica, Sarah, Lauren, Josh, and at her mom's and her dad's hopeful eyes. They were all waiting for some good news.

"I have some news I'd like to share." Kayla looked over at Gabe. "Correction — *we* have some news we'd like to share."

Gabe chuckled under his breath.

"We're engaged," she screamed.

The moment she said it, everyone stood and screamed with her. Sarah was the first to run up to them and hug them both, followed closely by Lauren. And then her parents and Matt and Jessica. Even Josh hugged her.

"I'd like to add one more thing," Kayla said while everyone sat back down. "Sarah will be taking on more duties at the store while I finish getting my degree online. Lauren, of course, will be there to help."

"And since our house won't be finished for another six or seven months, I'm going to be moving into Kayla's bedroom upstairs—unless that's uncomfortable for you, Lynne and Paul?" Gabe asked.

"Please, call us Mom and Dad. And we know what goes on behind closed doors. You're going to be intimate anyway, so you might as well not have to sneak around," her mom said with a big grin.

"I have to call Melody, and we have to call Gabe's family, too, but Mom...?"

"Yes, beautiful?"

Kayla started crying. She couldn't help herself. "When I told Nana about Gabe, right before she died, she gave me her blessing. I just thought you should know that."

With tears in her eyes, her mom placed her hands on Kayla's arms. "Nana would have been so proud. She also had unbelievable intuition. She must have sensed what a wonderful man Gabe is. I'm glad she blessed your marriage. I wish she was alive for this moment."

"And Pop, too," Matt added.

"Yes, and Pop. They loved each other deeply. They had their ups and downs like any couple. But they survived. I wish both of you as happy a life as Nana and Pop had." Her mom glanced over at Gabe.

"And us, too," her dad added. "I wish you a happy life like I have with your mom."

Kayla smiled. "I wish for that, too."

"I'm honored to be a part of this family," Gabe said seriously. "My main goal is to make Kayla happy."

Gabe grabbed her hand, and she moved into his arms and hugged him.

"Thank you for being patient with me. And thank you for giving us a second chance," Kayla said, holding him tight.

"Thank *you* for being patient with *me*. But the credit goes to my grandfather. He knew what he was doing by making me your landlord. He brought us together." Gabe kissed the top of her head.

Kayla looked down at the ring. "I hope your grandfather, Nana, and Pop are friends in heaven."

"They're smiling down on us, for sure. Now, let's continue to make them proud." Gabe kissed Kayla gently on the lips.

Kayla felt like the most blessed woman in the entire world. Life was always good, but now it had gotten a whole lot better. And even though she'd learned Nana had cheated on Pop, he had always been the love of her life. That was something Kayla and her grandmother had in common, as Gabe was the love of Kayla's life, no matter what.

She turned her head toward the television in the living room. "Did someone just put the TV on?"

"No...what the hell?" her dad said, bewildered, finding the remote control on the middle of the coffee table and turning off the television.

A loud bird was tweeting out on the back porch, and Kayla turned to look out the window.

"Gabe, your grandfather and Nana are here with us."

Gabe laughed as he held her tighter. Kayla and Gabe were the only ones who had read Melody's letter, so Kayla's family wouldn't understand about the television turning on and off, but she assumed her family would remember how Nana had loved birds.

"You see, honey," her mom said. "I *told* you Nana was proud of you."

Kayla missed Nana terribly. And with Gabe by her side, maybe she would finally have a chance to mourn the grandmother she'd adored. But for the first time in Kayla's life, she felt complete.

Finally, the pieces of her life were coming together. And they fit perfectly.

EPILOGUE

Two Years Later

WATCHING THE SUNRISE made Kayla's heart swell with even more love. Every morning at sunrise, she nursed her baby while welcoming a new day.

"I'm so glad I listened to you and built the sunroom here," Gabe said as he walked into the room and kissed Kayla, and then Emily, their baby girl, on their foreheads.

"You still owe me for winning that bet."

"I'll give you another baby," Gabe said with a twinkle in his eye.

Kayla laughed. "Emily's only three months old. Let's try to wait at least six."

"I'll try, but we'll have to use some type of protection."

Gabe was right. Other than the weeks following Emily's birth, they'd had sex nearly every day since becoming engaged. They really were making up for lost time. He'd moved into her room at her family's house for a few months as they'd planned. Everyone in the family knew what they were doing after dark, of course, but they pretended they didn't. Kayla loved them for that. They did try to stay quiet. Some nights were harder than others, especially when he touched that one spot.

They gazed out into the sunrise, just staring, for seconds, minutes, hours—Kayla couldn't tell. Baby Emily was fast asleep, and they might have sat there all morning if someone hadn't knocked on their front door.

Gabe sighed. "Do you think it's your mother or one of your sisters?"

"What time is it?"

Gabe checked his watch. "Five-fifteen."

"It's probably my mother. I'll talk to her and tell her not to come so early," Kayla said, as she walked toward the front door.

"Hey." Gabe grabbed her elbow to stop her. "I love you and I love your family. I knew what I was getting myself into the moment I proposed. And if your mom is coming here this early, something must be wrong. Your family has surprisingly learned to give us some space."

Kayla smiled. She loved him more and more each day. "Do you want to talk to my mom with me?"

Gabe pecked her on the lips, lifting Emily out of her hands. "Absolutely. I spoke with your dad yesterday. They seem to be compromising just fine, so it can't be about him."

"What did my dad say?" Kayla loved that he knew just as much, if not more, about what was going on with her family than she did.

"He said that your mom was mad at him for walking in the house without brushing his shoes off on the mat. They had a huge fight, but at the end, he told her to put a sticky note on the wall by the door, so he'll remember. That seemed to have done the trick."

Kayla laughed, before opening the door. Her mom stood on their porch, looking upset.

"Hey, Mom, what's wrong?"

"It's Sarah," her mom said as she walked past Kayla, lifted Emily out of Gabe's arms, and then took banana pound cake out of the bag that was dangling from her arm. "I'm sorry for barging in so early, and good morning. I baked you banana pound cake because I've been up since the crack of dawn."

"The crack of dawn is about now," Gabe said, as he looked out the window at the rising sun.

"You want to sit down?" Kayla asked.

"No, I have another cake in the oven, and I have to get ready to babysit little Zach. Jessica took the day off today to spend time with Matt alone. I think she's ready for another baby," her mom said. "But I needed to tell you about Sarah. She broke another man's heart. She didn't tell me, of course. But I ran into Bill Radman in town last night when I went to pick up some groceries. He told me Sarah dated his son, Lucas, for the last month, and then all of a sudden, she told him she never wanted to see him again. I've heard at least ten stories similar to this one in the last six months. But this time sounded the worst, so I thought I'd tell you."

"She has been a little unhinged lately," Kayla agreed. She knew Sarah was up to something. Kayla had heard the same stories in town as her mom had, but she wouldn't tell her mom that. A few days ago, she had confronted Sarah, but all Sarah said was she was looking for Mr. Now, not Mr. Forever.

But something didn't feel right.

"We'll go talk to Sarah," Gabe assured her mom.

"I'd appreciate that," her mom said after she kissed Emily on the cheek, then gave her back to Gabe.

"Thanks for the cake, Mom," Kayla said as she gave her mom a hug.

"Any time. I love you all."

Once she was gone, Kayla sighed.

"I've been going to Magical Toys every day this week to check on Sarah. She's been acting strangely. When I confronted her, she wouldn't tell me anything." Aside from Sarah's issues with men, Kayla thought Sarah was doing a wonderful job managing the store. All Kayla ever had to do was make sure everything was okay. She also liked spending time with her sisters there.

Lauren was happy and doing great, but Sarah was still a concern.

"You want to go see Sarah after your patient later?" Gabe asked.

Kayla answered as she walked toward the kitchen: "That's a good idea." She placed the delicious-smelling cake on the counter, grabbed a knife, and cut into it.

She had finished her degree, and Dr. Bosnie, a busy psychologist in town, had agreed to supervise her so eventually she could have her own private practice. It also helped him reduce his load by giving her some of his patients. Kayla loved it and knew without a doubt it was her calling.

"Cut a piece of your mother's amazing cake for me, too, and I'll put sleepy Emily in her crib," Gabe said as he kissed Kayla on the back of her neck.

"After we go see Sarah, do you want to grab an iced coffee and bring Emily to our rock?" she asked.

"I'd love that. And I still have the blanket in my car from the last time we went."

Kayla smiled softly and watched her gorgeous husband take the baby upstairs. She felt like the luckiest woman in the world. Gabe was an equal partner to her in every way. She had no doubt he'd help her figure out what was going on with Sarah.

By the time he came back down, she had cut two slices of the cake, almost finished hers, and handed the other one to him.

Gabe took a large bite and then looked at her with a twinkle in his eye. "Mmm, good, but I have a better idea."

From the look in his eye, Kayla knew exactly what his good idea was. So she took the last bite of the cake, swallowed it as quickly as she could, and then threw her arms around his neck.

"I love you, Gabe. But I also want you to know that I appreciate you and everything you do for me and our family."

Gabe winked at her. "Show me how much you appreciate me, beautiful."

He lifted her up, slid the cake to the far end of the kitchen table, and then placed Kayla right down on the center. Then he opened her bathrobe and pushed up her black silk nightgown, that, luckily, her mom hadn't seen because of that damn terrycloth robe. Gabe hated that robe, but Kayla was sure he had been grateful for it this morning.

He circled his finger over her clit and then used his delicious tongue.

"Wait a minute," she said. "I thought I was supposed to show you how much I appreciate *you*."

"You are." Gabe stopped licking and looked at her. "By letting me touch you in any way I like, you're doing just that."

Kayla didn't argue. She couldn't. His tongue was back at it, and she lost all thought.

"Well, I can't complain," was all she could think of saying.

Her family was back on their feet. They still had issues, but so did everyone. And Kayla was married to the love of her life. She really had nothing to complain about.

Gabe chuckled under his breath and continued kissing her in her most intimate place. She lasted all of three minutes before she came.

Gabe pulled down his sweatpants—he'd learned to get dressed the minute he woke in case the family popped in early, as her mother had this morning—and then thrust inside her.

"Every time I'm inside you, I feel like I'm in heaven," he said, his tone warm and seductive.

"I thought you were going to use protection," she said.

Gabe began thrusting in the tempo she liked.

"Next time," he replied in between breaths.

Kayla didn't respond. She didn't really care. She and Gabe had decided they wanted a big family to add to the chaos of hers. It would make life more fun, they decided. If she got pregnant, so be it.

This weekend, his parents were flying in to spend time with Emily. Although they were divorced, they got along great. Gabe spoke to them often.

Kayla's mom was throwing them a "Welcome to Bella Cove" dinner, even though they'd been there for the wedding. Gabe also invited Alice and her girlfriend, since Alice could tell his parents stories about his grandfather that they'd never heard. Even though his parents hadn't spoken to Gabe's grandfather in years, once he died, they'd missed him.

Kayla was the happiest she'd ever been. She was able to see her family and be there for them when she wanted. Every morning, she woke up to the love of her life. She was raising their beautiful baby girl. And she was fulfilling her dream of being a psychologist.

And judging from the way Gabe was thrusting inside her, she'd learned to communicate her needs. Lucky for her, she was married to a man who made sure they were always met.

The End.

Get More Romance in Your Inbox

For an additional free scene of Bella Cove, please go to:
www.RochelleKatzman.com/BellaCove

Acknowledgements

WRITING A ROMANCE novel is a huge dream of mine. I'd like to thank the following people who have helped me make it happen. First, I'd like to thank my family for their amazing support, and my mom who listened to me obsess about all the changes I made a week before the book was due in to the publisher. I'd like to thank Jody for reading each chapter and her invaluable critique. Thank you to Keidi Keating, for giving me the confidence to believe in my writing. To Jill N. Noble-Shearer, who is teaching me the craft of writing, to Tom Corson-Knowles, founder of TCK Publishing, who has taken a chance on me. And thank you to my dog, Henry, who has kept me company while I write.

Thank you for making my dream come true!

About the Author

ROCHELLE KATZMAN's first published romance novel, Risking Her Heart, became a #1 Amazon bestseller. She won her first two creative writing awards at age six. She loves writing about strong heroines who create the lives they are meant to live.

Rochelle is also an international yoga instructor and a life coach. When she's not traveling the world teaching workshops or helping women to achieve their dreams, she's at home writing books. She currently lives in New York, but she'd love to move to a beautiful land filled with playful fairies and magical castles. Rochelle enjoys spending time with her family, especially her dog, Henry, when he's not eating her favorite shoes.

Rochelle loves to hear from her readers!
For an additional free scene of Bella Cove, please go to:
www.RochelleKatzman.com/BellaCove

You can also connect with Rochelle online:
Website:
www.RochelleKatzman.com

Twitter:
twitter.com/Rochellekatzman

Facebook:
www.facebook.com/RochelleKatzmanAuthor

GET SPECIAL DEALS ON MORE BEST SELLING BOOKS

Get discounts and special deals on our best-selling books at

www.TCKPublishing.com/Bookdeals